The
Kindest Thing

The Kindest Thing

Cath Staincliffe

ROBINSON
London

Constable & Robinson Ltd
3 The Lanchesters
162 Fulham Palace Road
London W6 9ER
www.constablerobinson.com

First published in the UK by Robinson,
an imprint of Constable & Robinson, 2010

A copy of the British Library Cataloguing in Publication Data is available
from the British Library

ISBN: 978-1-84901-273-7

Typeset by TW Typesetting, Plymouth, Devon
Printed and bound in the EU

1 3 5 7 9 10 8 6 4 2

PEFC
PEFC/16-33-111
CATG-PEFC-052
www.pefc.org

For Tim

Many thanks to the people who were so generous with their time and knowledge: solicitors Robert Lizar and Nicky Hall; Joy Winkler, writer in residence, and the writers' group at HMP Styal. All the mistakes are mine. Thanks also to my agents: the late Kate Jones who encouraged me to tackle a different sort of novel and Sara Menguc for all her hard work.

Chapter One

It's my birthday tomorrow. Fifty. The big five-oh. I'm not having a party – I'll be in court. The charge is murder. More than one way to make the occasion memorable. Sorry. I'm being flippant. Fear does that to me. While it squeezes my insides and tightens my spine, my brain seizes on irreverent wisecracks and sarky comments. A defence mechanism, I guess. To hide how close I am to dissolving in terror at my situation.

The authorities find this verbal bravado very difficult to deal with. My lawyer soon cottoned on and told me to button it. Menopausal women with dead husbands are not meant to offer up smart remarks. Too bold. Too hard. It makes people uncomfortable – not least because for a nanosecond they share the humour. An expression of delight and hilarity flashes across their faces, chased away by frowns and winces. They wriggle in their seats, swallow and ease their stiff shirt collars with the hook of a finger. They expect a victim, all soft sighs and shame, begging for mercy. Not a backchatting bitch having a laugh. Different century and I'd have been fitted with a scold's bridle or floated on the village pond. Instead it's the Crown Court and the front pages of the nationals.

When the fear gets too large, when it threatens to devour me, like now, I drag my thoughts back to

Neil, to what we had, what we shared before it was all narrowed down to one infamous act. The good old bad old days.

I wish he were here with me. He could still me with a look. In his gaze I would find strength and love and an edge of amusement. No matter how dark things got, he always had that sardonic half-smile in him. And things got dark; they are dark. It's an illogical wish – if Neil were here, I wouldn't be. He's the reason I'm here.

I didn't like him the first time we met. Fancied – yes. Liked – no. He was beautiful but I mistrusted his confidence. Took it for arrogance. He was seated with his friends outside the pub. A hot September lunchtime. I was a fresher, heading back to the halls for something to eat. Feeling lonely and excited by the move to uni, unsettled and bound up tight, lurching from one event to the next and wondering how long it would all feel strange. He had his chair tilted back and he was talking loudly – no idea what he was saying but ripples and little explosions of laughter came from the people around him. There was a girl at his side, quirky-looking with a round pale face and shiny black hair cut like Cleopatra's. I assumed they were a couple. He caught my eye as I passed, just before I turned away, and I felt a little jolt of energy. Then he went on talking and there was more laughter and I'd a horrible fear they were laughing at me. Prat, I told myself, thinks he's God's gift.

The next few times I came across him, I made a point of ignoring him. I'd glimpse him out of the corner of my eye and force myself not to look his way. I'd see him around the arts faculty and eventually worked out he was studying history. I had expected something flashier: theatre studies or fine art.

Later that term, there was a house party in one of the big villas that the university let to students. A cold night, November or maybe December. The place filled up quickly; most of them were second and third years. Jane and I went along. She'd started seeing one of the second years who rented the place but most nights she came back to halls and slept there. Jane was ambitious and intent on getting good grades. Her three older brothers had all graduated with honours and she had a lot to live up to.

Friends from my course and I were sitting in a corner in the main room bitching about our lecturers and the essays we had to do – though none of us would have swapped it for the world. Neil came in with Cleopatra and a couple of blokes. One was small and wiry, he wore a duffel-coat, and the other was a lanky lad with shocking blond hair who always dressed in black. I turned away and pretended to listen to my friends, but when I looked back Neil's gaze was locked on mine. And I held it. Just a beat too long. Then I went into the kitchen, aware he'd be heading that way for a drink. I poured some wine into a plastic cup.

He was beside me then. 'Deborah Shelley.' He knew my name.

'And you are . . .?' Me trying to be clever, as if I hadn't made a point of finding out exactly who he was.

But he saw right through me, burst out laughing, a rich, throaty sound, and leaned closer in. 'Very pleased to meet you,' he said archly. 'Come outside, come and talk to me.'

3

'What about Cleopatra?'

He blinked; his eyes were the colour of green olives, his hair dark brown, almost black, brushing his shoulders. He realized I meant the girl. 'Jackie? She's gay. I don't think she'll mind. Not unless she's got her eye on you.'

I blushed, a little startled. I hadn't met any lesbians back then. Well, none that were out anyway, though at school we'd had our suspicions about the chemistry teacher. I drank some of the wine, cold and sharp. I hated blushing but he was kind and didn't tease me any more.

'Deborah.' He said my name again, slowly, like a kiss, all three syllables.

'It's freezing out there.'

'I'll keep you warm. Look.' He wore a greatcoat, a big heavy thing in grey, ex-army or something. It practically reached the ground. With his hands in his pockets he spread his arms out, flinging the coat wide open. An invitation.

I swallowed the rest of my wine.

He took my hand. His fingers were cool and long.

Outside, the garden was full of junk, old milk bottles, bakery trays and a broken dining chair, all frosted and glistening. There was just room to stand beside the door. I trembled. It could have been either the cold or the wine or the desire that flushed through my limbs and over my skin.

'Kiss me,' I said.

He raised a hand to tuck his hair behind his ear as he bent towards me.

I closed my eyes.

I fell in love.

* * *

The day Neil died, when he'd stopped breathing, I lay down beside him on our bed. Hoping, I think, that I might gain some equilibrium, some respite after the horror. Wanting to stay there till the soft June sunshine rolled into night. Keeping a vigil if you like. Not ready to let him go. But I knew I had to phone the ambulance and let Sophie and Adam know that their father was dead.

I kissed Neil again, told him I loved him and got up off the bed. Panic crashed over me. My stomach spasmed and water flooded my mouth. I ran for the bathroom and was violently sick, the vomit forcing its way down my nostrils as well as out of my mouth, scouring my throat. While I washed my hands and face and brushed my teeth, a lump of fear lodged in my stomach. Why had I ever agreed?

Fetching the phone from the hallway, I returned to our room, watching Neil while I made the call. 'He's stopped breathing, my husband. I think he's dead.' After I'd given my name and the address, I called Adam. His phone went to voicemail. 'Come home, Adam, as soon as you can.'

Sophie knew straight away. 'It's Dad?'

'Yes.'

'Oh, Mum.' Her voice broke. 'Is he in hospital?'

'At home.'

She got back before the ambulance arrived. Found me upstairs sitting on the edge of the bed. Her hand covered her mouth. The room stank. Her eyes flew to her father. 'He was fine this morning,' she said.

'Yes.' In the scale of things. Better than dead, anyway.

'Have you tried anything – the breathing space kit?'

I froze, tried to swallow. 'Sophie, it's too late. Darling, I'm sorry.' I walked over to her. She threw her arms around me and squeezed tight, sobbing into my neck. She wasn't often physically demonstrative. Not with me. With Neil – yes. 'Oh, Dad,' she wailed. After a minute or two she pulled away.

'It's all right,' I told her, 'if you want to sit with him or hold his hand or anything.'

She looked at her father again, then shook her head. She went out of the room. I'd misjudged it, perhaps. She was fifteen and we were constantly second-guessing her reactions. Sophie was always so practical and sensible that it was easy to forget how young she really was. Unlike Adam.

I followed her down. I hated to leave Neil on his own. Sophie was on her phone. She ended the call as I came into the kitchen.

'You didn't tell Grandma.' It sounded like an accusation.

'Not yet. I thought you and Adam – you've told her?'

She nodded. She was being so grown-up. I realized that this was how she would deal with it now. She'd throw herself into the arrangements and help me with the tasks that needed doing and find a way to be useful.

'Thank you,' I said.

The doorbell rang. There was an ambulance outside, a man on the step. He checked that he'd come to the right place and signalled for his mate to join him.

'He's upstairs,' I told them. 'He's been very ill.' I led the way and the two men followed. One crossed over to Neil's side and felt for his pulse. The other distracted me, asking questions: he'd been ill, what with, which hospital was he being seen by, how had he been earlier that day.

'He is dead,' his colleague confirmed. I nodded. The door went again. I heard voices. Then Sophie calling me. The ambulance man examining Neil gestured that I could go.

Downstairs there was a young policeman. Sophie had seated him at the kitchen table. He stood up as I entered the room. He was one of those men whose jaw is wider than his forehead, giving him the look of a comic-book hero. He introduced himself as PC Stenner, and explained he was following up on reports of a sudden death.

I sat down opposite him. Sophie was making tea.

'My husband Neil. He has motor neurone disease. I went to check on him this afternoon, about three o'clock. Anyway, he wasn't breathing.'

'Big shock,' he offered.

'Just a question of time, really. It's a terminal illness.'

'He's not in hospital?'

'There's no treatment.'

His eyes fell for a moment. 'I see. Well, the coroner will be informed, just a matter of routine. Any sudden death. But, like you say, if it was expected . . .' He wrote a few lines in his notebook, then stood and spoke to Sophie. 'I won't be needing that cuppa, ta.'

Her hands stilled and she flexed her fingers, a little signal of frustration. 'You can do one for me, love,' I put in.

The policeman left, and then the ambulance men came downstairs and explained that they would be fetching a stretcher to remove Neil's body. I tried Adam's number again but it was still on voicemail.

Typical. If he got back in time for the funeral it would be a bloody miracle.

Sophie passed me my tea and I took it upstairs to the bedroom. The smell caught me afresh; I'd probably have to chuck the mattress. We'd never thought about that. The way a body empties on death.

The sun was glancing off Neil's hair, turning the grey at his temples into silver and bringing out the shine in the rest, still dark brown. His skin tanned in spite of death's pallor. He'd loved the sun. Had inherited his father Michael's skin colouring, not his mother's. Michael had Spanish ancestry while Veronica was Irish, complexion pale as milk and prone to burn. They were both small, Veronica was petite really, and Neil had towered over them. They joked he was their cuckoo child.

His parents arrived as the ambulance men were manoeuvring the stretcher down our stairs. Veronica was weeping noisily even as she came up the path. Sophie ran out to meet them and Veronica pulled her close. Michael moved on into the house, looking older and smaller, curly grey hair, a thick moustache. 'Deborah.' I moved into his arms.

He caught sight of the stretcher, let me go and moved to support his wife. Veronica groaned as the men brought Neil down. As they stepped on to the hall floor and straightened, she gave a wail and moved forward. 'My boy,' she cried. A fifty-year-old man. Ridiculous, perhaps, but I recognized the passion in her cry, the depth of her grief. If this had been my boy, my Adam . . . I started to cry, too. She loved Neil. I loved him. And now he was gone. Veronica clasped Neil's hand between her own and kissed it.

'Where are you taking him?' I asked the ambulance men. 'Only my son . . .'

'He'll be at the mortuary. Once you've sorted out the funeral arrangements, you can arrange a viewing at the funeral home.'

Michael eased Veronica away and I bent forward and kissed Neil's cheek. I couldn't speak. I stepped back to let them pass and stood in the front doorway while they carried him down to the ambulance and slid him inside. I watched until they had driven out of view.

When we were at university open relationships were all the rage, and Neil and I were nothing if not fashionable. Neil had one-night stands with a stream of women when I was away or staying in to study. I had a few short-lived affairs. Most of the time we'd sleep together, either at his house or at the bed-sit I'd moved into in my second year.

One night I'd been visiting my mother and got back sooner than expected. The trip had rattled me. She and I had so little to say to each other that, for me at any rate, the visits were an excruciating mix of tension and boredom. We relied on banalities, talked about the weather, the increase in fuel prices, domestic mishaps and the ups and downs of acquaintances we cared little about. I went out of a sense of duty; I never could tell whether she got any pleasure from our encounters.

There was a disco on at the student's union that evening, and although I'd missed most of it, it would be more fun than sitting in getting stewed on my own. While I changed, putting on a vintage silk dress and dramatic makeup, I drank a couple of brandy-and-lemonades and smoked a joint.

Things were in full swing when I arrived, the air humid and smoky, the lights rippling over the crowd. Neil was in a corner, a pretty redheaded girl sitting on his lap. My guts clenched in reaction. I shot him a blazing smile and turned away. I wanted to rip her off him. I wanted him to dump her on the floor and come over to me. I wanted to kill them both. Not acceptable reactions. For the next hour I flirted with a group of lads at the bar before going off with the prettiest. It felt meaningless.

When I rolled up at my place the following afternoon, shivering in my thin dress, Neil was sitting on the doorstep. My heart burned when I saw him. He kissed me and followed me in.

I had a shower while he made bacon-and-egg butties. He was quiet as we ate and the tension was plain in the set of his jaw and the cast of his eyes. I put music on, rolled a joint. We lay on the bed smoking. He put the roach in the ashtray. I straddled him, let my robe fall open, traced his clavicle with my fingers. He stayed my hand and my skin chilled. He was leaving me. That was why he'd come round, why he was so wound up.

'Move in with me,' he said.

'What?'

'Or I'll move in here. I don't want anyone else.' He edged himself up onto his elbows, shook his hair back from his face. 'I don't want to share you.' His eyes were hot.

'Very bourgeois.'

'Deborah,' he warned me, his grip on my wrist tightening.

'Okay.'

He closed his eyes, a gesture of relief. Then looked at me again. Lay back down. I began to unbuckle his belt.

10

Living together. Monogamy. I wondered how long it would last.

We argued about housework: cleaning, shopping, cooking, washing. He tried to joke about it but I was deadly serious. There was no way I was going to become my mother; solely responsible for all that – even before my dad died. Life was too short and chores too soul-destroying. Neil was an adult, not a child, and I appealed to his political sensibility. 'You believe in equality – this is part of the equation.' I had little respect for a man who needed servicing. It worked both ways: I would shift rubbish and change fuses with the best of them. Not for me the helpless act, the little lady who hauls home the groceries then finds her muscles have melted clean away when faced with a flagstone.

Things weren't up to scratch for a long time but I'd seen my brother successfully use the excuse of incompetence to get away with doing nothing in the house so that wouldn't wash. We taught each other and weathered the ridicule of friends and family: *You the one wearing the apron, Neil?*

He became competent at cooking and cleaning and laundry. No more than that, but no more was expected. And I became a dab hand at DIY.

Chapter Two

The prison van comes for us at eight in the morning. We've eaten breakfast and are waiting in the reception area near the main exit. Four of us. A couple of the girls, who don't look much older than Sophie, are smoking and laughing, their nerves making them talk quickly. The other woman is silent. She wears Asian dress, a *salwar kameez* in a pale green. There's grey in her hair. I wonder what she's charged with.

The van is the sort you've seen countless times on television. Rectangular and white with the row of distinctive small windows. Any high-profile case and the news shows the van swinging towards the court and photographers running along, arms upstretched, cameras held to the windows, hoping for that lucky snap. I wonder whether anyone will greet my arrival. It's likely. The case, the ins and outs and the moral twists, have fed the papers and the discussion programmes for weeks. It appears mine is a *cause célèbre*. Not what we intended at all.

We climb into the van up metal steps located just behind the driver's cabin. The narrow corridor is lined with doors, a little cubicle each. Bare metal walls, a reinforced galvanized-mesh seat. The guard sends me into the first and locks me in. It is April and all I can see out of the little glass window is bleak grey sky. Nine months I've been in prison.

The journey takes about twenty minutes. Styal is a few miles south of the city centre. Before all this, it was somewhere we came walking, a place with woods and a river, an old mill and tea rooms. Where the kids played Pooh-sticks and Adam got stuck on a tree over the river and had to be rescued. Where Sophie got stung by a wasp and her ear puffed up and we worried it was an allergic reaction. The prison is less than a mile away from the country park.

Will they be there? Sophie? Adam? At Adam's last visit, I told him it didn't matter. That it would be horrible for all of us and I'd understand if he stayed away. I haven't seen Sophie. She's staying with Michael and Veronica.

Adam's looking after our house. That might be too strong a phrase. I expect he's treating it with benign neglect at best. If he's off the rails again, who knows? He might have trashed the place and sold the lead from the roof.

When I was first arrested Jane asked Adam if he wanted to move in with her. There's a box room in her flat he could squeeze into but he was happier at home. I asked him, too, just in case he was acting out of misplaced politeness. But he was quite clear: 'Jane's great, but move in? No way. I couldn't relax, you know?'

I nodded, picturing Adam sprawled on the couch, a game on the screen, dirty plates and discarded items of clothing strewn about. I'm glad he's comfortable at home, that there's some remnant of our family still there, that the house is not deserted. Jane keeps in touch with him; he can call her if need be. Adam likes Jane. I love her. She has been a constant for me, from those undergraduate days till now. A fast friend, someone I've shared my life with.

The vehicle speeds up and there are shouts outside, then a hard thump on the side. For me? For one of the others? Then we swing to the left and the van slows, the engine stops. We must be at the court. A ripple of panic courses through me. My skin chills but blood runs hot in my limbs. There's a rushing noise in my ears. The guard unlocks the door and leads us down the steps and into the holding area beneath the courts.

I don't want to be here. Anywhere else but here.

The summer of my graduation we went island-hopping in Greece. I'd studied photography at uni but, as the course went on, found myself less and less interested in the act of taking photographs and more and more fascinated with creating material to photograph. Concentrating on still life and found objects, I would spend weeks building up an environment or a collection of items or a scenario complete with figures, maybe a sense of narrative. The photographs became a way of documenting the creative process. Drawn to different themes and cultures, I researched avidly, reading everything I could find on Mexican and Aztec culture for a project entitled 'Day of the Dead' or experimenting with early dyeing techniques for a photo-essay on colour. Using my own urine to set dyes was one of the more scandalous elements of my second-year project.

Graduating with a 2:2, I knew I didn't want to work as a photographer. Perhaps I should have considered animation, though my drawing skills were average at best, or becoming a stylist, but at the start of the eighties there were precious few jobs for arts graduates.

Neil, who'd finished a year ahead of me, had gone on to do a teacher-training course. Jobs in history weren't ten a penny either. By rights he should have started a teaching job that September. But I'd talked him into our Greek trip. We both worked for a temp agency through July and August to raise the money, then had two months away.

We arrived in Athens in the middle of the night. The air was hot and full of dust, which left our skin feeling gritty.

There was no bus to the port at Piraeus till dawn so we sat in the scrub on the airport approach road waiting for sunrise. At one point a car drew up, airport security, and a man in a crisp uniform and peaked cap harangued us until we got up and dragged our rucksacks back to the building. There was nowhere to sit and nothing to eat or drink.

When the bus came we repeated the word 'Piraeus' to the driver, who took some drachmas and motioned us down the aisle. The front windows were framed with coloured fringing and sprigs of plastic flowers. Central on the dashboard stood a large plastic glow-in-the-dark Madonna, and rosary beads dangled from the rear-view mirror.

'My mother'd love it,' Neil murmured.

The bus juddered its way along winding roads and through the crowded jumble of the city, the muddle of apartments, small shops and businesses, to the port. When we got off, the place was quiet. Nothing open. I wondered where all the fishermen were. Hunger and lack of sleep were making me grumpy but then a corner shutter rose and a small, round, wrinkled man plonked a table and two chairs outside. We made our way over and stepped inside. There was a garish menu with photos of sickly-looking food. I pointed to a cheese roll, treacle cake, coffee. Neil nodded for the same. We ate outside at the rickety table and watched the gulls swerving down for debris on the quayside. The day was already warm and the food set me right. The sea was a pure deep blue and I took a long breath of air and watched Neil. Early on, I often feared he would leave me. That was what men did. I hid it well. He never realized. Of course, I imagined he'd betray me for another woman. Instead it was neurones crumbling and muscles wasting away that stole him from me.

We were the only tourists on the ferry. Well off the package holiday routes, Syra was, according to the guidebook, a thriving ship-building island with a strong local economy and deserted beaches. It was also several hours on the boat from Piraeus. The Greeks on board were all laden with parcels and packages. Most of them wore black or black and white. They seemed curious about us, eyes sliding our way. As they chatted, I wondered if we were the subject of their conversation – the scruffy hippies with their backpacks.

We set off with a clamour and the smell of diesel in the air. The engine clattered loudly and made it impossible to talk. But after an hour or so, the roaring noise cut out abruptly. One of the crew, a man with skin like an old satchel and grizzled hair, climbed down into the hatch. For several minutes he and the captain exchanged words. He emerged now and then to throw up his arms and grimace. One of the older women, dressed all in black, remonstrated with the captain.

How long were we going to be stuck there? My dreams of lunch in some small taverna followed by a swim and sex in the shade of a beachside eucalyptus tree shrivelled as the minutes ticked by. The sun was high and fierce now. There was no land anywhere in sight, no rocks, no other vessels, no lighthouse or buoys.

The crewman emerged, wiping oil from his hands onto a rag, and another noisy debate erupted with several of the passengers chipping in. After a few minutes of this the crewman spat over the side of the deck and lit a cigarette. The captain and a young lad, who I guessed was his son, began to lower a dinghy into the water. The crewman climbed into it and, after a few attempts, started the outboard motor. Most of the passengers retreated to the shade in the lounge area in the middle of the boat.

'He's going for help,' I said to Neil. 'Will he go to Piraeus?'

'Think so – there's nowhere nearer.'

I sat back down and closed my eyes, my face tilted at the sun. I savoured the heat. I could feel myself sliding into sleep, but struggled awake, aware of the hard iron struts on the bench biting into the bones of my back. 'I'm so tired,' I murmured to Neil.

'We could go over there.' He gestured to a corner under the stairs. It was in the shade and dry. There'd just be room to lie down. We left our rucksacks where they were and moved over.

We lay side by side, facing each other. The floor was hard; my hip bone soon ached. I used a hand to cushion my ear. 'I wish I could teleport.'

Neil smiled.

'Click my fingers and we'd be in our room.'

'With a very cold beer.' His T-shirt was crumpled from the journey, his chin dusted with stubble.

A picture of us making love formed in my mind:

Neil prone on white sheets, me riding him, his gaze blurred with desire. 'Touch me,' I whispered.

His eyes danced. He brought his face close to mine, I tilted my body towards him – I had my back to the few passengers on deck and hoped the run of the stairs and my position would shield them from seeing anything untoward.

He touched my lips with his, moved his arm slowly, brushing my nipple with his knuckles. If anyone was peering at us they would surely see my buttocks tighten and my back stiffen. Neil responded to my intake of breath. He kissed me again and shifted, trailing his hand down my body till it rested between my legs. My cheesecloth skirt was flimsy, my underwear close-fitting and I could feel everything as he made tiny circling motions with his thumb. The proximity of other people gave an added edge to my excitement. After only seconds I came, the sweet release rippling down my thighs and up into my throat, flooding me with heat. I tensed my muscles hard so I wouldn't flail about and managed not to cry out.

Opening my eyes, I stared at Neil. His face was flushed and sultry. I ran my tongue between his lips while I felt for his crotch and found the smooth curve of his penis, thick against his jeans. He stayed my hand. 'Later,' he whispered. I smiled. And closed my eyes.

The return of the dinghy woke me. I'd no idea how long I'd slept but my bum was numb and I'd pins and needles in my arm.

Whatever spare part the man had brought back did the trick and we were soon roaring and clanking our way onwards. By the time the island came into view, night was falling and a warm breeze came up, riffling the water and whipping our hair about.

The harbour was small. Coloured lights ran along the quayside in front of a row of tavernas. On dry land, we walked along the front, catching sight of shoals of fish close by, their scales flashing iridescent when the light spilled onto them. The smell of barbecued meat and fish and onions made my mouth water.

At the end of the drag the road forked; the right-hand turning led uphill and the other circled the bay. A few streetlights illuminated the buildings, many with boards advertising rooms. We'd started along the beach road when a voice called to us; 'Room? Room?' The woman was a few doors down and beckoned us closer. We reached the whitewashed block as she laid down her hose. The place was festooned with geraniums in oil cans and she had been watering them, the aroma of damp earth and vegetation strong. I caught the whine of a mosquito close to my ear.

The room was one of four on the first floor, overlooking the bay. With a location like that we'd have said yes to a cardboard box. It was clean and simple. Very simple. Bed, two rickety wooden chairs and a small table. A wardrobe that smelt of wax and contained heavy blankets. An ancient fridge, no fan, no kettle. Shower and toilet. Shuttered doors led on to the small balcony. We thanked the woman and asked the daily rate. It was reasonable. We asked her if she needed our passports and she shrugged. We weren't going anywhere. '*Kalispera.*' She left us and Neil shut the door. We grinned at each other in excitement and relief.

The bed, in a dark wooden frame, squealed as I sat back on it and eased off my rucksack. I used the bathroom; the water stuttered out of the tap as though it hadn't been used for a while. I'd caught the sun already, my nose and forehead bright. While Neil had a wash, I went out on to the balcony. The sea was close: I could hear the crashing sound of waves and just make out the water's edge.

Neil came out of the bathroom.

'I'm ravenous,' I told him, as I walked back in. He switched the light off. It was very dark. He cupped his hand round my neck and then walked me back until we reached the wall. The plaster was cool on my arms. His breathing, harsh and eager, mingled with the noise of the surf outside. He kissed me and then he fucked me, gripping the fabric of my skirt in bunches at my hips, his jeans puddled round his feet. I was ridiculously, sentimentally happy. I must remember this, I told myself, whatever happens. I must remember. He gasped when he came.

'Now take me out and feed me,' I whispered.

'Okay.' He kissed the top of my head. 'Then I'll fuck you again.'

'Promise?'

My solicitor, Ms Gleason, is here. She reminds me what the procedure will be in court today, what is likely to happen. It's hard to concentrate. Several times I find I'm agreeing with her and have no idea what she has been saying. It reminds me of a dream I have – they're quite common, most people dream something similar. In my version I am on stage and the curtain is about to go up and I have forgotten to learn my lines. I don't even know what the play is but I have a very big part and there is no time to find my script. It feels exactly like that as we wait for the usher to call us. And I know there's no waking up from it.

Chapter Three

The weeks of our Greek idyll passed in a daze of cheap local wine, fresh food, hot sun and sex. We were both constantly aroused. I was on the pill so we had no need of condoms. Those happy days before AIDS came stalking.

We travelled to Crete and went to Knossos, King Minos's palace; Neil told me all about the legend of the Minotaur. The site was vast, impressive, but what captivated me was the frieze of the dolphins, the vibrant colour, the energy in it, and the mosaic floors made of thousands of tiny tesserae, I loved the sophistication and elegance of the images, the harmony of composition.

We sailed to Rhodes, entering the harbour where the Colossus once stood. On the island of Kos we got the bus up to the Asclepeion, the first hospital in the world, built on wooded terraces. The place had an atmosphere of peace and tranquillity that not even the clusters of tourists could disrupt. Down in Kos town we sat beneath the plane tree where Hippocrates was said to have taught his principles of healing. Neil filled my head with stories of Greek gods and monsters and heroes. I came to share his fascination with the myths and legends.

Between our excursions to ancient sites we would walk up into the hills where the air was thick with the scent of pine resin and sizzled with the chirrups of crickets and the hum of bees. He would put his hand round the nape of my neck, a gesture that had surprised me at first but by then had become familiar, comforting. He would catch my neck and pull me close for a kiss or hold me like that as we strolled along. I was a head shorter than him.

'Deborah.' He'd stop me, circle my waist with his arm and steer me to a tree, the place dappled with shade and insects flittering in the golden pools of light. To the sound of cowbells in the distance, he would make love to me. His passion for me, his appetite, fed mine and the lust showed no signs of abating. On the beach, reading, swimming, roasting in the heat that softened my muscles and darkened my skin, my thoughts turned repeatedly to sex. Remembering what we had just done and what we might do next. Soon I would turn to him and whisper filthy words and sweet entreaties, teasing him until one or other of us caved in, stood, hand shading our eyes, and said, 'Let's go back for a bit.'

Neil had been dead for sixteen days and we still hadn't been able to make the funeral arrangements because the coroner's office hadn't released the body. The whole country baked in a heatwave. I barely slept, barely ate, close to nausea much of the time. But the warm nights meant I could roam about the house or my workshop and wait for sunrise. I'm an interior designer; my workshop is a converted double garage at the side of the garden. Most of the work I did myself: insulating the roof, dry-lining the walls and laying the floor, though I got contractors in to sort out the plumbing and electricity. I've a free-standing stove at one end that heats the place perfectly in winter.

The part nearest to the drive is an office and meeting area. Clients occasionally come to the workshop to check me out or go over some ideas. The rest of the space is for practical work, drawing table and plans chest, a messy area where I can experiment with paint and other materials: cork, plastics, ceramics. There are shelves lined with reference books and folders stuffed full of research. Some of the books I've had since university; others I acquired for particular projects, like the huge volume of nursery rhymes that I return to again and again when I'm considering children's rooms, or the *Gardens of Egypt* tome I'd bought when working for a couple who'd met at the Pyramids and wanted an outdoor room with the flavour of the Nile.

The length of the workshop that looks out on to the garden is all sliding glass doors, which gives me the natural light I need. There are plain hessian curtains for days when I want to shut out the sun's glare. I set it up the year I launched the business. I'd spent fourteen years working for a big design agency, mainly on corporate contracts: hotel chains and supermarkets. It involved more work away from home than I liked and less variety. I didn't get much holiday, and although Neil's teaching job meant he was available to look after the children in the school holidays, I wanted more flexibility.

It was a risk going self-employed but I knew if I crashed and burned we'd still have Neil's salary. We wouldn't starve. Accepting that productivity would come ahead of creativity until I'd established a reputation, I said yes to all comers. As it was, I struck lucky. One of the clients I'd worked with at the agency had heard I was going solo and recommended me to his boss, who had just won the contract for a new community hospital on the outskirts of Manchester. It involved me designing everything from the colour-coded seats in reception areas to the napkins for the meals service and the pictures on the walls. Eighteen months' work. After that I could pick and choose, and I built a portfolio of very different projects: hair salon, fusion restaurant, sixth-form college, as well as domestic jobs, refurbishments, loft conversions and the like.

So, sixteen days after his death and I'd spent the early hours in my workshop, awake but eyes closed to rest them, my mind lurching about like a drunk on a dance floor. Avoiding the quicksands of sleep.

At seven I went into the kitchen and made a cup of tea. Adam had stayed with friends, or so he said, but Sophie came down, got her lunch ready and left for school. She was very quiet and resisted my attempt to make conversation, returning only shrugs or monosyllables. This wasn't like Sophie but perhaps the silence gave her solace. In the aftermath of Neil's death someone had mentioned bereavement counselling to me: they offered it for children nowadays. If Sophie couldn't talk to me about her dad then perhaps she'd appreciate doing so with someone else.

I thought back to how my own mother had handled it when my dad drowned. Not very well. I was nine. We were on holiday, staying in an apartment in Mumbles on the Gower Peninsula. She sat me and my brother Martin down and told us in very simple terms what had happened: Daddy was missing. He'd been for a swim and must have got out of his depth. He wasn't a particularly strong swimmer and might have misjudged the tides or the current. He had left his clothes on the beach. I imagined them neatly folded, the grey and yellow check poplin shirt, grey shorts, covered with the striped blue towel. His watch in the pocket of his shorts. They recovered his body eight days later. Martin got his watch. I didn't get anything.

Once I had children of my own, every seaside holiday brought a moment of intense anxiety that rose like bile, then a falling sensation, a rush back to the numb panic of waiting for news while my mother spoke to strange men in hushed tones. The earth sways. I am flirting with disaster, I am tempting Fate, bringing myself, my children here, a sacrifice to the ocean. Neil had told me about Scylla and Charybdis when we were in Greece, the two monsters that sat either side of a narrow strait. If sailors managed to avoid the sucking whirlpool of Charybdis they sailed too close to the grotesque Scylla with her six heads, each with three rows of teeth, her loins girded by dog's heads. Scylla would drown and devour her captives. I imagined my father struggling against the pool of Charybdis, being pulled deeper and deeper, the water closing over his head, his limbs burning, heavy, feeble. Or Scylla, sated, cradling him in her loose embrace. Dad's bones clanking softly in the slow current, crabs in his eyes.

Determined to face down my monsters, I dandled the toddlers in the foam along the shore, showed them how to jump the waves. As they grew, I taught them to float and crawl and dive. Allowing myself to fear the worst, I pictured them gone, my eyes racing over the sand and the blue beyond. It's a talisman: if I dip myself into the foam of tragedy and coincidence, give rein to the dread, then it will not come to pass. Some superstitions are hard to shake.

After those first few days my father's death was never mentioned. And talk of his life was strictly rationed. Now and again my mother would mention how he loved to sing or recall watching him play cricket when they were courting, and I would keep still and hold my breath and long for more, so afraid was I that I would forget him. But she would always snap out of any reverie and if I asked a question, tried to keep her talking, she would feign forgetfulness or ignorance. 'I don't know, I can't remember. Now I must get on.'

One ill-judged day, at the age of twelve or so, I pulled out the photograph albums from the sideboard drawer. My mother was watching television. She saw me and tensed, straightening her spine against the sofa back and studying the magazine on her lap. I sat in the armchair and began to turn the pages, thick creamy vellum with black and white photographs carefully attached by corner mounts. This album ran from their marriage to our early childhood, and at the end the photographs were in colour: Martin and I in matching jumpers and tartan slacks, in romper suits on rugs, bundled up in woollen coats and tam o' shanters feeding the ducks. Our clothes so formal, like little versions of our parents', save the romper suits.

I turned the pages, longing for an invitation to share them with her but not daring to say anything. I was staring at a picture of my mother and father in evening dress. She looked vivacious, her lips dark with lipstick, her hair swept up in a chignon and her small figure stunning in a tulip gown. He gazed at her with great affection, his black suit and white shirt pristine. My mother laid her magazine aside and stood. 'I'll sort the ironing out,' she said. 'Turn that off', she nodded at the television, 'when you've finished.'

With everyone out, I listened to the house settle around me. The lack of sleep took me back to the days when Adam and Sophie were small. The same aching muscles, dry eyes pained by the light, a spine filled with sand, emotions horribly close to the surface. As a new mother I would eat to try to maintain some energy, some equilibrium, but now I couldn't. Instead I ran a bath and lay there until the water cooled.

Later, as I was hanging out the washing, I heard the doorbell.

A man and a woman are on the doorstep. For a moment I think they are selling windows or are Jehovah's Witnesses – something to do with the suits they wear even in this heat. But they aren't smiling. They flash ID cards at me and introduce themselves. All I hear is the word 'police'.

'Is it Adam?' My heart bucks and my skin crawls with dread. 'Oh, God, what's happened?'

'We're not here about Adam. If we could come in?' The policewoman flushes. I stand back, still swirling in the relief that Adam is okay, and they walk into the house. The ground tilts. I sense it then, a punch to the gut, the enormity of what's coming.

'We realize this is a very difficult time for you but there are a few things we need to clarify about the events leading up to your husband's death. We'd like you to come with us to the police station. Is now a convenient time?'

My throat is dry. I don't trust myself to speak. So I nod.

Like a zombie I put the answer-machine on, scrawl a note for Adam and Sophie, lock up the house and follow them out to the car. It is a plain vehicle, nothing to set the neighbours' curtains twitching and saliva glands drooling. Shame. Pauline-next-door would like nothing better than to see me bundled into a panda car. The officers are very polite; they seem completely relaxed. I will answer everything evenly, carefully, I tell myself, and it will be fine.

At the police station I am taken to the custody suite. Like some pastiche of checking in at a hotel reception I give my name, address, date of birth. They ask me about any medical conditions I might have – mad with grief? I have to leave my bag with them. A young policewoman spreads out the contents and lists them. They ask for my earrings, my locket. They take my wedding ring. And then I have to sign the list. My hand trembles and my signature looks fake.

They explain that I can see a solicitor before I am interviewed under caution. Have I any questions? Numb, I shake my head. They request a DNA sample and run a small wand along the inside of my cheek. This is sealed in a container and notes made on the label. They take my photograph. Then my finger-prints. The ink smells strong, metallic, and then I am given medicated wipes to remove the dark, oily stains.

A man takes me through a locked doorway and along a corridor into a small cell. He smiles cheerily and locks me in. I sink on to the bench that runs across the back of the room. There is nothing else in the space. They took my ring. I bite my tongue. Where is Neil's ring? In some sealed bag awaiting collection? What will they give me back? The clothes he died in won't be fit for anything.

The walls of the cell press in on me. My skin is clammy and there isn't enough air. I'm aware of my ribs locked too tight, my belly a fist of tension. I cup my hands over my nose and breathe out into my palms, eyes closed. I recall how I taught Adam to do this when paranoia made him hyperventilate, sitting beside him on his grungy bedroom floor, smoothing calm into my voice, talking him down. 'Breathe out nice and slow, let it empty out. Now wait, two, three, four, five. Very gently, little sips, that's it . . .'

His breathing was more regular, yet still when I tried to go to make us both a drink, he scrambled after me, eyes singing with panic, his fingers clawing at my sleeve. 'They're still there – they're still out there!'

Oh, Adam. I felt like snapping at him, 'They're not out there, they're in here, in you, and you're not the only one they're driving round the bloody bend.' Instead I shushed and soothed and stayed with him until Neil came to do his stint.

In the police-station cell, as I wait, my sense of time distorts. I don't know if it's hours or minutes. I feel so alone and it is nothing like the solitude I usually revel in but that awful sense of being isolated, left and forgotten. 'Left to rot', that's the phrase. They have locked me up and they will decide when I eat or sleep or pee, who I speak to.

The solicitor arrives. A black woman with a frazzled look as though she's been dragged from her bed after an all-nighter. Might worry some people but I find it reassuring – the messy black curls, creased suit and purple shadows beneath the eyes give her humanity. She introduces herself as Ms Joy Gleason in a ripe Bolton accent, and even though I guess her to be ten or fifteen years younger than me, there is a practical, no-nonsense, maternal style to the way she deals with the situation.

She describes her role and asks me to tell her about Neil. I explain: his illness, the deterioration, the last

29

morning, finding him dead; every so often she interrupts to clarify a point. She makes notes on a legal pad as she listens.

She frowns. 'The police have no obligation at this stage to disclose any information or evidence they have so we don't know what's prompted them to interview you. It may be that the post-mortem on Neil was inconclusive or they've found it hard to attribute cause of death. But I'm second-guessing and, in a situation like this, where we really don't know what they've got, then I strongly advise you to offer no comment.'

'Won't that make me look guilty of something?'

'That's what the police will tell you,' she smoothes her hands over her hair, 'because they don't like it. But until we know where they're going with this, I don't want to put you in a position of having to respond to questions.' She thinks for a moment. 'They haven't arrested you for anything but they do want an interview under caution. If you choose to answer their questions there's no adequate preparation I can give you. They will want an account from you and they will test that account very rigorously. It will be produced in court, if things ever get to court. I would only ever encourage a client to answer questions in the dark like this if I was a hundred and ten per cent sure that the account was absolutely watertight and that the police evidence wouldn't compromise it. But if I don't know what they've got, whether it's medical uncertainty or queries about the timing of events, whether there are suspicions of negligence or recklessness, then my advice has to be offer no comment.'

'All right.'

'It won't be easy. And it means you have to answer the same to everything they ask. Some of the questions will be trivial or mundane or obvious, but you still offer no comment. It will feel like a weakness, it will make you feel pathetic.' She looks up at me from under her eyelids, pressing the message home. 'Everybody feels like that. But you just persist. The police will be all sweet reason and they will make you feel ridiculous. They bank on that. And they will try to come between us. They might say I'm giving you poor advice, encouraging you to waste their time. Don't rise to the bait. You're recently bereaved so they know they must tread gently, but it will still feel horrible. Okay?'

Oh, fine and fucking dandy.

'I want to rehearse with you,' she adds.

I stare at her.

'The no-comments. It helps to try it out before you go in.'

She asks the questions and an edge of hysteria creeps up on me as I repeat, 'No comment,' each time. What if I laugh? Cackling inappropriately like some picture-book witch, that'd look really good, wouldn't it?

'Deborah?'

'Sorry, I drifted off.'

'You sure you feel up to this? I can ask for a few days' grace. It's just over two weeks since your husband died – we could raise that as an objection, that you're not fit for interview.'

'No, no, I'm fine.' Why am I so keen to have the interview? I think because it seems the quickest way to get out of the place, to be freed from the confines of the cell and the awful isolation. I will say my no-comments and they will let me go.

'Have you spoken to your children? Do you need to call anyone?'

31

I picture Sophie coming in from school, flushed with the heat, slinging her heavy bag down in the hall, drinking a glass of water, Adam peering into the fridge. 'No, I left a note. I don't want to worry them.'

'They may detain you overnight. They'd have to arrest you first but then you can be held for twenty-four hours.'

Shit. I cover my face with my hands. They are cool, though they feel grimy. If I were at home, I could take a shower, stretch out on our bed (new mattress in case you're wondering. Will that be held against me?) and let the afternoon unspool. Or sit in my workshop and gaze at the bees and the blue tits and the cabbage whites. Let their droning and swooping and flickering fill my mind.

'Don't worry about that yet,' she adds, but now she has warned me I feel it's bound to happen.

'I'll tell them we'll be ready in, say, fifteen minutes. I'll sort out a drink. Tea, coffee?'

I sit up straight, my back rigid like a slab, and take a deep breath, but the air is dry and stale and brings no succour.

Chapter Four

The interview takes place in a small, bland room with oatmeal-coloured walls, heavy-duty ribbed grey carpet and recessed halogen lighting – it could be in a hospital or a school, the same anonymity. The light is garish and makes us all look washed out.

The detective, DS Bray, explains the protocol for the session. He makes eye contact a lot and has an easy, confident manner. A little like Neil, in fact, though nowhere near as beautiful. This is how Neil would be when he gave his students' reports at parents' evening – friendly and open and a pleasure to talk to. The police say they will record my interview on video. The camera is already running. He reads the caution, the one from all the telly programmes, and asks if I understand it.

He begins commiserating with me on Neil's death, he understands what a difficult time it must be, sorry to intrude, but they would really like to hear my account of that day. Perhaps if I start from the evening before? How was Neil then?

I hesitate. 'No comment.' My voice sounds hollow. He's not put off by this: he must have been expecting it, though his colleague, a scratchy-looking man with dry skin, rolls back his shoulders, betraying irritation.

'Your husband Neil was suffering from motor neurone disease?'

'No comment.'

'How long since his diagnosis?'

A year and nine months. 'No comment.'

'How long had you been married?'

Had, as though the marriage ended with Neil's death. We still are, I want to tell him. If Neil had lived we would have reached twenty-four years this September. Twenty-four years and he's still my husband. I long to tell the man that, to prove the longevity of our relationship. 'No comment.'

Ms Gleason said it would be hard but there is worse to come. 'Was it a happy marriage?'

My throat swells. 'No comment.'

'You cared for him as his health declined.'

'No comment.'

'Was he on any medication?'

'No comment.'

'How was he that morning?'

'No comment.'

'Could he work?'

Neil, his lovely long legs, they could no longer bear his weight. He'd been so tall and strong, able to carry me. I'd revelled in his strength. My voice falters: 'No comment.'

'You have a son – Adam?'

'No comment.'

He makes me negate everything about my life. I hate him for it. And I feel craven. Unable to own the circumstances of who I am, what I am. His tone is measured and warm, but the process is brutal. Each question is a blow disguised as a caress.

'And a daughter, Sophie?'

Oh, Sophie, Sophie. My lovely girl. I should have cuddled her this morning – even if she didn't want to talk surely a hug would have helped. A pause, my mouth waters and my eyes sting. I can feel the pressure as the tip of my nose reddens. I swallow hard.

'This isn't really helping us, Deborah.' He is a sensible parent, a concerned form tutor. With ghastly inappropriateness I remember a joke Jane told me. About the inflatable boy who sticks a drawing pin in his foot and is called to see the headmaster. 'You've let us all down,' the head tells him, 'you've let me down, you've let the school down and most of all you've let yourself down.'

I blurt out a noise, a laugh or a sob. It doesn't matter, does it?

'If we can just hear your account of what happened to Neil it might help answer some of the inconsistencies we've come across. We're as eager as you are to see this sorted out.'

My solicitor chips in – can she smell me weakening? 'My client does not want to comment.'

'You said previously that you discovered your husband at three o'clock and couldn't rouse him. Is that correct?'

'No comment.'

How does he know this? Then I remember the comic-book-hero policeman, with the wide jaw and narrow forehead, who called while the ambulance was there, making notes at our kitchen table. What else did I say?

'No comment.'

'Did you give your husband any medication of any sort that day?'

'No comment.'

'Was he in pain?'

I don't like to think of Neil in pain. And it didn't often happen. The muscles became progressively weaker, turning from sinew to sponge as they lost the capacity to communicate with the brain. The pain wasn't physical.

'No comment,' I say tightly.

He takes a sip of water from the cup at his side. He's left-handed; he wears a plain gold band on his ring finger.

'I don't know whether your solicitor has explained to you how a jury might interpret your choice to remain silent.'

The word 'jury' sends my blood pressure sky high, a tightening of my skin, my pulse stammering. I want to run – I want to hurl my chair aside and fling open the door and pelt down the street, through the park, across the main road, on and on, away. Find somewhere safe, somewhere for Neil and me, where nobody can bother us.

Ms Gleason jumps in. 'My client is exercising her right to remain silent under advisement.'

'Did you love your husband, Deborah?'

He waits. My jaw is locked. My tongue stiff, pressed against my palate. My teeth imprinting scallops in the edges of my tongue. I force my teeth apart. 'No comment.' But I cannot hold myself together. I break down and Ms Gleason makes them agree to a break until I am less distressed. I'm crying for Neil because I miss him so. I'm noisy and messy and my nose is running and I don't give a damn.

'They seem interested in his medication,' Ms Gleason tells me, once we are alone. 'There may be something from the post-mortem that they've yet to disclose. Was Neil on regular medication?'

I want to say no comment. How much to tell her? Can I trust her?

'He'd been on anti-depressants.'

'He was depressed because of the illness?'

Stupid question. 'Yes.' I'd tried to keep my voice even.

'Anything else?'

'He'd become breathless, and had quite a lot of muscle pain. The GP had put him on liquid painkillers for that. Morphine.'

'He was self-medicating?'

'Yes.'

'Where did you keep the medicines?'

'His bedside.'

'So they were accessible to him. Is it possible Neil self-administered an overdose?'

'It's possible,' I say, my knees pressed tight together, toes curled, gripping the floor.

'You didn't give him anything that morning?'

'No. Just some wine at lunchtime.'

There is a knock at the door and she goes to see who it is. A respite. Exhausted, I slump in my chair. She turns back into the room and says she will be away for a few minutes. Do I need anything?

A *deus ex machina*, ta. I shake my head.

She is back in ten minutes. She takes a moment to settle her file and gather her thoughts. 'The police conducted a second post-mortem.'

I'm not sure how I'm supposed to react. Is this a good thing? She sees I'm confused, places her palms on her knees. She has large hands but slender wrists. In fact, she is scrawny, but for those mitts.

'They wanted to confirm the findings of the first. In a case like this we can opt to have an independent post-mortem carried out – if we don't trust their findings.'

What have they found? I don't trust myself to ask. She carries on talking but I'm imagining Neil, his

37

chest cracked open, his organs weighed and measured. Not twice but three times. Of course, he's not there any more: his body is a shell.

'Okay, we have partial disclosure of the postmortem reports. It's as I thought. Potentially fatal levels of morphine as well as alcohol in the blood. Now, we can get our own medical expert to interpret the results – it may be, for example, that motor neurone disease affects the body's ability to process the drugs. The levels may have built up over time – that's a fairly clumsy example but you see what I'm getting at?'

I nod.

'Right.' She puts her hands on her waist, straightens up. 'They want a second interview. It's half past six now. They have to allow you eight hours' rest plus a meal break so they can't go on very long. And I advise you to maintain your right to remain silent.'

I let my eyes close, hoping to summon some energy from somewhere. She touches my hand. 'I could do with another cuppa. You, same again?'

'Thanks.'

Sophie would be doing her homework in front of *Hollyoaks*.

'Will they let me go home tonight?'

'I don't know. It's hard to tell.'

'If I explain,' I begin, my voice shaky, 'give a proper statement . . .'

'I wouldn't recommend that. Any small variation in what you say could be catastrophic. We still don't have full disclosure. You'd be putting yourself in a very vulnerable position.'

'And I'm not already?'

She regards me for a moment. 'This could be

much worse. The caution's there for a reason. Anything you say, that means *anything*, can be used against you. To give a statement now would be nothing short of reckless.'

I surrender to her argument.

'Can you call my daughter, tell her I'm delayed, legal stuff to do with—' I can't finish.

'I'll be discreet.'

I know now. Something's tilted. Like the sheen on two-tone fabric shifting, the other colour to the fore. They are going to keep me here.

We are in the same interview room. I have been no-commenting for maybe an hour. All of me is weary from the soles of my feet to my scalp. The detective has maintained his cheery disposition but his colleague, scratchy DC Mercer, has been asking the questions this time. He has a more brittle edge to him. A note of incredulity taints his queries.

'And you have no idea how your husband could have administered such a high dose of morphine?'

'No comment.'

'You made no attempt to revive your husband. Why was that?'

'No comment.'

But it is DS Bray who weighs in with the next evidentiary disclosure. See how I'm picking up the jargon. A bombshell to you and me. 'The post-mortem shows signs of petechial haemorrhaging – that is damage to the blood vessels in the eyes – and fluid in the lungs. This is consistent with suffocation.'

The air in the room hangs still. The camera whirrs in the silence. I feel the pulse jump in my throat. The Furies have found me, the daughters of the night. They know I have blood on my hands and they are coming. With snakes hissing through their hair and blood dripping from their eyes, the three of them will hound me to insanity.

The detective tilts his head to one side, his eyes soft, open, inviting my confidence. If I talk, he's saying, if I just talk to him, then all will be well.

'I did not harm my husband. I love him.'

Ms Gleason scrambles to shut me up. 'Deborah! I'd like a word with my client in private, please.'

The detective agrees.

We leave the room and are taken into the adjoining one. She closes the door behind me. There's an astringent taste in my mouth, chemical, the smell of pear-drops. When did I last eat? I can't remember. Ketones, they call it, when the body is depleted and draws on fat reserves. I had it in my urine when I was giving birth to Adam. We'd bought glucose tablets to keep my reserves up but I couldn't keep anything down.

Ms Gleason takes a full breath and sighs it out. She stretches her arms up, clasps her hands behind her neck and stretches. Then drops them. 'We still haven't full disclosure,' she says, 'but the drugs in his bloodstream and the petechial hae-morrhaging are strong forensic evidence that this was not a natural death. Is there anything you want to revise from the account you gave me earlier today?'

'No.'

'Okay.' She nods. 'Then it's imperative that you do not offer any comment in there. Now more than ever.'

'Yes. Sorry.'

'You feel all right to carry on?'

They want to interview me a third time. Magic

40

number three – we all know that: sisters, princes, witches, curses, wishes, betrayals.

When we resume there's a change in the atmosphere, a sparkle of new-found energy from the detectives. Perhaps they've snatched a meal, taken a turn in the fresh air. Had an ice-cream or freshly ground coffee.

Detective Sergeant Bray leans forward. 'Deborah, we want you to tell us what happened in your own words.'

'No comment.'

'Did you give Neil morphine, with or without his knowledge?'

'No comment.'

'Did you do anything to deprive him of oxygen – for example, holding a pillow to his face?'

'No comment.'

He pulls a face, rueful, and sits back, his fingers flat against the edge of the table. 'Deborah Shelley, I am charging you that on the fifteenth of June 2009 you did murder your husband Neil Draper. You do not have to say anything but it may harm your defence if you do not mention when questioned something which you later rely on in court. Anything you do say may be given in evidence. Do you understand the charge?'

The words won't come.

He repeats the question.

There are wings beating in my chest and the chill of stone in my bowels.

'Yes,' I whisper.

'Is there anything you wish to say?'

'No.'

* * *

It was still light, the world gold-drenched with sunset when we arrived at the prison. I was stunned, a ball of static in my head that made it impossible to think clearly.

At the main gate, we were taken from the van one by one. The guards exchanged forms and I was asked to confirm my name and date of birth. The entrance to the complex was a big metal gate and gatehouse. Fences ran off either side, cream-coloured steel mesh topped with coils of razor wire.

A prison officer led me through to the reception area, unlocking and relocking a series of doors. There, I was met by two other officers, women. Again I had to give my name and date of birth.

'Have you been to prison before?' PO Vernon, asked me, various forms spread out in front of her.

'No.'

'Every time you enter or leave the prison we have to do a full search. Please put your clothes in the basket here. Socks and shoes in here. Your bag on the side there.'

My fingers trembled and I wanted to cry. I removed everything until I stood naked before them.

'Now walk in a circle.'

I did. My face burning, my pulse quick and uneven. I was so thirsty. And horribly aware of the eyes watching.

Everyone was very matter-of-fact and workaday about this process because it was their daily work. But me, I was drowning. Anxiety prickled my every pore. I was hot with shame and stiff with apprehension. My muscles twitched and shivered without control.

One of the women moved to my clothes and looked through them, holding them up to the light of the window, checking seams and pockets, shaking them. Then she examined my shoes.

The officer told me I could get dressed and asked my dress size. They gave me a change of clothes – briefs, bra and T-shirt, tracksuit bottoms and sweatshirt. Casual, anonymous garb. When I finished, they asked me to sit down.

'You get a towel and soap.' PO Vernon passed them to me. 'Do you need any sanitary supplies – Tampax or towels?'

'No.' It was two years since I'd had a period.

She poured the contents of my bag out on the table. 'There are some items that are prohibited,' she told me. 'They will go on your property card and be kept for you, until your release.'

She set aside my mobile phone, money and credit cards, paracetamol and lip salve. 'We can't allow any cosmetics in,' she explained. 'Some of the women conceal drugs in them. You can buy some here once you're settled.'

She also picked up the photograph of the four of us taken just before Neil got ill.

'Why can't I keep that?' I asked.

'Nothing allowed if it has your face on it. It could be copied, used to fake ID. You can have them send in some other photos from home. Everything will be checked before you get it.'

They let me keep my wedding ring.

'Do you smoke, Deborah?'

'No.'

She made a note on one of the forms.

'Are you a drug-user?'

'No.'

'Are you currently on any medication?'

'No.'

'Do you have any existing medical conditions?'

'No.'

'Do you suffer from any of the complaints on this list?'

She passed me a sheet, which I read through. It reminded me of the permission slips we had to fill in for the children's school trips. Asthma, diabetes, epilepsy.

'Sign here for the property we've taken.'

I wrote my name.

PO Vernon held out a plastic card to me. 'This is for the phone. There's two pounds' credit already on it. You can make a brief call to let your family know where you are.'

They took me through, locking and unlocking doors, and across the grounds to another building. There I waited behind two other women until I could use the phone. It was noisy: there were lots of women milling about, talking loudly, snatches of raucous laughter. People were glancing my way, a new face. I felt disoriented, shaky and exposed.

Adam answered the phone. 'Mum?'

'Adam, I'm . . . erm. Listen, love, I want you to call Grandma, okay? Ask her to come over.'

'Why? Where are you? Are you still at the police station?'

'I'm in prison, in Styal.'

'Fuck. Why? Because of Dad?'

Did I even answer his questions? I don't know.

'Is Sophie there?'

'She's in the shower.'

Disappointment weighed me down. I longed to hear her voice, picture her disconcerted but determined to manage. It probably wasn't fair but I was hoping she would make me feel better. 'Tell her I'm fine. You both look after yourselves. And will you ring Jane and explain to her? The number's on the thing in the kitchen.'

'Mum, it's going to be all right, isn't it?' Was he trying to reassure me or asking me? 'How long are you going to be there?'

'I don't know. I have to go to court in the morning. They might give me bail. I'd better go now. I love you.'

I was still in shock. People had to repeat things to me before I grasped what they were saying. My knees were weak and I worried that I might throw up, though there was nothing much to throw as I hadn't managed to eat anything for hours.

As a novice, I was put into a special unit called the First Night Centre. It was designed to give new prisoners extra care and support but I was so bewildered to find myself locked up that I was unable to pay much heed to such distinctions.

I shared a room with a slight, dark-skinned woman who spoke no English. I don't know where she was from, Africa perhaps. When I made attempts to find out her name, she just shook her head. We spent the time silent, each in our own cocoon of despair, numb and unresponsive. Everything around us was out of proportion, escalated like in a fever. The level of noise was debilitating: the hard surfaces amplified the sound of chairs scraping, gates clanging, coughs and shouts and canned television laughter. The smells, of women and food and unfamiliar toiletries, were overpowering. The ceilings were too low, the lights brash, the colours sickly and unsettling. When I touched the plastic chair in my room, an electric shock bit my fingers.

If they'd employed me I could have shown them how to use natural materials to absorb the sound and vibration, reduce the amount of static. Soften the lighting with daylight bulbs to give an easier spectrum, less tiring for everyone. Pick colours to soothe the eyes and ease the emotions.

The day after, I appear in the magistrates' court. There are three people sitting at the bench. I confirm my name and address and date of birth. The charge is read out and my solicitor says I am not entering a plea. She asks them to consider bail. The magistrate in the middle looks to her colleagues and a couple of whispers are exchanged. Then she straightens up, presses her lips together briefly before replying. 'Given the seriousness of the charges involved we will not be granting bail. The accused will be held on remand until the preliminary hearing next week.'

They send me back to prison.

Chapter Five

S o today, nine months after, I am being tried in the Victorian Court at Minshull Street Crown Court. There are two Crown Court buildings in the city. This one's not far from Piccadilly station. Handy for spectators, if popping into town for a shot of criminal justice is your thing.

As the name implies, it's a traditional set-up: a raised gallery for spectators, dark wood benches and panelling, a high, vaulted ceiling. The combination of pomp and circumstance that the Victorians loved and their careful workmanship. You can see evidence of that in the carvings on the ends of the benches, the crest with the lion and the unicorn high on the back wall.

Being a prisoner, I enter the court up steps that lead from the cells beneath. When I hear the clatter of our shoes on the marble, my thoughts seem to fly apart in fragments, like spilled beads rolling into the shadows, under furniture, out of sight. I cannot remember what the solicitor said. There's an urge to run, to flee or buckle.

The room bristles with attention as I appear. Afraid, I do not dare look round yet. I need to place my feet one in front of the other and turn so as to reach the dock. The usher nods that I may sit and I do, letting my gaze fall on the warm, worn wood of the ledges around me. My cheeks are aflame and my pulse thrums heavy in my neck. There are whispers and muttered conversations and the rustle of papers – all the lawyers have great big folders. They march around with them, in one arm, all importance. Well, it is important, the reports and records and documents that speak to liberty or incarceration.

Little by little, I raise my eyes, glancing to my left, across the people seated in the main well of the court. My barrister, Mr Latimer, the one in charge of my defence, is a bullish man with an unfortunately appointed nose and beefy skin. He stammers but he has a technique for overcoming that in public, a sing-song delivery that reminds me a little of the comedian Kenneth Williams stretching out his time on the radio quiz *Just A Minute*, though Kenneth was way more camp. Beside Mr Latimer is his junior. And beside them my messy solicitor, Ms Gleason, takes her seat. She's the one who's held my hand for all these months. Today the hair has been pulled back in a barrette. She smiles across and nods. She is watching me and the others are talking shop.

Beyond them is the prosecution table. I have already been told about their team but the names escape me now. The main prosecutor is a woman and she has a male aide.

My heart squeezes as my eyes light on Adam in the public gallery. My boy. I am so glad he has come. That seems bizarre. What mother wants her child to see her tried for murder? Next to him, Jane. Jane and I are the same height but she's a bigger build. More padding, she says. She's on a diet every few months and shifts a few pounds. Then it creeps back on. She can't stop smoking either. She's done the lot, everything from patches to acupuncture.

48

I try to smile but my lips jerk about in some ghastly jig. Adam bows his head suddenly, close to tears, I think. Jane gives a wry smile. She has always been there for me. Have I been as good a friend? Jane is giddy, gregarious. She's never really left the hubbub of her childhood, competing with her three brothers for a spot in the limelight. The phrase 'good for a laugh' comes to mind. Not that she is frivolous or shallow, more that she has a ripe sense of humour. She sees the funny side and points it out. People mistake her comic vision for happiness but Jane has had a hard time of it. Since Mack left her she's never found the right man. And she's very lonely. She's a manager in the NHS, her working life a mire of reports and strategies, evaluation and targets. She and Neil had plenty to moan about together, swapping anecdotes of bureaucratic lunacy and governmental folly.

Sophie isn't there, or Veronica or Michael. There are other faces – I'm startled to see two of Neil's colleagues, and people I don't recognize. The gallery is full. I'm quite a draw. Who are all these strangers? What brings them here?

The team have dressed me in mumsy clothes, Marks & Sparks, a plain light blue blouse, navy skirt, opaque tan tights. The skirt rustles against the tights when I walk. I hate these clothes. I'm a fraud. I've never worn things like this in my life. School uniform came closest. But I will do whatever they tell me now. At their mercy. They even brought earrings, small gold studs. My fingers seek out my wedding ring. I twist the familiar smooth metal.

We bought our rings from Lewis's. It's hard to remember now why we got married. It certainly wasn't part of some shared dream of white silk dresses and pageboys and speeches. And we didn't do it to stock up on toasters and tableware, either. I did wear silk – and taffeta – a gorgeous cherry red cocktail dress that I found in a dress agency in Stockport. Neil wore a black suit and shirt and a bolo string tie. He still had his hair long and looked like an extra, a pioneer in some Wild West movie. We got hitched at the register office and only told our families afterwards. They were hugely disappointed. My mother gave a little 'Oh!' of regret on the phone, as though I'd punched her in the stomach, which perhaps I had. And Veronica was furious: the register office ceremony wasn't a union in the eyes of God. But I was a non-believer, with no intention of converting, and Neil had been lapsed for years. Neil told me they tried to keep it all secret from their Catholic friends.

I'd had boyfriends before Neil, I'd even had some after, but sooner or later they had irritated me. The reasons varied, the timescale too, but eventually their childishness, the way they held my hand or their taste in music, the smell of their skin or the pattern of their conversation would pall and then rankle – like grit in my shoe, producing a blister, not a pearl. Soon everything about them would be wrong and I'd be planning my farewell speech.

'You want perfection,' Jane had said, when I was dumping my first boyfriend at uni. 'It's impossible. Give him a bit longer.' She finished rolling a joint, lit it and sucked hard.

'No, I feel trapped. When I think of carrying on I feel panicky.'

She'd shaken her head. 'He's so sweet.'

'It's not enough. I know he's sweet and pretty good-looking, and he's not dumb but ... I can't change how I feel. I can't unthink what I've been thinking about him.'

'Unthink?'

I held out my hand for the joint, the first two fingers splayed. 'Exactly, not possible.'

So when I asked Jane to be a marriage witness for Neil and me, she reminded me of how picky I was. 'What if you go off him?'

'We've lasted six years.' I laughed. 'It's him going off me I'm worried about.'

'You love him more than he loves you.'

'Do I?'

Had that been true? Back then or as time went by? Had the power in the relationship shifted? I wasn't sure. Rather, I thought, the intensity of feeling we had, the desire for love and the need for independence, ebbed and flowed between us like a subtle tide.

Jane was one of our witnesses and Tony Boyd, Neil's old school friend, the other. Tony was a lovely man who could consume more illegal drugs then anyone I've ever met and still acquit himself decently. He'd got hold of cocaine for our wedding party. It was pretty rare then and more expensive too.

We'd all booked into a hotel in the Derbyshire peaks, and once we'd checked in we took a picnic out into one of the deep valleys, still in our finery. The four of us got stoned and went paddling, drank champagne and rolled about in hysterics. We've a handful of photos left from the day – I had my camera with me – but there's only one with all of us in. We roped in a passing hiker who did the honours. I look so young; we all do. The dress, its strappy top and flared skirt, glows against the green of the grass, the colours acidic.

When friends heard we were married, some were quite shocked. They'd assumed we had rejected the institution, that we'd live together in defiance of hidebound rituals. If Neil hadn't proposed perhaps we would have. But I liked my new status. I think I needed the conspicuous commitment, though I kept my own name. And bank account.

Jane once asked me whether I thought Adam's troubles might have been made worse because we'd taken a relaxed approach to drugs, never hiding our own history of experimentation. I gave her question some thought. Had he needed limits that we'd failed to provide? Had he needed different boundaries? But in the end I couldn't see it. If we'd hidden our views and adopted a rigid just-say-no stance, his dabbling would have been even more covert and we'd only have learned later how the drugs were affecting his mental health.

I look across the courtroom at Adam again and try the smile. A little better, perhaps, though Ms Gleason frowns. I am to be the grieving widow for the duration of my trial, a hollow shell of a woman. They have warned me against sly remarks or clever answers. I must show some humility. It's not me, at all.

My brother Martin is not here. I didn't know whether he would come or not. We've grown apart – not that we were ever that close. There was a flurry of contact when Mum was sick. Adam was only a month old when she first saw her doctor about her weight loss. She was dead before he was three. He was a wonderful baby but he never slept and he couldn't bear to be alone. He'd be up at five every day and happy as Larry if he was carried everywhere. It was exhausting. We had a baby sling, and for the first year we lugged him about in it constantly. I remember hoovering with him strapped to my back. Then we bought a back-pack with a frame. Those years were a blur of broken nights and driving back and forth to my mum's, Martin and I conferring over who would do the next hospital visit.

Neil and I were both shattered, ill-tempered with each other, bickering about the chores – all the new ones that came with parenthood. I didn't cut him any slack; he would do everything bar breastfeeding or die trying. I knew other couples where the advent of a baby seemed instantly to dissolve any intentions of domestic parity, to rob them of political intelligence and plunge them back into the stereotypical gender divisions of the fifties. The man was working harder than ever, all the overtime going, quickly losing faith in his skills as a parent; the woman did all the housework, the shopping, cooking, cleaning, the baby. She was up night after night, simmering with resentment and careful not to disturb him because he was tired and he had to go to work the next day. As if child care wasn't twice as demanding.

No, Neil and I worked at it. Some days I'd wait at the front door for him coming in from school, ready to thrust Adam into his arms so I could set off to see my mum – or even so I could just get out into the garden and have ten minutes' peace. I went back to work part time after six months and we took turns dropping Adam at the child-minder. It was shaky for a while, the parent thing, but we made it work. Not rocket science, just a little social engineering. Oh, I know I can be a smug bitch but, hell, I didn't drop my beliefs when I dropped the placenta. I'm proud of what we did. I'm proud that

Sophie and Adam can look at us and know we were both fully involved in their care, their schooling; we both wiped and fed, changed and scolded. We both did the fun stuff too, and there was plenty of that: Play Doh and puddle-jumping, castles made of cardboard, bedtime stories. Huge pleasure. Having children gave me glimpses of my father, rare flashbacks to his whistling, letting me sip the whisky from his glass (it smelt like wee and tasted horrible), him playing the piano in a honky-tonk style and me plonking the black notes, him watching me master my pogo-stick one Christmas morning.

Sophie was born in the shadow of my mother's death and the clamour of Adam's toddlerhood. Either she was born self-contained or she immediately adopted that as a strategy in the face of the competition. As long as she was fed and her nappy was clean, she would watch everything around her with steady interest.

There were times when I felt ripples of guilt that she got so little attention and I would engineer it so Neil could take Adam off somewhere, leaving Sophie and me to ourselves. I would lie down on the floor with her and sing and play. She'd give a gummy smile and gurgle or make little shrieks as she flailed her fists about, but I got the sense that she was just playing along. That it didn't matter to her whether I was giving her my undivided attention or not. That she'd have been exactly the same with a babysitter or Grandma Veronica.

When I tried to explain this to Neil, he gave me an indulgent smile. 'She's a baby! She's just a different character from Adam, thank God. You're used to him, the way he has us running round in circles. She's the second child.'

'Like me. But they're usually more difficult. What if she turns out to be some wilting feeble, Barbie doll, all inept and fluffy?' I speculated.

'By way of rebellion, you mean? I think that's pretty unlikely,' Neil said.

And he was right. She's a little solemn but she's bright and articulate and ferociously independent. As soon as she could dress herself she chose her own clothes. As a four-year-old on holiday she always picked a seat away from us on the coach or bus, quite happy savouring the view.

She made friends at playgroup and nursery but not with the passionate attachment that Adam brought to his alliances. She did well academically and was reading by the time she reached Reception. She seemed to soak it all up effortlessly, while Adam became mute and mutinous if we tried to get him near a book. We had countless meetings with his teachers about his lack of progress.

My girl thrived and I was buoyed by her success and always felt the lifting of my heart, that lightening sensation, when I clapped eyes on her, but I knew she loved her father more than me. Or perhaps her love for him was less complicated. I understand. I made the same differentiation in my feelings for my own parents. My love for my father was visceral, unsullied, simple, direct. But the emotions my mother called up in me were contrary, critical, double-edged. I hated her at times but never my father. Did Sophie learn these patterns from me, or discover them for herself? If Adam had been any different would it have changed the dynamics? Sophie thinks I love Adam best. I don't. I just love him differently. Is it because he's a boy? Or because he's Adam?

None of that differentiation was going to happen when I had children. Boy or girl, they would be treated equally. No gender-based toys or colour-coded outfits, no breastfeeding a boy for longer or over-protecting a girl when she headed for the climbing frame. Any girls I had would be tomboys like me, any boys sensitive and caring. Of course, there's another side to the equation that I hadn't factored in – Adam and Sophie as individuals with personalities and predilections fully formed.

I miss them so. And how much harder must it be for them? Losing Neil and then, before they can get their breath back, I'm gone too. Locked up. It was never meant to be like this. I rage at Neil, floating around in the bloody ether. Well out of it. You're off in your Elysian Fields, mate, but look at us. See where we are? You sacrificed us all. You sorry now?

Chapter Six

It was just before Easter 2007 that Neil first complained of stiffness in his hands and arms. I wasn't very sympathetic. It's the sort of reaction I get myself if I've been doing something that involves a lot of manual work: cutting tiles or screen-printing, repetitive movement that strains the muscles. I said as much but he replied he hadn't been doing any physical jerks. Try paracetamol, I told him.

He didn't go to the doctor until the summer. The GP gave him a course of anti-inflammatory drugs and asked him to come back afterwards. They didn't help.

After his next appointment, when he came home, I could see straight away that something was wrong. His face was sallow and he'd an artless, vulnerable look in his eyes. Sophie was in the kitchen, sorting out ingredients for her food-technology class – pineapple upside-down cake.

I sent a warning glance to Neil, not that he needed telling, and walked after him into the lounge.

We sat down. He looked at me, gave a little 'huff' and swallowed. 'They want to do tests.'

My guts clenched. I assumed he was talking about cancer.

'It could be . . . the weakness, losing control . . .'

I stared at him, the cup he'd smashed, the plates he'd dropped now sinister.

'. . . it might be motor neurone disease.'

Stephen Hawking on *The Simpsons*, wheelchair, robotic voice, head lolling to one side.

'Oh, Neil.' I wrapped my arm around his shoulders. 'It'll be all right,' I said. 'Whatever it takes.'

'There isn't any cure.'

My heart stopped. 'But the treatment, there must be something.' I refrained from mentioning Stephen Hawking – he'd lasted years. Or had he got a different illness?

'Not really,' he said quietly.

I kept still. My mind was scrambling, trying to unpick what he was saying.

'It just has to run its course.'

A deluge of fear, my heart thudding in my chest. This wasn't happening. No. It wasn't true. It was a mix-up, that was all, a silly misunderstanding.

'Oh, Neil. These tests,' I said tentatively, 'it might be something else.' A condition they could treat, a disease they could cure.

'Yes.' He took a shaky breath and then another. He was crying. I'd only ever seen Neil cry three times in our years together: at the birth of our children and when I'd told him about my affair. The sound of him crying was alien to me, the rhythm unfamiliar. I climbed on to his lap, wrapped my arms tight around him, raised one hand to cradle the back of his head. He put his face in the crook of my neck. His tears soaked warm into my T-shirt. He was going to die. How long? I was screaming inside. How long? Ten years? Five?

People talk of a bolt from the blue, of being thunderstruck, and that was how it felt. As though Zeus had hurled his lightning bolts at us, a sickening crack to the skull, a galvanic shock, paralysis and the sun stopped in the sky.

'It might be fine,' I said.

And the lie, the false hope, lay leaden between us.

At the first opportunity I had, when everyone else was out, I went online to find out about the disease. Doctors did not know what caused some people to develop it. It was not a virus and there was only a hereditary link in a very small minority of cases. Each site I logged on to reported the same stark facts: for those people with the most common form of the disease, life expectancy was between two and five years from diagnosis. Neil's muscles would weaken and waste – he would lose ability in his arms and legs first; then chewing, swallowing and speaking would become difficult. As his chest muscles also weakened he would only be able to sip shallow breaths. Eventually his breath would fail.

On the upside, he was not likely to become incontinent or impotent. He could go down fucking, then. He wouldn't go senile either. Although the disease affected the motor nerves that connected the brain to the muscles, the brain itself wouldn't be affected. He'd be fully aware until the end stage. MND is not a painful killer, not like the cancer that riddled my mother and rendered her insensate with pain. MND sounded sly and swift and wilfully random.

As with any new project, I flung myself into research hoping understanding might make me better able to deal with the situation. I read and read, surfing link after link, waiting for obscure medical abstracts to load as pdf files, sussing out books on the disease, startlingly few. But all it did was reinforce my anger, my alarm, each new web page breaking over me, a cascade of rapids, cold and treacherous. Without hope.

Neil's next appointment was with a hospital neurologist. Apparently it isn't easy to diagnose MND in the early stages: the symptoms may be due to other problems, which have to be ruled out. After an examination, a muscle biopsy and an electromyography test to measure muscle strength they might be left with MND. A matter of elimination.

We agreed not to say anything to Adam and Sophie until we knew one way or the other. We were worried about Adam's reaction. Sophie would be devastated but Adam's state of mind was fragile and a shock like that could see him in meltdown again.

As it was he beat us to it.

That Friday night, a few days before Neil had to go for tests, Adam didn't come home. He was sixteen then and had just started back at school. Part of the deal he'd made with us and the counsellor was that he'd be home by midnight or get in touch if not.

That night we lay in bed longing to sleep, taking turns checking the clock. I tried Adam's mobile at twelve fifteen, one thirty and two forty-five. I got up at five. The house was chilly. There's a convector heater in my workshop. I went to get it, half hoping that Adam would be there, spreadeagled on the rug or even huddled on the bench in the garden. A lost key, reluctance to disturb us, the explanation.

There was no Adam. Back in the kitchen, I made coffee with hot milk, then dragged out my breadmaker, dusted it down and sprinkled in dried yeast, filled it with wholemeal flour, adding sunflower seeds, chopped dried apricots and walnut pieces, salt, sugar, olive oil and water.

Neil came down at seven. 'Adam back?'

I shook my head.

'Should we try Jonty?' He was one of the friends who still hung out with Adam.

'It's very early, I'll try at nine.'

Neil stood behind me, wrapped his arms around me and stooped to kiss my cheek. 'He probably got pissed and stayed at someone's house.' He straightened up.

'And lost his phone?' I was more sceptical. And also, if I thought the worst, as I had done all night – the body broken beneath car wheels; the figure, beautiful and bare-chested, falling as he tried to fly; the knife fight after some silly comment; the beating dished out by a gang of hard lads who had sniffed out Adam's middle-class softness – it would not come to pass.

The phone rang. It was Manchester Royal Infirmary. Adam had been admitted to A&E. Unconscious. He'd ingested a cocktail of drugs washed down with vodka. They were pumping his stomach.

When we got there he was awake but very drowsy, looking sheepish and then plain sad when I asked him if he was okay.

'I'm sorry,' he said to us both. There was defeat in his tone, a note that sent a chill through me, as though he'd accepted that it would always be like this. Him messing up, him hurting us, scaring us.

He claimed not to remember anything about the hours before he collapsed.

'Nothing?' Neil said incredulously. 'Not where you were, who you were with?'

Adam shook his head and looked away, his lips parted slightly, his tongue up behind his front teeth: a trick he uses to fight tears. Had he taken the drugs to get off his head or had he wanted to harm himself? The question bored into my brain. It didn't seem fair to ask him yet and I guessed he'd be more likely to lie now, in the immediate aftermath, eager to reassure us and be forgiven. I knew all that but I was so upset I wanted to shake him.

'You promised,' I heard myself saying, 'that if you ever felt at risk . . .'

'Mum, I got trolleyed,' he said. 'That's all, honest. I'm sorry.'

The rest of the weekend I found myself watching Adam, looking for signs of deterioration: was he hanging around the kitchen so he wasn't alone? Was he feeling anxious again? When he stayed at home all day Sunday, was that because he wanted to chill out after Friday's scare or because he was too fearful to leave the house? I asked him if he wanted to see the GP but he shrugged a no. He gave the same response when I offered to contact the counsellor.

Once Sophie knew he was okay, she dealt with the situation by ignoring it: he wasn't going to get any of her attention with his dumb behaviour. She had spent her life being frustrated by Adam, playing together and invariably falling out. Adam always pushed things too far, rebelled; he'd grow bored with whatever game they were playing and want to change the rules; he'd get distracted and start playing something else. Sophie would end up incandescent, in angry tears, vowing never to play with him again. Till next time.

His chaotic behaviour sucked up our attention while her diligence, hard work and successes won way too little recognition. Neil and I often talked of it, as things grew difficult in recent years: how to care for Adam without neglecting Sophie. He saw the same thing with some of the kids at school: that gap between achievement and recognition when another sibling is acting up.

We tried to talk to Sophie about it when Adam first saw the psychiatrist, to explain the situation and apologize for the upheaval, for our distraction, maybe our neglect.

'It's okay,' she reassured us. 'I'm fine.'

'We love you, Sophie,' Neil said.

'I know, Dad. And I'm not a little kid any more. I can see that Adam needs your time.' She was relentlessly self-reliant. But the truth was somewhat different.

One day I found her weeping in her room, face blurred with misery. 'Sophie, what's the matter? What's wrong?'

'I'm sick of it, sick of everything, and Adam and living here. It's all so shitty,' she cried, the words a snarl of hurt.

'What's happened?'

'Your precious Adam happened. I know you love him more than me.'

My heart tore. 'Sophie, that's not true! I swear to you, I love you both. More than anything.'

She gave a shuddery sigh, sniffed and wiped her face. 'I hate it, Mum. Why can't he just be normal and stop messing everything up?'

'Adam—' I took a breath, meaning to try to answer but her question was rhetorical.

She went on, 'They're all talking about it at school. I'm not me any more, I'm just Adam Shelley's saddo sister.'

'Sophie, you are not a saddo. You're a wonderful—'

'Mum, don't.'

Tears burned in my eyes. 'Hug?' I offered, my voice too squeaky by half.

She gave a little shrug, noncommittal. I moved in and wrapped my arms around her. Kept quiet. In a few moments she spoke: 'When's Dad back?'

'Soon.' Could he make it better? 'I'll tell him to come up and see you?'

'Yeah.'

'Okay. It won't always be like this, you know. It'll change. Everything changes.'

She nodded. 'Yeah.' A small voice.

'You want anything? Hot chocolate?'

'No, just tell Dad.'

'I will.'

She always wanted her father. He was her rock. And now he's gone. I have taken him from her.

Neil persuaded me not to hang around while he was in having the tests done. He wouldn't get the results then, and most of the day he'd be sitting about waiting. He promised to call when he was done.

It was late afternoon when I picked him up. He didn't say much about the day, just some quip about hospitals being no place for sick people. He had a little plaster on his arm where they'd taken the biopsy. They wanted him back in a week's time for the results. 'I'll come with you,' I said.

Did the days go fast or slow? They rippled, concertina-like, altering speed. The sooner the days passed, the sooner we would know.

That winter I was working on a refurbishment project for a health spa. They were building an extension and it was a good time to revamp their interior, which was looking jaded: Roman mosaics and friezes, pillars and arched doorways. I'd been playing around with something minimalist, using Japanese influences. Any materials would have to be high spec, to cope with the heavy traffic and, of course, the effects of steam and chlorine in the pools area, without looking industrial. Calm, comfortable and clean: these were the words I used with the client during my first presentation.

The day of Neil's follow-up appointment I drove out to the spa, near Knutsford, for a meeting and spent the morning with the manager and the architect. It was frustrating: the manager was eager to shave off costs but not happy to compromise on quality, and the architect was dying to get away.

I tried not to get too sharp even though I felt the manager was wasting our time. At one point I suggested he redraw his budgets and give me a new figure to work to, if he was having second thoughts, which prompted the architect to complain about delays. The manager backtracked and blethered on. My husband might be dying, matey, I thought. I don't give a flying fuck for your yardage problems. But I smiled thinly and did my job. After all, if Neil was dying, I'd need all the work I could get.

Of course, the proper jargon, as I learned on the Internet, is living with MND, not dying from it. Like AIDS. Adam had a T-shirt around that time, black and voluminous with a slogan in scratchy white lettering: '*Life – a death sentence*'. That soon got lost in the wash.

At the hospital, I saw Neil before he saw me in the waiting room (ghastly orange chairs designed to deaden the bum and weaken the spirit). He was reading, his head tilted to the side, legs stretched out, ankles crossed. Beautiful. If I hadn't known him, I'd have thought the same: the shape of his face, his frame, dark hair, inherently attractive. I didn't need to get close enough to smell his pheromones.

He sensed me watching, looked up and smiled, closed his book. Unhooked his ankles and sat up straighter. I reached him, sat beside him, unbuttoning my coat, unwrapping my scarf: I was hot after the frosty air outside.

'They're running late,' he said.

'Great – gives you a bit more time, then.' I thought I'd gone too far but his eyes crinkled at the joke.

'Good meeting?' he asked.

'Crap. He wants to cut corners without it showing. I told him we need to move forward by next week or he'll lose the slot, another client waiting, bigger.'

'Have you?'

'Nope.'

'Neil Draper,' the nurse called.

The consultant, Mr Saddah, was a really nice man. He took his time, answered all our questions, even if most of the answers started off with *it's hard to say* or *it varies a great deal.* He said eminently sensible things about support and resources and dealing with it as a family and how MND progressed.

His words streamed past me, lapping around me like channels of water carving the sand. I gripped Neil's hand and tried to stop time.

The judge comes in and everybody stands. A wave of panic washes through me, blurring my vision. I blink hard. Jane is saying something to Adam. It's lonely here, lonely and exposed. Did Martin think of coming and decide against it? If my dad had lived would he have come to show support? I'm glad my mum's not still around, not here today, anyway. Because her reaction to all this, her eloquent unhappiness would give me more of a burden to carry. Happy birthday, Deborah. Happy bloody birthday.

Chapter Seven

'Call Deborah Shelley.'

I stand in the dock, beside me a guard from the court. The clerk asks, 'Are you Deborah Shelley?'

'Yes.'

Do they ever get it wrong? No, not me, mate. Whoops, sorry, you should be next door with the traffic offences . . .

'Deborah Shelley,' she reads from a notepad, 'you are charged that on the fifteenth of June 2009 you murdered Neil Draper at 14, Elmfield Drive, contrary to common law. Are you guilty or not guilty?'

'Not guilty.' My voice sounds thin, swallowed by the space.

The judge is exactly how you would imagine a judge to be: old, white, male. The only deviation from the stereotype, a northern accent. He has wild white eyebrows and a pleated face. He leans forward slightly and asks the clerk to fetch the jury. They file into the court and make their way to the jury box. Here they are sworn in, each person putting their hands on the Bible (no one chooses the Qur'ān even though two are Asian and one is black) and promising to try the case faithfully and reach a true verdict on the evidence presented. Three of them choose to affirm rather than use a holy book. I find it depressing that nine are believers. But perhaps their faith is the church-once-a-year variety, the sort of people who tick 'Christian' on the hospital admission form because they can't bear to tick none. If any of them are fundamentalists, rabid right-to-lifers, it bodes ill for me.

The clerk repeats the charge against me to the jury.

The judge explains to the jury and the court that we will hear first from the prosecution who will make an opening statement. He consults with the barristers about a probable time to break for lunch. The exchanges are eminently civil and the reality that I am in the dock for murder seems preposterous set against this mannered chat. I detect warmth in the judge's voice, perhaps down to those Lancashire vowels, and a benign paternalism in his manner. It shouldn't make a difference: he is meant to be impartial, his role simply to apply the processes of the law, but had he seemed waspish or frosty I would have been more fearful. After all, the jurors will look to him for guidance, they will drink in all his non-verbal communication. And if I am not acquitted he will set my sentence.

The prosecuting barrister stands up and introduces herself. 'Your Honour, ladies and gentlemen of the jury, my learned friends, I, Briony Webber, appear for the prosecution, and my learned friend, Mr John Latimer, appears for the defence.'

I guess she is in her early forties. She's extremely tall, like a seedling gone rampant, but she carries it well. No stoop. Her wig looks fresh and tidy, whereas Mr Latimer's has the appearance of a scrap of sheep's wool caught on barbed wire.

Miss Webber has a clear voice, a fluency with words as she lays out my crime for the court.

'In the dock today stands Deborah Shelley. She is here accused of the gravest crime, that of murder. The murder of her husband Neil, a loving son, a caring father, a valued colleague. The case for the prosecution is that Deborah Shelley set out to kill Neil Draper, in the full and clear knowledge that what she was doing was wrong. We shall show how she attempted to cover up her crime, lying to her family and lying to the police. We shall show how, faced with incontrovertible evidence that she had poisoned and then suffocated her husband, she continued to lie. Neil Draper was unwell. He suffered from motor neurone disease. He had a limited life expectancy. It is our contention that Neil Draper asked his wife to help him end his life prematurely and that she complied. We shall call witnesses who will testify that Deborah Shelley was functioning well in the days before this tragic death, witnesses who will report her being in good spirits, able to socialize, to work. We will call a psychiatric expert who has examined Ms Shelley and who will tell you that the defence of diminished responsibility is a sham. Ms Shelley knew exactly what she was doing that day last June.'

She gives the word 'Ms' a little buzz, a hornet's touch.

'She set out to end Neil Draper's life and she succeeded. She then covered her tracks, employed deceit and a web of lies to try to convince the world that this was a natural death. There was nothing natural about this death, there was nothing natural in her behaviour. This woman lied to her own children, to the parents of the man she killed, to the authorities, and she persists in her lies even as she stands before you today.'

Holding my head high, fighting the urge to bow, aware of the tension in my throat and my jaw, I watch the jury, their eyes flicking from the prosecutor to me. Examining my hair, my clothes, making assessments already. Forming first impressions. Snotty cow, not even a Mrs, unnatural, how could she do that?

The day the magistrates refused me bail and remanded me to Styal, I rang home again. The desire to hear their voices, to make sure they were coping, was all-consuming. Sophie answered the phone.

'Sophie, it's Mum. Are you all right, darling?'

There was a pause and then she said in a low, trembly voice, 'You shouldn't have done it, Mum.'

My heart racketed in my chest. I felt the blood drain from my cheeks and the cold steal into my bowels. 'Sophie, I never meant to hurt—'

There was a clatter as she let go of the phone. She believed what they were saying. She trusted them, not me. I longed to call her back to the phone, to try and explain. Her censure was understandable: she'd adored her father and now she thought I had taken him away from her. I felt unsteady, the love and concern I'd anticipated from Sophie snatched away. The chance we might console each other shattered.

A few seconds later, Adam came on. 'Mum?' He was subdued.

'Adam, I'm sorry for all this. I need you to be strong now, look after yourself.'

'Yeah.'

'You can go to Grandma and Grandpa's.'

'I'll stay. Sophie's going.'

I'd a mad image of Adam opening up the place for a house party. It'd be great weather for it, tents in the garden and a barbecue, giant spliffs and too much booze.

'Talk to Jane, if you need anything.'

'Cool. Can I come and see you?'

I couldn't speak for a moment. Tears burned the back of my eyes. I didn't want to break down on the phone, didn't want him to have to cope with that on top of everything else. 'Yes, please. I'll find out what we have to do. You'll need to go shopping – make sure you eat something.'

'Course.' There was a pause. Then he went on, 'Jonty's going to this festival in Spain – there's a load of them going. I . . .' He offered it as something to talk about, then realized it might seem tactless.

'That sounds great. You thinking of going?'

'Maybe.'

'When is it?'

'Middle of August.'

'Good.' I'll still be in here, I thought. Ms Gleason had told me it would be between six months and a year till my trial started. 'You could take the little tent.'

'Yeah.'

'Well, I'd better go. I love you. I'll ring you about the visit.'

'Cool.'

'Bye-bye.' My hand ached from gripping the phone.

That night as I lay in my bed, Sophie's words tore through me, again and again. *You shouldn't have done it, Mum.*

The prison isn't one big building, as I'd imagined. Instead two rows of large red-brick villas slope down avenues lined with oak and lime and beech trees towards the wing at the bottom. Most women live in the houses, which were built as Victorian orphanages. Nowadays the villas all take their names from venerable women, good role models for us: Brontë, Gaskell, Pankhurst. Though when I think about it Pankhurst spent quite a bit of time behind bars, being force-fed for her trouble.

The more dangerous prisoners, those with chronic addiction problems and those in for the most serious offences, live on the wing. Although my charge was up there with the worst, once I had been assessed and deemed to pose no threat to the other women, I was allocated a room in one of the houses near the bottom of the hill close to the wing.

The majority of the women 'pad up', two or four to a cell, in the houses. When they sent me to Shapley House – this villa is named after a pioneering radio broadcaster who lived in Manchester – I was put in one of the small single rooms, a privilege, and I was hugely relieved that I didn't have to put up with someone else's taste in television night after night, that I didn't have to lie awake listening to another woman breathe and dream.

We share a bathroom, one to each floor, and I can't get used to sharing with strangers, never time to indulge in a long shower or a hot soak, someone always knocking on the door. I dart in and out when I have to and never linger. The single cell gives me the option to retreat. That's all I want to do. To withdraw into my shell like a hermit crab. To creep back along the crevices of memory.

My 'pad', as I learned to call it, measures ten foot by eight. Beneath the protector, the mattress is plastered with graffiti, crude and poignant: *Cilla4Shawn, I suck cock, help me, Kimberley Smith died age 3 my angel in heaven.* There is a moulded block covered with a speckled rubber coating for the mattress to rest on. I once used some of the same material for a maternity unit. It copes well with heavy human traffic, is fireproof, will easily repel blood or urine or vomit and withstands accidental or malicious damage. An important aspect in prison. My pad also has a set of built-in shelves and a cupboard made of the same tough material, a chair, a telly and a sink. Its redeeming feature is the big lime tree outside the window. Its limbs sashay in the wind. I lie on my bed and gaze at it. Listen to the rooks cawing, the 'teacher teacher' song of great tits and the roar of jets. We are close to the airport, below the flight path, and the planes overhead are a reminder of freedom, of escape, of holidays. And beyond all those sounds are the haunting calls of women yelling from the wing. Like a chorus of sergeant majors, their plaintive conversations bellow across the spaces between the cells, between the wing and the houses. That sound more than anything is Styal. I can never make out the words. No one ever calls for me. But through the mangled yells and shouts, news travels: of private affairs and public tragedies. Of the woman who set her hair on fire and the one who's got a release date and the one whose child has been taken away in the mother and baby unit.

And at night, at the bottom of the hill, I am close enough to hear the clamour that erupts at intervals from the wing. The sudden alarms and bursts of activity, shouts and feet kicking at doors – 'Come on, Keely, come on, girl, come on' – as Keely or Jen or Emma or Kim is discovered hanging or bleeding or comatose. Night after night, the same deadly dance.

* * *

74

Ms Gleason came to see me the day after I had been remanded without bail. She told me we would be back for a preliminary hearing in a week – and that a timetable would be set for the trial. Then we had six weeks until the plea and case management hearing. This sounded like so much jargon to me. I asked her to explain. 'That's when you enter your plea to the charge, guilty or not guilty. It's also when we adjust the timetable and agree on dates for the exchange of papers, the preparation of reports and so on.'

She placed her palms against the edge of the table, fingers splayed, edged forward towards me. 'We need to run a defence. It'll be my job to prepare a brief for your barrister. That will include our instructions, what we want them to do for you and all the information they need to fight your case. The barrister will be there when you plead and again for the trial. Between now and then I expect them to come and see you to go over statements. And I'll chivvy them if they don't.'

'Don't they always?'

She gave a little snort of amusement. 'You'd be surprised. I've had plenty of clients meet their brief on the day the trial starts. But a serious case like this, they'll want to put the time in. There's a QC I know who'd be excellent. Meanwhile we need to consider your defence. The prosecution have substantial medical evidence, which they will produce to back up the murder charge. But we can use our own medical experts to raise doubts about each element of that evidence. Considering the drugs, for example, we might argue that Neil took the medication himself, without your knowledge.'

This was our fall-back position but now I wonder if it's going to fly. The police asked me about smothering. If they can prove I did that, they will see he had help. Should I tell Ms Gleason the truth now? It's hard to think clearly. I almost miss what she is saying.

'Or that his condition led to a build-up of toxins in his system. If his metabolism was impaired then the drugs might not have been processed as quickly as in a healthy person.' She held up her hands in warning. 'These are just examples off the top of my head. Medical advice would help us formulate the best defence.'

The prison meeting room where we sat was pleasantly warm and brightly lit but I felt feverish, as though I could no longer maintain my temperature. My skin was clammy and my back ached. From somewhere else in the prison I could hear the banging of doors and the occasional voices raised in greeting or farewell. Guards coming and going, I thought, or inmates going for their recreation. Are we inmates? Or prisoners? What's the correct term for us? There was a glimmer of hope in what she was telling me: if we could use science and doctors to explain away those post-mortem results then I might have a chance.

'We would also need to produce expert testimony to give alternative explanations for the lung damage, perhaps as a consequence of the drugs, or his condition. He had trouble breathing?'

'Yes. We knew it would get worse.'

We had a kit from the Motor Neurone Disease Association for just such an eventuality. When I first read about them in the literature that, more than anything else, brought home the inexorable horror of Neil's future.

'And it may well have,' she said. 'Then there's the haemorrhaging in the eyes. I've had a quick look into this and I think we can easily dismiss that – in some people a heavy sneezing fit can cause the same outcome.' She smiled and sat back. 'We have a number of options. At one end we have a clear not-guilty defence that relies on us countering the medical evidence – and it's crucial for you to remember that we do not have to persuade the jury of how Neil died. We simply have to cast doubt on the prosecution's version of events.'

I tried to grasp this: she was saying they could argue away the symptoms of suffocation. So, if I told her Neil had taken the overdose, that I'd found him and hidden everything . . .

'To convict you, the jury must have no doubts about the prosecution case.'

'What are the other options?' I asked.

'Reckless or negligent manslaughter. We would argue that you administered the drugs to Neil but without any malice aforethought. You increased the doses or gave extra tablets for the best of intentions, not realizing the risk.'

I shook my head. This muddied the waters. And it's not me – I'm not some ditzy wife who gets the pills mixed up. 'I didn't do that.'

Ms Gleason nodded. 'Good. I'm confident we can cast doubt on the forensic evidence, which would leave us with witness testimony.'

My stomach spasmed as I imagined Veronica on the witness stand, talking about Neil, rewriting the story of our marriage from her perspective. Veronica, who believes unflinchingly in the sanctity of life. There had already been features in the papers, laden with assumptions, portraying me as some euthanasia campaigner and Neil as some martyr to the cause of assisted suicide. A knee-jerk reaction to news of my arrest and Neil's condition. It was not a mantle I wanted.

I didn't help Neil die. I found him dead. I'd no idea. It wasn't a mercy killing. That was what I'd been telling everyone. Even my lawyer. What happened was personal, and particular to the two of us, to our situation. I could hear Neil teasing me: 'You used to think the personal was political.' But I didn't know any more. I didn't know whether what I had done was right, you see. And it was certainly not something I was prepared to wave banners and go to gaol for.

'I don't know yet who they are calling as witnesses,' Ms Gleason went on, 'but I'll set the wheels in motion for our medical experts and I'll have a think about who we call for the defence. As soon as I have any news, I'll be back. Have you any questions?'

I was wordless, out of my depth on the high seas. Was silence the safest option? She sounded so confident. Would she find a medical expert who could explain away Neil's death? Perhaps we could win this and I could keep my secret. I hesitated and missed my chance.

She let the guard know we were finished and said goodbye. She hoped to get back to me in a few days' time.

She was back within twenty-four hours. I was in the common room – feeling awkward and horribly lonely, trying not to make eye contact with any of the women around who all seemed more at home than me, a situation reminiscent of waiting for Adam and Sophie in the school playground – when one of the warders called my name. My cheeks burned as I got to my feet and I saw one young woman nudge her neighbour and whisper something. It only occurred to me then that they knew who I was, why I was there.

The warder took me through to the meeting rooms where I found Ms Gleason. She looked solemn and tired. My stomach knotted.

'Deborah, I have some news, some difficult news. Regarding witnesses.' I stared at her. How could this be any worse?

'Your daughter Sophie is appearing for the prosecution.'

There was a massive thump in my chest. The shock made me cry out. My girl, my Sophie. 'No,' I moaned. 'I don't want her to.' I looked across at Ms Gleason. 'She shouldn't have to. She's sixteen.' I imagined her, brave and scared, in front of all those people. Hurting from her father's death, hurting because she thought I helped him leave her. Angry and mixed up. What would that do to her, to us? 'I don't want her to,' I repeated. 'She's a minor, I'm her only parent.'

'We can't do anything about it, Deborah. Sophie's already made a statement. She contacted the police with her grandmother, on the twenty-fourth of June.'

I froze. Stared at her. Nine days after Neil's death. Before I was arrested. Sophie went to the police. And then they arrested me. Oh, God. The phrase 'turned me in' came to mind. I imagined Veronica fuelling that grief, not from malice, for all we have clashed, but out of her genuine sorrow and outrage at my sin. At my going against God's will and robbing her of Neil. I will lose Sophie, Adam will lose her. How do we ever come back from this? I imagined Sophie's fierce determination, her moral certainty. The way she raises her jaw and stares you down, all conviction and courage. All that ranged against me when I'd had unspoken hopes that she would come round, see sense and deploy that passionate belief on my behalf. Tears slid down my face. I wiped them from my chin. Took a deep breath.

'If I plead guilty, say I did it, that Neil begged me to help him – would she still have to testify?'

Ms Gleason stilled, her face became a mask. 'Probably.'

Oh, no.

'Deborah, you need to be very careful. I can only run a defence based on the account you give me. If you're changing that account then the whole of our defence needs re-examining.'

'But if I say Neil wanted to die, that I did what he wanted—'

'No defence. That's an admission of guilt and a mandatory life sentence.'

'He was terminally ill.'

'They'd lock you up, a life sentence. No alternative.' She said this crisply, surprised I think at my naïvety or maybe at my *volte-face*.

All those myths of lovers torn apart by death: Dido so bereft she stabbed herself and leaped into a pyre, Hero throwing herself from her tower when Leander drowned, Orpheus, torn to pieces, his head severed from his body yet still calling for his beloved Eurydice as he floated down the river. But I'm not going anywhere. My side of the deal is to stay, to hold my resolve, to protect the children from the fallout. And I never imagined this.

'I don't want to stay in prison,' I begged her. 'I don't want Sophie to be a witness.'

'We can't do anything about Sophie. I'm sorry. If

you're changing your story, if you're admitting that you deliberately gave Neil the medication, then there's only one defence possible and that is guilty to manslaughter due to diminished responsibility.'

'What would that mean?'

'We wouldn't need to challenge the medical evidence, the post-mortem report and so on. Our argument would rest exclusively on your state of mind at the time. We would argue that you didn't know what you were doing.'

I wanted to laugh. I'd known exactly what I was doing. 'So, I pretend I was disturbed?'

'No pretence. You were disturbed. The strain of caring for him, other stresses in the family . . .'

She means Adam.

'. . . the situation drove you to behave irrationally, to break the taboos, to break the law.'

'He asked me.'

'And the fact that you did what he asked is proof that you were out of your mind at the time.'

I was Alice in Wonderland. 'And if I stick to denying it all?'

She frowned and ran her hands through her hair, then looked at me directly: her eyes, a caramel brown, a freckle of gold in each iris. Her gaze stark. 'You've given me two versions of events. I cannot lie to the court. I cannot represent you if I believe you intend to lie to the court. If you revert to your original statement and deny involvement I would have to advise you to get a new solicitor.'

She can't leave me! I was as panicked as a small child. I couldn't bear to start again with someone else. 'I want to tell the truth. Neil asked me to be there with him, to help. We talked about it many times. I finally said yes.'

81

She nodded gravely. Sighed. 'One thing you need to be aware of is that the prosecution will make a meal of your change of story. They will use the fact that you lied as a stick to beat you with, to undermine your credibility. But if we know that from the outset, we can do our best to counter it.'

'I'm sorry.' Maybe I should have told the truth straight away but I was hoping they'd let me go, that if I repeated the version of events that Neil and I had settled on often enough, the children would never know he had chosen to leave them and I would not risk prosecution. But it had all fallen apart.

Chapter Eight

B riony Webber calls her first witness. It is our GP, Andy Frame. I like him a lot: he was great with Neil, sensitive but not too sombre. A good bedside manner. He looks a little uncomfortable as he catches my eye on the way to the witness stand. After he has sworn to tell the truth, and confirmed his identity and his role as our GP, she asks him about Neil.

'When did you last see Neil Draper?'

'At the beginning of June last year.'

'And you were sharing his care with the hospital?'

'That's right.'

'How did he seem?'

'He complained of breathlessness.'

'Were you able to help him?'

'I prescribed some morphine. It helps to relax the patient and is often used in the treatment of this disease in its later stages. It is also used in pain management, and in May Neil had reported a worsening of pain in his shoulders.'

'So you had prescribed it before to Mr Draper?'

'Yes, in May.'

I see where she is going now. Laying out how we hoarded the drugs.

'Did you administer the medicine?'

'No, it comes in a liquid form. Neil found that easier to take and he could use it when he felt particularly anxious.'

Or when he was planning to top himself.

'And I'd also supplied an emergency dose in the breathing space kit.'

'Can you explain to us what the breathing space kit is?'

'It's a pack supplied by the Motor Neurone Disease Association. It has instructions for use and drugs to help in an emergency – if a patient is choking, for example. The carers learn how to administer it, so they can use it while waiting for a doctor or nurse to come.'

I examine the jury. Twelve people are an awful lot to get to know. I decide to assign them nicknames or jobs to help me. I christen four of them, all on the front row. Dolly is the woman with too much makeup and a brassy hair-do. The Prof wears tweed and specs and has trouble fitting his long legs into the space. Besides him sits Callow Youth: he can't be much older than Adam but he dresses very conventionally. I imagine he does a job where he has to conform and not frighten the customers; perhaps he goes door to door trying to get people to switch fuel suppliers. Next to him is Mousy, she's middle-aged and has given up: shapeless clothes and lank hair. Trinny and Susannah would have a field day giving her a TV makeover. She looks tired – I wonder if she has a hard life.

Miss Webber turns Andy Frame's attention to me. 'You were also Deborah Shelley's doctor?'

'That's right.'

'And when did you last see Ms Shelley?'

'In October 2008.'

'You didn't see her at all in 2009?'

'No, not on her own behalf.'

I stiffen, waiting for him to mention Adam's name. This is one of the worst things – not being able to insulate the children from it. But he continues: 'I saw her on occasions with Neil.'

'As her GP, what would you deduce from her lack of visits to your surgery?'

Mr Latimer stands, but before he can say anything the judge speaks. 'No deductions, please, Counsel.'

'Sorry, Your Honour. Dr Frame, did Deborah Shelley come to you with any health problems in 2009?'

'No.'

'Had she ever come to you for help with psychiatric problems?'

Andy Frame nods. 'Yes. In 1993 she was under a lot of stress. I prescribed Prozac.'

'But not since then?'

'No.'

'If she had been under stress again would you expect her to come to you for help?'

He hesitates but what else could he say? 'Yes.'

'And she didn't. Thank you, Dr Frame.'

The implication hangs heavy in the air. I wasn't off my rocker when I helped Neil. I was as right as rain.

Mr Latimer has a few questions of his own for Andy Frame. He asks him about my medical history. Was I a frequent visitor to his surgery?

'No.'

'How often did Deborah Shelley come to see you, on her own account, in the years between 1993 and 2009? How many times a year?'

'I don't have the exact figures here.'

'A general idea?'

'Perhaps twice a year.'

'And when you prescribed the Prozac for Deborah Shelley in 1993 this was in the aftermath of her mother's death. Is that right?'

85

'Yes.'

'How long did she take the medication for?'

'Six months.'

'She could have taken it for longer if she wished?'

'Yes.'

'But she chose to come off the medication. Why was that?'

'She didn't like the side-effects, and she didn't really feel it was helping.'

Mr Latimer pauses, turns a page of his notes and examines something.

There's a juror on the second row, a weather-beaten man with long grey hair. I call him the Sailor. I imagine him salted and sozzled at ports around the world. He sneezes into a big white handkerchief, interrupting the thick weight of the silence.

Mr Latimer returns to the task in hand. 'And in the years between 1993 and 2009 did Deborah Shelley ever seek your advice for help with stress?'

'No.'

'For depression or anxiety?'

'No.'

'Did she ever ask for a psychiatric referral?'

'No.'

'The appointments she made were to discuss physical ailments?'

'That's right.'

'So, even after her husband's diagnosis, or in the time when there were other family troubles, she did not come to you with any emotional problems?'

'She didn't.'

'Thank you.'

The questions end abruptly and the jury look a little perplexed. The Prof rearranges his legs. The Sailor glances at his neighbour, the eldest of the two

Asian men who is very plump. He has a little gesture, pinching the corners of his mouth together – it makes me think of someone savouring food so I nickname him the Cook. The other Asian man is much younger, with collar-length hair, and wears a colourful handmade jumper. The sort of thing from a designer stall rather than an unwanted present. He will be the Artist.

At this stage Mr Latimer can't explain what's significant about the GP's answers. He will get his chance later. But he has told me already that he wants to show how unlikely I was to seek help, how Prozac hadn't really helped me before so I wouldn't bother asking for it as I became increasingly unhinged caring for Neil.

The prosecutor asks the judge if he has any questions for the GP. He does not. He thanks Andy Frame and tells him he may go. As he leaves there's a little surge of activity among the lawyers, notes referred to, gowns straightened, water poured. As soon as the door closes behind the doctor, Miss Webber announces her next witness.

'Call Mr Byron Wallis.'

He is one of the ambulance men. He's wearing a nice suit, a white shirt and green tie. I don't recognize him but I realize he is the man who tended Neil while his colleague asked me questions. He confirms his identity and affirms he will tell the truth.

'Mr Wallis, you are a paramedic.'

'Yes.'

'You attended an emergency call on June the fifteenth at 14, Elmfield Drive.'

'That's right.'

'Can you please tell the court what you found on your arrival?'

'We went upstairs and there was a man in the bed. I checked for vital signs but he was dead.'

'Did you carry out any procedures for resuscitation?'

'No.'

'Why not?'

'It was too late. There were already signs of lividity.'

'Can you explain what lividity is for the jury?'

'After death, blood settles and pools. With a body lying on its back, like this one was, it's visible in the underside of the limbs, the back, the fingernails. It's the effect of gravity.'

'What would it look like?'

'Discoloration, like faint bruising, purple.'

'And you observed this where on the deceased?'

'On his fingertips.'

Oh, Neil. Unexpectedly, grief clasps my throat. I think of his fingers, long and slender like a pianist's though he only ever played a guitar and that with little real skill. Just good enough to strum a few tunes round a campfire.

'How long after death would lividity appear?'

'From half an hour or so.'

'And did Ms Shelley say anything about her husband's condition?'

'She said he had motor neurone disease, that he had been very ill.'

'Do you recall seeing any medicines in the room?'

'No.'

'Did you look for any?'

'No. We didn't think it was a poisoning.'

'A poisoning?'

'An overdose.'

'It was a sudden death?'

'Yes.'

'But at that point, judging by the information you had from Ms Shelley, you believed it was a natural death, occurring as a result of Mr Draper's illness.'

'Yes.'

'No further questions.'

The first time Neil had raised the prospect was a few weeks after his diagnosis. We were still reeling from the shock and trying to find a way to interact. It was as if our old routines rang hollow, as though a new sun shone light on habitual gestures and exchanges, painting them false.

But what he hated, what we both hated, was that for a while, every smile and glance and touch was heavy with the burden of his prognosis.

One night we got drunk. We'd eaten late and shared wine with the meal and more after. We were looking through old photographs. Sophie was doing an art project and wanted pictures of celebrations. Neil and I ferreted our way through packets of prints, reminiscing about the phases the kids had gone through, the faces of people we no longer saw, birthdays and holidays and all the in-between days when I'd got my camera out. I remained chief photographer in the family.

When Neil opened another bottle, I raised my eyebrows.

'Well, I'm not exactly bothered about liver cancer any more.'

Giggling, I held out my own glass. 'Silver lining.'

He poured and began to speak. 'When things get bad, I want to be here. Not some hospice or hospital.'

'Yes,' I agreed, without hesitation.

He sought my eyes. 'Deborah, if I wanted to choose when it happened, if I needed help . . .'

There was a spurt of fear in my stomach. His words sobered me up but I pretended to be pissed still, hiding my panic and slurring my words. 'I'm sure the doctors'll sort you out. They do that nowadays.'

He wouldn't let me go, his eyes clamped on my face. 'I'm not asking them,' he insisted.

I was scared, scared by what he was asking and by my own cowardice. I wanted to say no. My first instinct was to say no. I closed my eyes, tilted my head back to escape his scrutiny. When I recovered and opened my eyes he was looking down at the coffee-table, his fingers tracing a line with the spilled drops of wine.

After a while we resumed drinking, sifting through the photos, but the wine tasted acidic, our recollections were superficial, going no deeper than the obvious anodyne memories: Adam loved that trike, the time Sophie ate the sand.

That night I woke in the early hours, shaky and hung-over and feeling dirty.

Back then, I thought he'd taken my silence as refusal. That the question wouldn't arise again. Whenever I allowed myself to envisage the outcome of his illness, the inevitable, unstoppable end, dread reared inside me. Not just the dread of losing him, of bereavement, but the dread that he would ask me again. If I refused, what would that say about my love for him, my compassion? That I wasn't prepared to stand by him and let him control the event? And if I agreed, what would it mean? How would I weather the reality of killing him? How would I bear breaking that taboo?

It was another six months before we spoke again about the manner of his dying.

'Call PC Stenner.'

My neck prickles and I sense a frisson of interest from the jurors: a policeman – maybe now we'll get to something juicy. He comes in, wearing his uniform, and is sworn in. His blocky head and wide jaw are as I recall. He has an angry rash on his neck.

'PC Stenner, please take us through your notes from the fifteenth of June, when you attended 14, Elmfield Drive.'

'Yes. I had a report of a sudden death. An ambulance was attending and I was in the vicinity. On reaching the premises, I found the ambulance service already in attendance. I spoke with Mrs Deborah Shelley, who reported that her husband had been terminally ill and she had been unable to rouse him that afternoon. She also stated that it had been only a matter of time.'

'What did you think she meant by this?'

'That he could die at any time, that it was expected.'

'At that point did you make any further enquiries?'

'No.'

'Can you recall for the jury Ms Shelley's demeanour at that time?'

'She was quite calm.'

'Thank you, PC Stenner.'

Mr Latimer gets to his feet. Some of the members in the jury box rearrange their positions. Are you sitting comfortably?

'PC Stenner. Did you meet anyone else at the house that afternoon?'

PC Stenner looks blank. I wonder if his mind is working furiously or whether you get what's on the tin. 'The daughter.' He's got there at last.

'Yes. And can you describe her demeanour for the court?'

The constable hesitates. He knew they'd want the low-down on me but he hasn't done his homework on Sophie. 'I don't remember.'

'R-really.' There's a hint of Mr Latimer's stammer but then he gets going. 'You recall clearly the demeanour of Deborah Shelley but have no recollection whatsoever of the demeanour of her daughter, Sophie?'

'That's correct.'

'I suggest to you that the reason you cannot recall Sophie's demeanour is that there was nothing remarkable about it.'

'I don't recall.'

'I suggest, like her mother, Sophie appeared calm. Do you remember she offered you a cup of tea?'

'Yes.'

'Hardly the actions of an hysteric. Let us return for a moment to your description of Deborah Shelley. She seemed calm. Would it be fair to say she conducted herself with dignity, as did her daughter?'

There is a squawk of protest from Miss Webber. Mr Latimer cuts her off: 'Let me rephrase that. Did Deborah Shelley behave in an undignified manner while you were at the house?'

'No.'

'Thank you.'

Mr Latimer has planted the notion of dignity, altogether a different image from the woman who had just calmly seen off her husband. Not cool and calculating but brave and dignified. Mousy gives a little nod and that spark of hope tickles in my chest.

Chapter Nine

The judge suggests we break for lunch and the jury file out. Mr Latimer comes over. 'Everything all right?'

I nod, a little dazed. The tension in my body is suddenly evident to me, running the length of my limbs, coiled round my spine.

'Good.' He smiles.

I wonder why he doesn't invest in a new wig – or is the tatty relic some sort of statement? The legal equivalent of a Hell's Angel's dirty denims.

The guard escorts me downstairs and, after using the facilities, I sit in my cell. This is a windowless box with whitewashed walls and a bench seat across the narrow rear wall. Hundreds of people have sat here, waiting to be called, to be tried, to be sentenced.

The guard brings lunch, a cheese-salad sandwich, bag of crisps, a pack of round shortbread biscuits and tea in a plastic cup. I eat half of the sandwich and one of the biscuits. The tea is tasteless, an odd grey colour with little discs of oil visible on the surface. I sip it and close my eyes. My bones feel weak, my muscles feeble. I'm like a puppet that has had its strings cut.

My case had already made the national press and television, so when I got up the courage to go into the prison kitchen and meet some of the women I'd be sharing the place with, they all knew what I stood accused of.

There are eighteen of us in Shapley House; perhaps eight were in the kitchen that day. 'I couldn't do that,' announced one of the women, flatly, arms crossed and staring at me as I fumbled about trying to find the things to make a cup of tea. 'Drug someone up, then hold a bag over their head and watch them die.'

The room was quiet and I stilled, not knowing how to reply. I set aside my cup and turned to leave.

'You got any burn?' the same woman asked. She had a crude tattoo on her neck, small, hard eyes. 'You, Mrs Mercy Killer, you got any burn?'

Some of the other women laughed but I sensed unease riddled through it. The nickname was to stick. I became known as Mercy.

'Any baccy?'

'I don't smoke.'

'What bleedin' use are you, then?'

I fled to my room. 'Burn' was short for Old Holborn, the rolling tobacco of choice that the women wound into needle-thin cigarettes. It was the top currency in Styal, prized even higher than the methadone given out to the addicts three times a day. Some of the addicts sold their methadone to buy tobacco.

Fleetingly I considered taking up smoking in order to have something to trade.

I don't know why Gaynor, the loudmouth in my house, took such an instant dislike to me. I guess I was an easy target, different from nearly everyone else, different class, different background, different accent, room of my own. It was like being in a foreign country: I didn't understand the culture or the language. 'The sweatbox' was the name for the van that transported us to and from court. People would say, 'I'm in on a section twenty,' and I'd need it explaining – assault inflicting grievous bodily harm. There was no neat little number for me. Murder is murder.

In prison there are sheets to fill in for everything: phone credit, CDs, shampoo, tampons, lip salve. For some reason all the toiletries have to be from Avon. We fill in our menu choices ahead of time and these are sent to the kitchen. At the top end of the prison, along from the main gate, there are old vegetable gardens. Long abandoned, the poly-tunnels are ragged with holes; weeds grow waist high among them. It's a shame we don't grow our own fruit and veg – they'd be a welcome addition to the meals. I don't eat much. The food reeks of institution, tray-baked for too long. The women constantly complain about the portion sizes.

I was allowed to have things from home, and I made a list to give to Jane. Clothes and sketch pad, pencils, some of my earrings (nothing larger than a ten-pence piece allowed) and a decent pillow. Neil's denim jacket. When Jane sent stuff in it was examined, then added to my property card.

'You could have told me,' Jane said, when she first visited. It wasn't a reproach, there was no glint of that in her eyes: she was stating fact – you could have told me and I'd have stood by you.

'I couldn't.' I shook my head.

'I might have been able—'

'It was part of the deal. With Neil.'

She took that in, her face shorn of artifice or the usual glimmer of mischief. 'Would you have told me eventually?'

If they hadn't found me out? Would I? I'd said nothing in the days between Neil's death and my arrest even though Jane came whenever she could, day or night. With food and wine and the comfort of her presence. 'I don't know.'

I think she was hurt. I would have been. We'd never had secrets. But it will not come between us, I trust in this. We have come too far to lose each other now. I've known her longer than I knew Neil – just. I know her well enough to see beyond the public persona, the humour, the upbeat take on everything, the endless energy. Over the years we have revealed ourselves to each other, peeled back those social layers, the poses and façades, sharing the bad times, the languors and doldrums, the storms and ship-wrecks that punctuate our lives.

'Well, thank God you didn't – I might have been done for aiding and abetting,' she said ruefully. I grinned. With the quip she forgave me. I wish she would stop smoking. I won't grow old with Neil but I would like to share whatever's still to come with Jane.

Once I have Neil's jacket, I wear it every evening. It's big on me, I have to roll the cuffs back, but it smells of him; it feels like him.

The only thing I sketch is the lime tree. Again and again, charting its journey from high summer into autumn and on. The glow of its large soft leaves from bright green to sherbet yellow. The little ball-shaped fruits dancing in the winds. The same fruits that Sophie used to collect and paint red as miniature cherries for her teddy bear. In the winter months the tree is often shrouded in mist in the morning, its stark trunk black, branches reaching up and out. On grey days it is wreathed in fog, which settles along the avenues muffling what we can see and adding a spookier quality to the noises of the prison.

The days are strictly regimented. Set times for meals, for work, for breaks and association. The roll is called at the beginning and end of the day and also at random times. We all have to stop what we are doing while the officers count us and relay back the numbers to Security. Everyone in the prison has a 'job', from working in the laundry or the gardens to piecework in the textile factory or helping in the office. As soon as I opened my mouth and demonstrated I was well educated and literate, they suggested I work in education. Many of the women can't read or write more than their name and those of their children, and there is a constant demand for people to tutor those wishing to learn.

I thought the work might be like the miserable sessions we had trying to teach Adam to read, the leaden silences, his restlessness, one foot kicking against the chair, but the women are not sullen or resistant. They're greedy to learn and when they do make progress I share their sense of pride. Our sessions are short, twenty minutes at a time; little and often is the best way. As the weeks go by, I get to know them: we exchange titbits of information, the small victories and defeats of prison life and the life outside that they yearn for – the excitement of visits and parole hearings, the bad news about children with problems and illnesses, or husbands getting into trouble.

When the court resumes the pathologist takes the witness stand. He is a gingery man with a beard and a Canadian drawl. I guess it's Canadian because his initial qualifications are from Toronto. In answer to Miss Webber's questions he tells us he has been a practising pathologist for twenty-three years, that he has conducted thousands of post-mortems and that he performed a post-mortem on Neil Draper on 23 June 2009.

'Please summarize your findings for the court.'

'The deceased was in an advanced stage of motor neurone disease and muscle wastage was apparent in the limbs. The external appearance of the body was otherwise unremarkable save for petechial haemorrhaging, which was visible in both eyes.'

Miss Webber asks him to describe this for the jury.

'This presents as broken capillaries on the whites of the eyes.'

'Comparable to broken veins?'

'Smaller, but the same principle.'

'Please continue,' she says.

'Internal examination revealed trauma to the alveoli of the lungs and the presence of fluid in the lungs. The stomach contents contained alcohol and I ordered a toxicology report.'

'Am I correct in saying that the report establishes what, if any, drugs or poisons are present?'

'Yes, that's right.'

'And the results?'

As the pathologist begins to talk of negligible amounts of Zoloft but morphine present in so many parts per million, Dolly blinks and a look of boredom steals over her face. In the row behind her the Cook folds his arms and tilts his head, eager to give the impression of someone taking it all in, but I suspect the pose is a disguise for being completely at a loss.

Thankfully, the pathologist then simplifies the dizzying numbers by telling the court that this level of morphine would invariably result in death. So our calculations weren't that far out.

'A fatal dose?'

'Yes.'

'In a healthy person of the same age as Mr Draper what effect would this have?'

'Metabolisms do vary a great deal but in most people such an amount taken with the alcohol would be likely to precipitate depression of the central nervous system.'

Callow Youth frowns: he doesn't like the long words, or maybe he just doesn't like being here. Me neither.

'How would that manifest itself?'

'Tiredness, dizziness, loss of motor faculties, then a slide into unconsciousness.'

'Were you able to establish cause of death?'

'Brain failure.'

'Due to the drug and alcohol?'

'No, the evidence, the state of the lungs, the petechial haemorrhages, suggests that the deceased was suffocated, which deprived the brain of oxygen.'

'Would the drug and alcohol have contributed to the death?'

'Yes.'

'Can you summarize for us the most likely scenario based on the physical evidence you observed?'

Someone over on the benches to the right is scribbling. Ms Gleason has told me that's where the press sit. Something spicy for tomorrow's readers.

The pathologist clears his throat. Dolly sits forward and rolls back her shoulders. Behind her the row of jurors shuffles about too. In the back row of the jury, the two oldest women, who are neatly turned out – blow-dried hair, colour co-ordinated scarves and cardigans, looking for all the world as if they have strayed in from doing a bit of shopping in St Ann's Square and will head off for a cuppa at Marks & Spencer's any minute – exchange a glance. They are probably Veronica's age, maybe a bit younger. The upper age limit for jurors is seventy. I dub them Hilda and Flo, old-fashioned names that may be coming round again.

'My conclusion would be that the deceased imbibed a mixture of morphine and alcohol and that he then suffocated.'

The room is quiet. Miss Webber leaves it hanging there for a few beats while everyone absorbs the hard facts. 'Were you able to ascertain how he suffocated?'

'No. We swept the nasal passages and examined the trachea but there was nothing conclusive.'

'Could it have been a pillow?'

'Yes.'

'Or a plastic bag?'

'Yes.'

The detail drills through me. What must it be doing to Adam?

We will not contest this evidence because I am admitting to all of this. Yes, I fed him the morphine and the booze. And, yes, when he still wasn't dead, I smothered him.

Nevertheless the way the pathologist has set it out for us, the stepping-stones that Miss Webber has laid down, lead to a picture of ruthless intent, not one of a person pushed to extremes, and I wonder if Mr Latimer will cross-examine. Is there any finely phrased question that might redeem me? Any image he can elicit to show me as crazed and demented rather than efficient and cold? I catch my breath as he rises, but then he turns to the judge. 'No questions, Your Honour.'

The first time Adam came to me in Styal was the worst – the unfamiliarity of it all, I suppose, the institution, the room full of bustling families and women prisoners all used to the parade.

My expectations bristled with iconography from the movies and American crime drama series on the box. Would we be allowed to touch? If we betrayed any emotion would a guard with a scowl and a nightstick yank us apart and slam me in solitary?

As it was there were no hands pressed palm to palm either side of a Perspex screen, no screens at all, no sadistic screw ready to pounce or cakes with nail files. It was all a little shabby and terribly depressing. The visiting lounge had all the atmosphere of a coach station – perhaps the shadow of parting and separation was similar.

'Mum.'

We hugged and I wanted to hang on to him for ever. Adam isn't as tall as Neil was but he's got the same build. For a dizzying moment Neil was in my arms and when I opened my eyes we would be back home.

'Did you find it all right? Did they tell you what to do?' I made small-talk as we sat.

'Yeah, cool. Miss Gleason sorted it out. There's a bus from town.'

A moment's pause and then we both spoke at the same time. I heard him say, 'Sophie,' and stopped. 'That is so wrong,' he went on.

'Adam, I know it's hard but . . . she's not doing it to be mean . . . Something this serious—'

'You could go to prison.'

'I am in prison.'

He half smiled. 'Mum.'

'I've got good lawyers. They will do everything they can.' I studied him a moment. I owed him a bit of gravity. 'I never wanted you to find out like this.' I felt uncertain; should I continue to talk about the situation, explain everything that had gone on or steer us into safer territory? My concern was that the strain would tip him into a reprise of his own destructive behaviour. 'We can talk about this later,' I offered.

'I'm all right, Mum. It's just Sophie – I hate her. Why's she doing this?'

'Adam, even if she hadn't gone to the police there would still be enough evidence to put me here.'

He was surprised.

'The medical stuff,' I elaborated.

'Even so—'

'Have you seen her? Has she said anything?'

'I got some fuckin' lecture from her before she went to Grandma's. Dad wanted this, right?'

I nodded.

'Then what is her problem?' His face was intent, his eyes blazing.

'She's hurt, she's missing him, and I know we all are, but Sophie must feel that this is the right thing for her to do.' It was ridiculous. There I was defending her when she was lining up to throw stones at me – but it hurt me so much that they couldn't rely on each other to get through this.

'Like I care? You did what Dad wanted, why can't she just accept that?'

I rifled through platitudes and homilies, discarding them. Nothing fitted. I put my hand on his arm and smiled. 'Tell me about the festival.'

He raised his eyes, aware of the clumsy change of subject, but went along with it. As he talked, various practical questions occurred to me. Things I needed to ask Ms Gleason about. How could the kids get money while I was inside? Did I need to give anyone power of attorney to deal with the house stuff? And Neil's will? Would that be in abeyance until the trial was over?

'The house is okay? No problems?'

There was a spark of irritation in his eyes. For my asking? Was I undermining him? I began to explain but he cut across me: 'Fine except for Pauline. She keeps trying to ambush me – she waits by the bins.' I laughed at this image of our next-door neighbour. We don't get on and there have been a few run-ins over the years. She's big on complaints. One of her better offerings was a request that we ask the children not to make so much noise when they were playing out. They were nine and six, playing out the best thing they could be doing. Noise came with the territory, and it wasn't late at night.

'They're kids, Pauline, they need to let off steam,' I tried to reason with her.

'They make such a racket.' She glowered. She hadn't any kids of her own and I did wonder if there was some sadness there, grief that hearing Adam and Sophie and their friends at play tapped into, resulting in irritation.

'You could try ear-plugs,' I suggested.

She had snorted with annoyance and bustled back inside.

'Just smile and ignore her,' I told Adam now. 'Any other news?'

'I've got an interview tomorrow,' he said. 'A club in town.'

'Bar work?'

He nodded.

'How many hours?'

'Don't know yet.'

Adam had worked in a few pubs and bars in the previous year but never for very long. He was a poor timekeeper. I was glad he had the prospect of work, something to structure his time. He was all alone in the house. The fallout from our seismic shift in fortune struck me again. A month ago the house was home to a family of four; now the sole occupant was a teenage boy.

'You seeing anyone?'

He grinned. Another flash of Neil in the alignment of his features and the warmth of that smile. 'No chance. We're notorious, aren't we?'

Christ! I hadn't thought. People in the city know each other. They gossip and chat in shops, on the corner, at work. My murder trial was front-page material. Draper and Shelley – the names must now be synonymous with sinister deeds, a savage end, a lying spouse. 'No telling what you might do,' I said darkly. Wit seemed to be the best defence. He laughed. I loved to make him laugh.

My mind rolled back over the years to previous scandals or tragedies that had touched our circle of acquaintances: the teacher caught downloading porn, the priest at Veronica's church done for drink-driving, a colleague of Neil's who ran off with a sixth-former, a friend of Adam's whose father beat his mother and broke her jaw. We'd tittle-tattled along with the best of them, sharing our latent suspicions or our complete surprise.

And, of course, now all our friends and acquaintances, all Sophie's mates and Neil's colleagues would be swapping their reactions. All over Manchester Neil and I and our children were being picked over like so many bones.

Chapter Ten

It is Detective Sergeant Bray's turn to talk about me. He makes an excellent witness: the same disarming manner and friendly approach as when he questioned me at the police station. The lawyers all have transcripts of my interviews and DS Bray holds one too.

Miss Webber establishes the date and time of the first interview and then asks, 'DS Bray, is it true that when you questioned Deborah Shelley she offered no comment?'

'That's right.'

'And in the second interview, which commenced at sixteen forty, that is twenty to five in the afternoon, she again offered no comment?'

'Yes.'

'And in the third interview Ms Shelley refused to answer any of the questions put to her but said only, "No comment"?'

'That's correct.'

Miss Webber nods along with him, both sharing disapproval at this monstrous display of un-cooperative behaviour. 'DS Bray, you've many years' experience in the police force?'

'I have.'

'How many?'

'Seventeen.' He gives a rueful smile, like *how did I get here?* And the Prof smiles too.

'In your experience, why do people choose to reply, "No comment"?'

'To avoid saying anything that may be used against them.'

I wonder if Mr Latimer will object to this: even though Bray's answer is strictly true, it makes me sound like I had something to hide but he makes no move.

'Ms Shelley failed to give an account of the circumstances surrounding her husband's death?'

'That's right.'

'Did she answer any questions about his illness?'

'No.'

'About the family circumstances?'

'No.'

'About her own movements on June the fifteenth last year?'

'No.' His tone doesn't change: there's a steady, slightly downbeat note to it, implying he was saddened but not surprised.

'When you conveyed to the defendant the forensic evidence that gave rise to concerns, did she offer any explanation?'

'No.'

'Please will you explain to the court what effect refusing to answer questions has on the interview?'

'It makes it uncomfortable for everyone. It is frustrating for us, the police, but it is also difficult for the person being interviewed.'

'It requires a degree of determination?'

'It does.'

'Have you interviewed people before who have found it impossible to sustain offering no comment?'

'Yes, on many occasions.'

'Did Ms Shelley answer any questions at all in the course of three separate interviews?'

'Not directly but she did say—' Bray looks down at the transcript to check he gets it right. '"I love my husband. I would never harm him."'

'On the second of July last year you received notification that Ms Shelley was changing her story?'

'That's right.'

'That she was admitting to manslaughter due to diminished responsibility?'

'Yes.'

'Is it the case that if Ms Shelley was found guilty of murder she would face a mandatory life sentence whereas manslaughter carries no mandatory sentence?'

'That's my understanding.'

'In your professional opinion what would be the reason for Ms Shelley changing her story?'

'The forensic evidence we have is compelling. It is hard to see what other defence might be accepted by the court.'

'Thank you.'

The jury have hung on his every word but there is no flourish of pride in DS Bray's evidence. That is why he is so dangerous.

Mr Latimer picks up the transcripts and grins wolfishly at DS Bray. 'Thank you, DS Bray. Please will you turn to paragraph three on page four of the transcripts. Will you please read that for the court.'

DS Bray turns the pages. He looks across at Mr Latimer when he's found the right place. His eyes lose a little of their sheen, or maybe that's my wishful thinking.

'"Ms Shelley distressed. Interview suspended,"' he reads out.

'Do you recall this?'

'Yes.'

'In what way did Ms Shelley demonstrate her distress?'

'She was crying.'

'She was crying.' Mr Latimer repeats the answer and looks sad, as if he might too. 'Was she calm?'

'No, she was upset.'

'Were you surprised?'

'No. It was a distressing situation.'

'In what respect?'

'She was being asked questions about her husband's death.'

'Did you ask a doctor to attend to Ms Shelley?'

A slight hesitation, just a nanosecond but loud as a fart. 'No.'

'Even though she was so distraught that you had to stop the interview?'

'If her solicitor had requested it we would have given any medical care required.'

'Thank you. No further questions.'

Mousy looks disappointed. She liked DS Bray. Could have listened to him for longer.

The judge decides to call it a day. The jury rise and wind out of the court. He gathers various folders from his table and disappears out of his own door at the back of the room. Adam catches my eye, attempts a smile. I wink at him and he screws up his mouth as if he's fighting a guffaw. Winking might send the wrong signal but I reckon with the jury out of the way it's not going to affect my profile. The guard approaches and we set off. I'm taken downstairs and straight out to one of the vans parked on the side street. And back to Styal.

There are privileges with living in the houses – no official lights out, a kitchen where we can get drinks and make snacks and associate. We are not locked into our rooms at night – only the main door to the house is locked – and we are left alone then, though we can summon help by pressing the emergency call buttons. We are 'free-flow': trusted to move around specific parts of the prison complex without an officer escorting us. Women on the wing are escorted everywhere, their every movement checked. They have set times for exercise in their own concrete yard.

I saw inside the wing one day, accompanying an officer who was returning one prisoner and collecting another to come and work with me on the reading programme. The rectangular building is two storeys high; the cells run the length of each wall on both levels. The metal cell doors are thickly painted in garish primary colours: red, yellow, blue and green. It reminded me of a car ferry, the same preponderance of metal and the tough wipe-clean materials. Bad behaviour could see any of us sent to the wing and subject to an unforgiving system of reward and punishment: red and green cards. Red cards are issued for the slightest infringement of rules and if you accumulate three you are put into isolation, holed up in your cell day and night. Most of the suicides occur on the wing.

Some prisoners I never meet, the ones who are segregated in the modern block beyond the wing. These women never mingle with the general population. They are deemed either too dangerous or too vulnerable. They are escorted everywhere, many on twenty-four-hour suicide watch – they can't even pee in private. Some are sex offenders who would be recognized. When possible the prison mixes 'nonces' with the general population, though, of course, the women know to lie about the crimes they've committed. Those who might be recognized, their faces familiar from news coverage, stay in segregation.

There are days when the whole prison feels pitched on the edge of hysteria. Four hundred and fifty women close to explosion, half of them suffering from PMT at the same time. A vertiginous mood. Though there seems no bent to riot. When the dam breaks it is usually individuals falling off, losing their tenuous grip, feeling their nails tear and their feet flail for purchase. They're more likely to descend into madness or take a blade to their own flesh than attack their gaolers.

One night I woke to shouting. This was not the echoing chorus of women calling from building to building but something close and urgent, with the rhythm of violence. Before I had opened my door the alarm sounded, a deafening shrill in my ears. Someone had summoned the guards.

On the landing Gaynor was red-faced, screaming at Stephanie, the pretty young Afro-Caribbean girl she was sleeping with. There were plenty of trysts inside and they were tolerated by the staff. Stephanie's face was swollen, one eye puffed up and bloody. Her nose was bleeding and her nightshirt patchy with dark stains.

'Teach you a fuckin' lesson,' Gaynor continued to shout. Her fists were smeared with blood.

The guards burst in and we were roll checked, then sent to our rooms. There was more shouting, and banging as Gaynor was taken downstairs. From my window I watched them walking her down the hill to the wing. She was still cursing and voices began to call back in response from the black windows of the wing, the telegraph already spreading news of the attack.

My life got a little easier without Gaynor's jibes to deal with. I expected Stephanie to relax now her assailant was locked up, but two days later she too was shipped off to the wing. The rumours were that Stephanie had sexually assaulted a girl in the gym.

On my wall there are two birthday cards, one from Adam and one from Jane. Nothing jokey about being over the hill or still up for it, thank God. For a while I distract myself remembering earlier birthdays, the surprises I had, the homemade gifts when Adam and Sophie were little, many of which found their way into my workshop when I couldn't bear to throw them away. The time I'd been working away and come home to find the house full of flowers and a birthday tree (a yucca) hung with presents.

Sophie turned sixteen this February. I wanted to send her a present. In prison I am only allowed to order things from the Argos catalogue. I pored over the pages wondering what her grandparents would get her, wondering if she had bought herself any of the things that I was considering. Although I have some money here, earnings from my job, they don't amount to much at 15p a session. I asked Jane to get Sophie's present for me – I'd try to pay her for it later. Our bank accounts had been frozen. Jane has had to go to the Citizen's Advice Bureau to help her sort things out with the bank so our direct debits continue to be paid and money made available from our savings for the children. The bank's not really geared up for this sort of thing – one account holder dead and the other on remand. Not what's expected of their platinum reserve customers.

I got Sophie a camera, a digital SLR. She was talking about doing photography at A level. There was a workshop in the prison stocked with graphic materials and computers where we could make cards and calendars. I designed a card and sent it to Jane to include with the present.

I didn't hear whether Sophie liked the camera. Would she shun it because it had come from me? I didn't probe Adam when he visited. He sees her a couple of times a week but he finds it very difficult, and if I mention her there is always a flash of resentment in his eyes.

I am lost in this chasm between Sophie and me. A trench so wide, so deep, filled with choppy water, sunken rocks. Her insistence on justice is familiar. When she was twelve I mistakenly accused her and Adam of running up the phone bill, and told them they couldn't make calls to their friends, especially not to the mobile numbers that cost so much more. Sophie's face hardened. She'd stuck out her hand for the bill and disappeared. She returned later and she had highlighted the calls she made. The cost of them was negligible. It was all down to Adam. She had been furious at the unfairness of my accusation. My paltry 'Sorry' and my backtracking weren't enough. She refused to speak to me for days.

And now here we are estranged. Two pinprick figures either side of a canyon. I ache for the sight of her face turning my way, the break of her smile, the tune of her laughter, the brief weight of her embrace.

Tonight I lie awake spinning headlines and worrying about the children. When I sleep I dream of sinking sand: it is dark and I am out alone in a vast estuary, being sucked under, my legs leaden in the mud, my nostrils filling with the cold, gritty stuff until my lungs crave breath and my heart climbs into my throat.

Chapter Eleven

The jury file in and I watch the parade as they walk through the court to their seats. Mousy moves with her eyes cast down, her shoulders rounded; Dolly has strappy shoes, which cause her to wobble a little; the Prof strides along and the Callow Youth bobs after him. The Cook and the Artist and the Sailor take their places in the second row. The only woman on this row is young and trim. She wears her hair scraped back into a ponytail and she has lovely skin – either that or she's a makeup wizard. She reminds me of a PA we had at the big interior design firm so I'll call her PA. Hilda and Flo settle in on the back row, sandwiched between the only black juror and an overweight woman with ginger hair. The man wears a crisp blue shirt and a suit and has been following the proceedings with an intent and unchanging expression. He looks a bit flash – estate agent or media man, perhaps? Yes, Media Man. Earning plenty, I guess, with a canal-side apartment, a beautiful girlfriend and all the latest gadgets.

At the other end of the row, the last juror couldn't be more different from him. She's probably in her early twenties, her hair is long and she wears an Alice band. Alice has a wide, freckled face and her large size is emphasized by the tight clothes she wears. She smiles a lot, laughs a lot, nods as if she agrees with whoever's speaking.

When they go home at night, these twelve peers of mine, do they confide in anyone? Does any of them have an audience clustered round the family tea-table, clinging to their every word, or are they alone with their thoughts from the day, or oblivious, shrugging off my case with their courtroom clothes and heading out to see friends?

The court usher calls Sophie Draper and my bowels turn to water. I would give anything to stop this, to shield her from the amphitheatre. I had asked Latimer if he would refrain from cross-examining her. He gave me a pitying smile, murmured some words of sympathy and assured me he would be gentle with her. There would be nothing to gain if the jury witnessed him ripping into a tender sixteen-year-old.

Sophie had the option of giving evidence by video link but only the real McCoy would do for my girl. My jaw is clamped so tight I think my teeth will shatter. Saliva clogs my throat.

She comes in and I am so happy to see her. How daft is that? My maternal instincts kick in and override all other considerations. She is here, my girl is here. It is almost six months since I have seen her. That was at Neil's funeral. This flush of pleasure, the quickening of my heart, is swiftly replaced by a bitter sadness, an impotent desire to protect her.

She steps into the witness box and tucks her hair behind her ears. A gesture that betrays her youth. The sympathy emanating from the jury box is almost palpable. I wonder if any of them have children, teenagers, and daughters. Can they make sense of this rift?

Sophie's hair is different, longer, layered, the highlights bolder. By this time of year her hair has usually darkened to the colour of toffee. She wears clothes I don't recognize: a plain cornflower blue long-sleeved top, black boot-cut trousers. Who went with her to buy them? A wave of jealousy grips my neck. Did Briony Webber have a hand in it? Counselling her witnesses as to what apparel would best create the right image? The prospect that Sophie and I might never do these things together again, shopping, ordering things online, that she will never wander into my room and ask me if she can borrow my eyeliner or if she should put her hair up or leave it down, kicks me in the belly.

All I have lost.

Sophie does not look at me; she does not look at her brother in the gallery. She concentrates on Miss Webber and the jury.

'You are Sophie Draper?'

'Yes.' Sophie's voice is small but not timid.

Neil chose the name Sophie. I wanted to call her Rachel but he wasn't keen. He'd gone out with a girl called Rachel at school; she'd been horribly clingy when he broke up with her. All those years later the name still conjured her up. So we settled on Sophie. Adam had my surname and we gave Sophie Neil's. We had no plan for how we would name a third child.

Sophie affirms, which I'm relieved about. She'd had a religious phase as a younger teen and challenged Neil and me when we made any anti-religious comments. I think I'd been worrying that staying with Veronica might have sent her looking for comfort in God.

'You are the daughter of Neil Draper and Deborah Shelley?'

'Yes.'

116

'And on the twenty-fourth of June, nine days after your father's death, you made a phone call to the police?'

'Yes, I did.'

'What did you tell the police?'

My throat is tight and there's a burning around my ears. I concentrate on my breathing, taking air in slowly through my nose.

'That I thought my mum had something to do with my dad dying.'

There are gasps and sharp intakes of breath from around the court. Dolly puts her hand over her mouth in shock. Sophie blinks, tightens her lips with resolve.

'Please can you tell us what happened on the afternoon of June the fifteenth?'

'I was on my way home from school when Mum rang me, to tell me Dad had died.'

'Were you surprised?'

'Yes, he'd been fine that morning.' There are tears in her voice and my heart rips. Resentment ripples through me. I want to leap across the space and gag Miss Webber, free Sophie from the ordeal.

'You'd seen him earlier in the day?'

'I said goodbye before school.'

'You got the phone call. What did you do next?'

Her voice is firmer. 'I went home. Mum was there and we went upstairs.'

'You saw your father?'

'Yes.'

Callow Youth is following Sophie's testimony carefully. Perhaps he relates to her because she's closer to his age than any of the other witnesses. And she's gorgeous, of course.

'And then?'

'I asked her if we could do anything, like the kiss of life and she said it was too late. There was an ambulance coming. Then I rang Grandma and Grandpa to tell them.'

'Your mother hadn't called them?'

'No.'

I am neglect on legs.

'And your brother?'

'She said his phone was off.'

I sense rather than see Adam flinch. It had been another few hours before he had come barrelling home to find the sky had fallen. His absence he saw as another failure to carry with him, another brick in the basket.

'How did your mother appear?'

'A bit upset.'

'She was crying?'

'A bit.'

'Did she tell you anything about events that day?'

'Just that she had gone upstairs and couldn't wake him.'

'Nine days later you called the police. You told them you suspected your mother of involvement in your father's death. Why did you think that?'

'Well, he died really suddenly. He was okay when I went to school. They'd told us about MND and what would happen and it wasn't like that at all.'

'Was that the only reason?'

'No. I knew Mum had been looking on the Internet at sites about assisted suicide, euthanasia.'

'How did you know this?'

'She never deletes her browsing history.'

Flo narrows her eyes; perhaps she's not a silver surfer. But Miss Webber is prepared for this and has a follow-up question. 'So when you went on the computer you could see a list of previous websites that had been visited?'

'Yes.'

'Perhaps your father had been looking them up?'

Not unless he'd regained the use of his legs, got himself down there without help.

'It's her computer – it's a Mac for her work. He didn't really go on it.'

'And was there anything else that alerted your suspicions?'

Sophie swallows. She licks her lips. My hands hurt: my fists are bunched, my nails cutting into my palms. I uncurl them, clasp my hands tight together.

'Well, when I first got back and I wanted to know if we could do anything I asked her if she had tried the breathing space kit – I thought maybe that might help. She just said it was too late, but later when I went to look for the breathing space kit I couldn't find it.'

'You knew where it was usually kept?'

'Yes, in the kitchen, in the middle cupboard. We all knew where it was and what to do if Dad was choking or couldn't breathe.'

'And this kit was missing?'

'Yes.'

'Do you know what drugs it contained?'

'It was morphine, I think, and something else, a sedative but I don't know what it was called.'

Midazolam. We hadn't used that. If Neil had taken it as well, might the end have been different? My mind veers away from the memory.

'What did you think had happened to the kit?'

'I thought she'd hidden it, my mum.'

'Why?'

119

'Because she'd given him the drugs but she didn't want anyone to know.' Her answer is fluent, logical.

'Can you tell us what happened after you phoned the police?'

'They wanted to talk to me in person.'

'And you agreed?'

'Yes.'

'You made a visit to the police station the following day?'

My mind flew back, dipping around dates and memories. Ten days after – she'd have still been at home, wouldn't she? But everything became hazy in those days after Neil's death. What had she told me? That she was going into school? I couldn't recall.

'You spoke to the police and they asked you if you would be prepared to make a statement?'

'Yes.'

'They asked you whether you would be prepared to testify, if the case came to court?'

'Yes.'

'You agreed to those requests. You are here today. Can you tell the jury why you decided to help the police?'

'It was the right thing to do.' She is simple in her certainty, steadfast. My Antigone. I could use exactly the same words in my own defence – except I have to pretend that what I did was very much the wrong thing. And as for Antigone, after defying the authorities to honour her dead brother with a burial she was walled up and hanged herself.

'Sophie, can you tell us how your mother seemed in the months leading up to June last year?'

Sophie hesitates a moment. I don't think she's unsure. I think she's choosing her words carefully. 'The same as usual.'

'Did she complain of strain or stress?'

'No.'

'Did she seem withdrawn or depressed?'

'No.'

We are getting to the heart of the matter. This is what the trial pivots around – was I off my trolley or not? Ms Gleason summed it up: battle of the shrinks. And Sophie is the opener, the first line of attack who may be sacrificed but serves to expose chinks in the enemy's line, root out weaknesses and gaps, to illuminate the pattern for the next assault.

'Had she exhibited any signs of anxiety, any panic attacks?'

'No.'

'Did your mother behave in any way that made you think she was mentally ill?'

'No.'

Each 'no' rings out calm and clear. Sophie tucks her hair back again.

'Did she continue to care for you and your brother in those months?'

'Yes.'

'And she was working?'

'Yes.'

'And running the house?'

Isn't that little lot reason enough to go doo-lally? Or are we running along the lines of the Protestant work ethic here? Busy hands equal a healthy life.

'Would you say your mother coped well with your father's illness?'

Stupid question. How can anyone know how I coped? That's what coping's about, isn't it, swallowing the trouble and soldiering on?

'Yes.'

'Thank you.'

As Mr Latimer rises to his feet, adjusting his robe around him, I push my feet into the floor and grip the edge of my seat. Some of the jury stiffen too. Mousy's chin goes up, her expression sombre, and Media Man straightens his shoulders, uncrosses his legs.

'Miss Draper, is it true that your mother suffered from insomnia?' Mr Latimer jumps in without any preamble, though his tone is soft enough. He even stutters a little on 'insomnia'.

'Yes.'

'Was this a constant problem?'

'No.'

'But your mother had insomnia in the months leading up to your father's death?'

'Yes.'

'In your estimate, how often did your mother have broken nights?'

'I'm not sure.' There's a trace of a frown. Sophie is always so concerned to be honest, to get things right.

'Once a month?'

'More than that.'

'Once a week?'

'At least.'

'And after sleepless nights how did your mother seem?'

'Tired,' Sophie says drily, and a little ripple of laughter runs around the room. Dolly snorts and Alice smiles and I feel a rill of pride at Sophie's wit.

'Did she ever snap at you?'

Did I? Well – yeah!

'Yes.'

'Lose her composure?'

'Yes.'

'Can you remember seeing her distressed during this period?'

'No.'

That's not what Mr Latimer hoped for and he changes tack. 'Is it true your brother Adam has had mental-health problems?'

'Yes.'

'This pre-dated your father's diagnosis?'

'Yes.'

'And Adam also has a history of drug abuse?'

Adam's face has reddened; the spots on his forehead look angry. Jane's expression is heavy with disappointment. I am grinding my teeth.

'Yes.'

'Can you tell the court how this impacted on the family?'

'It was difficult. They worried about him – they never knew what would happen next.'

'A stressful situation?'

'Yes,' she says quickly, aware that he's getting close to what he's trying to prove.

'Miss Draper, does your mother usually confide in you about her problems?'

Sophie blinks, swallows. 'No, not really.'

'She is quite a private person?'

'Yes.'

'So, it might be hard for you to know how circumstances are affecting her.'

Sophie doesn't know what to say and I hate it. 'Maybe.'

'Did you discuss your decision to go to the police with anyone?'

'With my grandmother.'

'Veronica Draper?'

'Yes.'

'Did your grandmother encourage you to go to the police?'

'Not at first – she didn't believe me. Then, later . . . Well, she didn't push me.' Sophie is a little defensive and in the note of protest is the chime of a different truth.

'How was your grandmother in the aftermath of your father's death?'

'Very sad – she couldn't stop crying. She had to see the doctor.'

'And you moved in with your grandparents shortly after your mother was arrested?'

'Yes.'

'You live with them now?'

'Yes.'

My skin prickles as I sense him circling my girl. A sharp pin after a winkle.

'Did your grandmother talk to you about your father's death?'

'Yes. She couldn't understand it, like me. It was so fast. We never got a chance to say goodbye or anything.' Sophie's face flushes and crumples and she squeezes tears away. 'Sorry,' she says. My own throat locks in sympathy. Oh, Neil, what have we done?

Chapter Twelve

Some of the harshest criticism I've faced, on television and in the newspapers, came from disabled people. Many with life-threatening illnesses have spoken out about the risk to human rights when carers and relatives make judgement calls on a person's quality of life. Members of the MNDA have issued several persuasive statements about the misleading portrayal of the disease by the pundits and the very real possibility of a dignified and peaceful death if people seek out the appropriate resources. Some of these arguments are familiar to me. I raised them when Neil asked me the second time to help him die.

We'd gone away to Barcelona for a weekend – three nights actually – to a resort a few miles north of the city. It was almost a year after his diagnosis and we had all been adjusting to the new situation. Neil now had 'foot-drop' – he was dragging his left foot, which made walking and stairs hard work. It also ruined his shoes (well, the left ones). He used a cane, a rather stylish carved affair with a snake on the handle and a silver tip. He was still working. School had been brilliant and had offered him an early-retirement package for the following year, along with an understanding that he might need to take long-term sick leave before then if his condition deteriorated.

We often talked about how lucky we were: we had read so many horror stories of people plunged into debt and fighting for benefits, their last months a nightmare of the battle for recognition and support.

We had a ground-floor beachside apartment with a veranda. The place had a pool and a restaurant, a small shop and a beauty suite. There was air-conditioning and satellite TV in our room and a super-king-size bed. The complex catered to people who expected a little extra luxury from their holiday. Neil and I were like children exclaiming over the complimentary bathrobes and state-of-the-art wet room. Arriving, I felt the thrill of adventure – daft, perhaps, given how cocooned we were in our four-star comfort.

We walked down the few yards from our veranda to the strip of beach. The bay was fringed with palms and pines and the edge of the sand was scattered with old fronds and cones. The sea stretched calm and vivid cerulean out to the horizon. No children to worry about but the thought of Neil, weak in the water, drifting away, shadowed my mind. He wouldn't do that to me, I reassured myself. He wouldn't.

Neil grinned at me and edged forward to the shallows. I slipped off my shoes and walked after him. Underfoot the sand felt hot and gritty, finer near the shore, then the water silky cool. Neil caught my hand and we paddled slowly along the water's edge, his lazy foot leaving an arc in the sand with each step.

'Good, eh?' He'd picked the resort.

'Perfect.'

We soon turned back – he was tired.

'Fancy a lie-down?' I asked.

He turned, a sparkle of interest in his eyes.

'To sleep,' I said, 'and then a little lunch. And afterwards I'll shag you stupid.'

I dozed beside him for an hour, the room densely black with the shutters closed. I showered and changed into a sun-dress and went exploring. There was a road at the rear of the complex that ran through the resort then up to the main coast road. About half a mile along, a mini-market sold everything from lilos to cheese. I bought a selection of tapas from the deli section and some fresh rolls, a bottle of chilled white wine, a couple of squat glasses, sparkling water. We could have eaten at the restaurant but the prospect of lunch on the veranda and falling back into bed was more romantic.

Strolling back, I soaked up the little details of being in a different country. The whitewashed walls draped with honeysuckle and splashes of bougainvillaea, the lizard that scurried away at the edge of the road where rough concrete met dust, and water pipes emerged from the scrub. Tall, striped grasses hung with snails. The smell of hot resin from the pine trees and the tang of rosemary and thyme baking in the heat. The sky was unbroken blue and some sort of larks dipped and spun above the fields, mirroring the cadence of their song.

While Neil showered, I laid out our little feast. Olives with herbs, chunks of chorizo and cheese, a pot of green salad, saffron chicken.

We ate and drank, the wine still achingly cold, with an appley taste and a slight fizz. We gazed at the sea, gazed at each other.

When the food was gone, I went inside and brought out our books. I stood beside Neil and passed him his *Homage to Catalonia*. He squinted up at me, the sun high and bright. He ran his hand up between my legs, stroked me. I took a shivery breath. His face darkened with excitement and I bent and kissed him roughly before returning to my chair. While he read, I scanned the bay, followed a little motor-boat and its silver wake, observed an elderly couple with faces like dried fruit, who walked down from one of the other rooms to the beach and watched the insects, hornets and butterflies dance around the potted plants along the walkway.

I took the last of our wine inside and Neil followed. The shutters were adjustable (only the best) so I fiddled with the rods until they admitted little slits of sunlight, enough for us to see what we were doing.

We kissed. I unbuttoned his shirt, slipped it off his shoulders. Bent and pulled down his shorts, helped him step out. His balance was delicate, and simple things like undressing were harder for him now.

'Lie down.'

He stretched out on the length of the bed: still slim, his skin smooth, his penis erect. I undressed myself, savouring his eyes on me. Making love was easier with me on top. I kissed him and stroked his arms and his chest, his belly and his thighs before guiding him inside me. I rode him slowly at first, relishing the languorous movements, the way my own body responded, swelling and quickening. He played with my breasts and my nipples. Our breathing became harsher, ragged. He called to me, dirty entreaties, words he knew would arouse me more, then placed his hand so that as I thrust up and down the pad of his thumb pressed against my clitoris. Panting and moist with sweat, the tension of sexual excitement washed through me, growing and retreating, ocean pulses that gathered depth and speed until I came, sighing loud with sweet relief and setting him off too.

We spent the afternoon lazing on the beach, on loungers under a big blue parasol that flapped in the breeze. Time and again, as I rubbed oil on his back, as we waded into the cool water, as we considered where to eat that evening, the realization that this might be our last holiday together swept over me. Like gusts of wind knocking everything about. Hating myself for the maudlin sentimentality, I struggled to live in the moment. To savour the pleasures we were sharing, not to look ahead. To focus on the details: the scent of coconut from the sun cream mingled with the kick of brine, the particular colour of aquamarine at the end of the bay, the fine dark hairs on Neil's knuckles, the crisp texture and honey taste of melon bought from the beach vendor, the feel of grit between my toes and the thready whine of a motor-boat on the horizon. But Cassandra had my soul and her talons gripped my head and held my eyes wide, one bony claw pointing to the future. The prospect of death stuffed my ears and nose and throat with dread. Perhaps, I thought, the holiday had been a mistake: stripped of our routines, there was too much time to think.

Neil knew me so well that he likely guessed at my melancholy. We'd had a couple of sessions with a counsellor who worked with terminal patients and their families. The general guidance was not to try to deny or hide the gamut of emotions: the savage embrace of anger and fear and guilt were normal and to be accepted. Neil seemed calm. Why couldn't I smell his fear? If our roles had been reversed I imagined I'd have been noisy, needy, bitchy. Making the most of my remaining time by having tantrums. But he seemed to find a stoicism within, a steady centre for much of the time. A legacy, perhaps, of his childhood faith – the sweet resignation to God's will, the certainty of an afterlife of love and grace. Even though he didn't believe it, or so he told me, might it still be a comfort to him? He had been angry at times, once the initial shock had worn off, turning to me one evening after brushing his teeth, face trembling, eyes ablaze, telling me, 'I'm so fucking pissed off, so fucking—' before he broke, a sob deep in his throat. (The books said crying more, or laughing more, was a symptom some people experienced, probably to do with changes in the frontal lobe so that these responses were ratcheted up. I don't think that happened to Neil: his crying was always correctly proportioned to the situation.) His anger seemed to seep away over the next couple of weeks. When I asked him about it, his answer startled me: 'I'm desolate, there's no room for anything else, but there's moments of, I don't know, euphoria, too.'

'Euphoria?' The guy's dying and he's getting high on it?

'Everything's so intense, and still so ordinary.' He smiled, shaking his head a little because it sounded weird. 'It's amazing.'

'But desolate?'

'Oh, yes.'

Any illusion I had that our Barcelona trip was going to be an escape from real life shattered on the second night as we sat on our patio after dinner. My skin had that taut sensation from the sun and the salt, I was tired from the heat and the sea air and the wine and surprised that Neil hadn't already flaked out. Our books lay on the table. I was too sleepy to read and he'd set his down when he topped up his glass.

'It's beautiful,' I murmured, staring out at the inky night, the sea's dark pierced by half a dozen fishing-boat lamps, the sky by thousands of stars flickering magnesium white.

'Can you see Orion?'

I laughed. Neil had taught me some of the constellations, the Greek heroes flung into the night sky for eternity.

'Yes. And there's Cassiopeia.'

'Deborah,' he said quietly, 'I want to choose the time.'

My skin contracted. There was the sensation of a blunt blow to my stomach, a blur of rage in the back of my skull. How dare he ruin all this with his unreasonable requests? 'I don't—'

'Listen.'

I sighed and turned to look at him.

'It's going to happen, we know that. I don't want to wait until I'm choking—'

'It doesn't have to come—'

'Just listen,' he interrupted. 'I want a good death. For me that means choosing when.'

He paused, inviting me to respond.

'I won't stop you.'

'But will you help me?'

I didn't speak. A flutter of black swooped past near the roof – a bat. I studied my nails, the ridges and grooves, the cuticles ragged. My mind tangled. 'You might not need any help,' I fudged. 'Look, there are organizations, aren't there, people who go to Switzerland . . .?'

'I don't want to go to Switzerland. I want to be at

home, with you. I want you there with me, Deborah.'
His voice shook with emotion.

A thousand questions skittered in my mind: how
would you do it, what would we say, what would I
have to do?

I stared up at the stars. They were cold and
brilliant. My eyes watered, making each prick of
light a pinwheel, the jet sky now full of silver
dandelions.

'We can manage the disease,' I tried. 'The association, there are so many things we can do, you won't
be in pain, you won't choke . . .' My words were
running on like panic, filling the hiatus.

'Deborah?'

'I'll be there,' I said slowly.

'And you'll help?'

What could I say? No, I'd rather you did it,
actually, all by yourself, so my conscience will be
clear. Now I'll just pop down to the shore and wash
my hands of you.

'I don't think I can.'

'When you had Adam,' he said, 'you wanted to be
at home. I thought you were mad.'

'Your mother didn't help.' Veronica was a nurse
and firmly toed the line that first babies are best born
in hospital. She'd tried to talk us out of it even
though Dr Frame and the community midwives were
completely at ease with the idea.

'Maybe not,' he said, 'but I trusted you, I went
along with it. It was fine, Sophie too, even with the
cord, but you chose.'

'It's not the same,' I protested. 'In fact, it's the
opposite. I wanted home births to avoid interven-
tion, if possible. I wanted it to be as natural as
possible. What you're talking about is *not* letting

nature take its course. It's interfering.' I could feel my tears rising.

'I want it on my terms.'

'No. I want to keep you here as long as possible, not help you slope off early. I don't even know whether I want you to die at home – I want the safety of knowing you can go to a hospice where people know the score, where they can help us.'

I began to cry silently. I wasn't looking for comfort but the anxiety inside was too strong to contain. 'It's not fair, you shouldn't ask me. I don't want you to die. Why should I make it happen any sooner? I'll do everything I can to help, Neil, but not that.'

The silence burned between us. I could hear the suck of the sea. I stood up then. Mumbled something about a walk. When I returned Neil was in bed, asleep. And the final day of our holiday, our very last holiday, was brittle with resentment. My throat ached, my stomach cramped. Neil was remote. The beauty of our location, the gorgeous weather only served to highlight our shared misery.

A question swung to and fro in my head like a pendulum. Had I refused because I loved him or because I didn't love him enough?

Chapter Thirteen

They have finished with Sophie. The judge thanks her, warmth in his manner; the creases in his face deepen as he smiles at her. She walks down from the witness box, a blur of colour in her cheeks now. The urge to cry out to her is visceral, a fist in my chest eager to punch its way out. What can I say? Forgive me. If I had only known ... I'm sorry. I love you. We never meant to hurt you.

She does not look at me, or anyone, but makes her way steadily to the doors. I watch her back, her hair flowing down to her shoulder-blades, honey-coloured against her top. When will I see her again? Will I see her again? My girl. I do not speak, I barely breathe. My cheeks are wet.

The judge calls an end to the day and we all stand. The jury are solemn, subdued. Media Man rubs at his face and sighs, and Alice is fiddling with her hairband but she's gazing off into the distance. I wonder if she is thinking about what Sophie has said.

I force myself to look at Adam, to suck the grief from my face and give him a nod of reassurance. He dips his head and casts down his eyes. He, too, is on the verge of tears. My expression must have changed because Jane, catching my eye, blanches with consternation and turns to Adam, says something. He nods at her enquiry. Who is comforting Sophie? Are Veronica and Michael waiting for her out there?

The court empties. Jane lifts her hand, a wry farewell as they troop out. The recorder and the barristers are exchanging comments. Bits of business that they need to share before tomorrow. Miss Webber piles her files high, scoops them into her arm, sings a cheery goodbye to Mr Latimer. She is riding high on Sophie's testimony. The jury loved her. Who wouldn't want to believe a young girl prepared to bear witness in such raw circumstances? Her youth and courage sound a clarion call to truth.

Mr Latimer gives me no false hope when he stops beside me on his way out. 'Early days,' he says. He sighs. 'We'll get our turn, r-remember. Always difficult for the defence at this stage.'

Ms Gleason comes up after he's gone. 'How are you holding up?'

'It was hard.'

'Yes. Try to rest tonight. Is there anything you need?'

I shake my head. Whatever I need, freedom, absolution, a night down the pub chewing it over with Jane, my home and children, is way out of her provenance.

On Adam's third or fourth visit to Styal he was very subdued. He had returned from his trip to the Spanish festival, which I'd insisted he go to, and seemed to have survived it intact. He was working at the club in town. He said it was a bit boring but the people were 'cool'.

I worked hard at the conversation, trying to find out if he'd changed his mind about Jane's place, even if just for a while. 'It must be lonely, there on your own?'

'I don't mind.' He shrugged. Then his face collapsed, his eyes reddened. 'I miss you – and Dad. I miss him so much.'

My heart thumped. I lurched across the low table separating us, wrapping my arms about him. 'I know.'

The guard called for me to sit down. I glared at him, furious.

'Adam, I'm sorry.' I moved back a little, my hands cupping his face. 'I'm so sorry.'

'No – what you did . . . that was right. It was what he wanted. You did the right thing.'

My breath caught and I waited. His belief in me was so precious and I was afraid that perhaps it was not warranted. 'He loved you so much,' I told him. 'Don't ever forget that.'

Adam nodded, rubbed at his face with his hands. I was sorry and scared at what it would mean for him when we went to trial. I took a breath and leaned close again. 'I've been talking to the solicitor,' I said. 'We have to argue that I was disturbed when I gave your dad the overdose.'

'But he wanted you to?' Adam frowned.

'Yes, but if I say that I did it to help him and I knew what I was doing they will find me guilty of murder.'

'That's mental – that's totally cracked.'

'I know. But that's the law. The only chance I've got is to plead guilty to manslaughter and argue that I was in such a state by then I can't be held responsible.'

He shook his head, bemused.

'The thing is, it means that in court I have to talk about everything that contributed to my state of mind, all the stresses . . .' I paused, hoping he'd make the leap, but he watched me, waited. 'Adam, I'm

136

going to have to tell them all about you being ill, the overdose, everything.'

Embarrassment swept his face and he reddened. 'It's cool,' he said. 'You did the right thing – that's all that matters.' And he shrugged again.

I made an effort to smile but I wasn't sure I agreed with him. The consequences of doing the right thing were very wrong: my family scattered, our grief choked off and sullied by the investigation and the trial. Right for Neil, but for the rest of us?

It is dusk as they take me from the back door of the court building to the prison van. The air is cold and damp and from somewhere there is the smell of fat and onions, fast-food. One of the trams gives a melancholy hoot and I catch a glimpse of figures hurrying along the street at the end. People making their way home for tea, carrying shopping or laptops, looking forward to a hot soak, a TV dinner or the ritual of bedtime stories.

Neil hated weather like this. Before we had Adam, at weekends the dull drizzle, the mottled sky would see us cocooned. Wearing woolly socks and jumpers in bed, reading the papers and snacking, getting high and making love, our hands grubby with newsprint, faintly sticky with marmalade. He couldn't bear a dreary Sunday; he said it reminded him too much of the aching boredom of his childhood days, the weekly ritual of no breakfast before mass, the tedium of the service, the long dull afternoons when the whole world seemed shut, the visits to his grandparent Drapers' graves. He said that wasn't every week but it felt like it.

Once the children came along we had two strategies to redeem those miserable days. One was

137

to cocoon them too, to make a feature of being trapped inside, building dens from big cardboard boxes or making a tent with the clothes horse and sheets, passing them in picnics to share. Whitewashing one wall in their playroom and bringing out chalks for hours of scribbling and drawing. Or 'making mess', setting out the kitchen with Play Doh and food colouring, water and sieves at the sink, glue and paper and glitter. All four of us mucking about with the curtains drawn and the lights on. The other technique was to cock a snook at the gloom and go out in it. But far out – to the hills, sealed in waterproofs and wellies, where even the dimmest day was enlivened by the sights and smells of nature, and puddle-jumping or mud-dancing was *de rigueur*. The promise of chips and cocoa when we got home. Clothes steaming on the radiators, smelling of fresh air and grass and earth.

It was weather like that when we buried Neil. Fitting. They let me out to attend the funeral. It was October, four months after he had died, and six months till my trial. Everything had been delayed because of the post-mortems. Prison guards escorted me; I was handcuffed lest I do a runner at the graveside. I hadn't had much input into the arrangements. No doubt Neil's parents had thought bumping him off was more than enough of a contribution from me. I'd provided the body, they'd see to the rest. Thank goodness they included Adam in the process: he reported back to me with youthful disdain. The notice in the paper asked for donations to the Motor Neurone Disease Association rather than flowers. I remembered from burying my mother that there are so many decisions to make when someone dies: which coffin, what service, who will read, lilies or a wreath, where to go afterwards, which clothes to dress them in.

'His suit.' Adam snorted. 'He hated suits.'

'He didn't, actually.'

Adam stared at me.

'He made fun of people who acted like suits but he quite liked that last one, the charcoal, soft wool. He looked good in it.' Neil had bought it in the sales. His old suit was showing its age. There were times at work when he wanted to look smart and a suit in the wardrobe was always there if you had to attend a funeral. His own would be the first funeral he'd worn it to.

Adam was a little taken aback, his memory of Neil compromised by mine.

'I hope you held out against a tie,' I said. 'Ties he really did hate.'

'Yeah. No tie.'

Another visit and Adam was bubbling with resentment. 'They're going to do a mass,' he blurted out. 'At St Theresa's.'

I resisted the prick of anger. Neil had specified nothing in his will about the arrangements. He'd had clear desires about the manner of his leaving but not about what came after.

I played peacemaker. 'The service is for the people left behind more than anything. Grandma and Grandpa – it'll mean so much to them.'

'It's hypocritical,' Adam said. 'Don't you mind?'

'No, not really.' Choose your battles. Allowing Neil's parents the comfort of a mass, the support of their congregation, in the same place where they had christened him seemed the decent thing to do. And, after all, what choice did I have? I could hardly mastermind a coup from my prison cell, snatch the coffin and sneak everyone off to some atheistic woodland burial.

'When I come home,' I said to Adam, the words dangerous, preposterous in my mouth, 'we can have our own ceremony if we want to, to celebrate Dad.'

'Do you want cremating?'

His question startled me. 'I couldn't decide,' I said, with a shrug, 'so I'm leaving my body to science.'

'Are you?' He looked worried.

'Yes.'

'What if they use it for something you don't agree with? Like cloning or something?'

This was the sort of discussion I might have with Sophie. Adam had never been given to ethical debate.

'You don't get to cherry-pick.'

He blew out a breath, a noisy sigh, a youngster again, tired by it all.

'So, have they bought you a suit, yet?' I teased him.

'No,' he growled.

'What will you wear?'

'I've got a shirt, my black trousers.'

'It'll be fine,' I told him. 'We'll just go with the flow.'

With Neil being an only child, lapsed from his faith, I hadn't been to many Catholic services; there were no brothers and sisters asking us to their ceremonies. I'd probably been to wedding or two, a christening. What struck me most at Neil's funeral mass was the theatricality of it all – the vivid language, the dramatic gestures, like the throwing of holy water and the swinging of the incense lamps, the way the pungent reek filled the space.

140

We all sat in the front right-hand pew: Michael, Veronica, Sophie, then Adam, me, cuffed to the guard, and Jane. It felt bizarre, the proximity of this burly stranger. Perhaps I should have demurred and sat at the back in purdah, but I wanted to be there with my children even if it did scandalize people. The church was almost full, though I recognized few faces. Some of Neil's colleagues were there but I think most of those attending were friends of his parents.

My temperature was all over the place, chilled inside but hot and moist on the surface of my skin. Locking my eyes on the coffin, I imagined Neil inside: long and slim and still in his suit and shirt. He was a manikin. No heart, no pulse. He had gone four months before so why did I find my spine tightening and feel burning behind my eyes?

Among the prayers and responses, the chants, kneeling and rising, there were hymns, each chosen for their sentimental heart-wrenching qualities; three-hankie numbers. The singing was buoyed up by a group of two women and a man who stood by the altar and led us with robust voices. They helped compensate for the people who fell by the wayside, sniffling and gulping with sorrow, burrowing in hankies. Me among them. It was Adam who set me off, the little huff as his shoulders rose and fell. I put my arm round him and pulled him close and let my tears come, warm rain on my cheeks. Jane reached across in front of the guard and squeezed my arm. I turned to her, saw her smile through the blur. Grateful that she was there, her friendship unwavering, her reliability never doubted.

Veronica looked older; we'd been quite near each other as we entered the church. Other people moved slowly past her and Michael, Sophie and Adam, offering condolences, murmured phrases, touching an arm, a shoulder, clasping hands, brushing cheeks. I did not know my place, aware that I wasn't exactly up for a Widow of the Year award and that people had no idea whether to speak to me or not. I was hungry for a gesture from Sophie, a look, a smile, some reprieve from the terrible silence between us, but she concentrated studiously on everyone else. I hadn't lingered then, just moved ahead into the church, but I had noticed that Veronica's hair was greyer, thinner, her foundation paler, the lower half of her face around her mouth and jaw wrinkled and saggy. Still an attractive woman for her age. Neil had shared the same fine bone structure and dark hair. I always thought there was a look of Elizabeth Taylor in Veronica; not that striking, of course, but a similar type, a petite version.

Kneeling, when we bowed our heads in prayer, I slid my eyes to watch Sophie and saw Veronica's hands, sky-blue beads strung between them. They were shaking uncontrollably. We did not speak to each other at all that day. And Michael avoided me. I was disappointed in him. We had always got along well, though I suppose our contact was buffered by the children. Perhaps I should have expected it – I'd never heard him gainsay Veronica. He was like a satellite, really: she was the centre of the relationship, or that was how it seemed. He was a quiet man. An ambulance driver who had found the job too traumatic and become a warehouse manager instead. He shared Neil's love of history and the two could talk for hours about the past, about boys' stuff. Michael was always a kind man but I wondered what he thought about me now, whether he had any more understanding than Veronica about what had driven me to honour Neil's wishes.

At the crematorium I felt as though I was in a glass cylinder. The service there was swift and I watched, dry-eyed, as Neil's coffin slid away. The funeral party were going back to the church hall for refreshments. I was going back to prison.

In the car park outside the crematorium, I said goodbye to Adam. Jane gave me a hug and told me she would see me in the week. I drank in a last glimpse of Sophie climbing into the funeral car. I ached, wanting to hold her, touch her. It drove off. As I made to go, someone touched my arm. It was Tony Boyd, Neil's old friend, who'd been a witness at our wedding. He'd lived in Portugal for years, had a wife and family there, twin girls. We still exchanged Christmas cards and once every couple of years, when he was visiting his parents, he would call Neil and we'd meet up for a night of reminiscing and catching up. He was one of the people we had phoned in the days after Neil's death but I'd had no idea he'd be coming to the funeral.

'Deborah,' he looked me in the eyes, 'I'm so sorry.' He hesitated, glanced at my minder, gave a shake of his head and opened his arms. He pulled me close and his generous embrace made me weep. I closed my eyes and savoured the warmth from his body and the breadth of his shoulders and the peppery smell of his cologne.

I pulled back and surveyed him. He was almost bald, his hair cropped close, his eyebrows grey. He had a paunch too, tight against his shirt. We are so old, I thought. We've all got so old.

'I've got to fly back tomorrow,' he said, 'or I'd have come to see you.'

'That's fine. Keep in touch.'

'I will. He was a lovely man,' he said, 'and he was so happy with you.'

The compliments meant so much to me that day and for a few moments I was an honestly grieving wife, not a murderess.

Chapter Fourteen

I don't know why I had an affair. I couldn't explain it back then, either to myself or to Neil. It hasn't got clearer with hindsight. Was I just bored? Flattered by the attention?

Adam was seven, Sophie five. My business was expanding. The other man was a client. When we first met, I felt a swell of pleasure at the sight of him. The same reaction that I'd had when I'd first seen Neil. With this man I concealed it. I was happily married, a mother. I wasn't in the market for an affair. It wasn't an option. He was married, too. His wife was at that first meeting. Jeremy and Chandi. They were doing a new-build and staying in a rented apartment while the project took shape. It was an exciting design they had planned, no Barratt home. A two-storey dwelling on a brownfield site in a redevelopment zone. There was a canal nearby and Jeremy wanted a modern, waterside feel. There would be glass-and-steel patio doors along the back overlooking the canal, an open-plan living area, and central stairs to the upper floor. The couple wanted my input into the kitchen design and also a scheme for the colours and soft furnishings in the other areas.

Disconcerted by my attraction to Jeremy, the way my stomach contracted when I made eye contact with him, the pleasing timbre of his voice, I made a point of focusing on Chandi as we talked. She was a hospital doctor; he worked as a translator of educational books; together they had enough of an income to build their dream home. I went away with a clear idea of their likes and dislikes, their specifications and a copy of the architect's drawings for the site, promising to return in a fortnight with initial designs.

At the second meeting there was no sign of Chandi. Had he engineered it like that? When I asked if she didn't want a chance to comment, he told me she had to be at the hospital during working hours and would give me any feedback via him. Jeremy smiled and offered me tea. His teeth were white, his lips the colour of raspberries. He was shorter than Neil, stockier. I busied myself laying out my portfolio while he made the drinks. Their rental flat was part of a warehouse refurbishment, very eighties with bare brick walls and wooden floors, recessed lights. The ceilings were surprisingly low, and the décor neutral colours, easier to rent out than something distinctive. The couple's own furnishings were more eclectic, and included a monster of a couch with a geometric Scandinavian print in turquoise, white and orange clambering all over it. But the piece was too large in the space.

Nervously I talked Jeremy through the plans. Once in my stride I was able to quell the sexual feelings but whenever he asked a question or bent closer to examine a sketch everything shifted and I became clumsy and self-conscious. The encounter was like a badly executed dance: we'd speak at the same moment, or interrupt each other after awkward pauses. Slowly it dawned that it wasn't just me who was off-kilter.

Eager to leave, I ran through a brisk summary of which options he would discuss with his wife. The Belfast sink and central island with a butcher's block (salvaged rather than new) were key to the kitchen design and other elements would tie in. He and Chandi would consider whether to accommodate an Aga or go for a smaller oven and hob with a separate wood-burning stove. The latter were quite rare back then and Jeremy appeared to find my enthusiasm for them amusing. He had samples of fabrics for curtains and upholstery to show Chandi and a style board I'd put together.

Finishing my spiel, I gathered up my portfolio. Silence hung in the air, and I looked up to find his eyes locked on me, his face serious, his lips slightly parted as if on the brink of speech. Clearing my throat, I looked away and got to my feet. He caught my wrist and stood up. My heart galloped. He came closer. I let him. He kissed me and lust flared through me, hungry, needy. I dropped my papers. When he began to pull at my clothes, I made no protest. In fact, my hands were running over his shirt, and down, touching his erection through his clothes and feeling myself grow moist in response.

He pulled me over to the couch and I lay down. He ran through to the other room and came back with a condom. He stripped off his pants, slid on the condom. With our clothing half off, he knelt above me, nudged against me and I lifted my hips to meet him. Neither of us spoke and the sex can't have lasted more than five minutes. Touching myself, I came as he climaxed, his face contorted and dark with blood.

He withdrew and edged down beside me. I wriggled over to make room, keeping my eyes closed. I waited for my heart to slow, my breathing to return to normal. He was still and I thought perhaps he was dozing but when I opened my eyes he was gazing up at the ceiling.

'I've never done anything like this before,' he said.

'You're a virgin!' My joke punctured the tension and we burst out laughing. Part of me was horrified. How could I laugh at a time like this? What on earth had I done?

'Let's not talk,' I said. 'I've a marriage, children. You have a wife. We just forget this . . .' I halted and tried again. 'There are other designers, people I know . . .'

He shushed me. 'This can mean whatever we want it to. I didn't set out to . . .'

'Fuck me?'

'I don't regret it. And I don't want anyone else to do the design.'

He was calm and articulate while I felt confused, dizzy as if someone had punched me. 'I don't know.' I gathered my clothes together, began to dress.

'Debbie.'

I resisted the impulse to correct him; I hate being called Debbie. I'm not Debbie. Perhaps I thought that if he didn't use the right name it would negate some of what had happened, that I could splinter off this Debbie woman into some cubby-hole – distinct and unconnected from Deborah.

'I don't know,' I repeated.

'Are you sorry it happened?'

I didn't answer.

'It needn't happen again, if that's what you want. But don't run away.'

I shivered. Finished pulling on my clothes. 'I need time to think.'

'Fine. Call me?'

* * *

At home, I showered and changed my clothes, my mind racing over what had happened. A voice in my head laid out all the reasons to quit the job and avoid seeing Jeremy again.

When Neil got back from school, I was terrified he would sense a change in me, smell my treachery. He didn't.

The next morning I sat in my workshop, the plans for Jeremy and Chandi's house spread out around me. I would ring him up and decline the work. There were Neil and the children to think about. I was happy, wasn't I? Why risk it all for a fling that might be exciting but certainly wouldn't lead to any greater happiness? I wasn't the girl in the black vintage silk dress any more, reckless and disinterested. I was a wife and a mother with a business to run.

I dialled his number. And listened to myself arrange a rendezvous for the end of the week.

The sex was always the same: passionate, fast and greedy. Always at his house, always with the pretext of a meeting about the project. We never made small-talk or ventured to suggest meeting anywhere else, to do anything else. We used the couch, sometimes the bedroom. On one occasion I was so eager, aroused with the anticipation as I drove over there, that I grabbed him as he let me in and we screwed standing up against the front door.

Neil never noticed. But Jane did. Jane was newly wed herself then and living across town. We habitually met for a drink and a talk. I didn't like her husband Mack very much so we had never developed the habit of going out as a foursome. Besides, our friendship pre-dated our marriages and without our partners there we could confide in each other better.

'You look good,' she said, as she slipped off her coat and settled opposite me. 'Very good.' She took another appraisal. 'Oh, God, are you pregnant again?'

'No.' Then I told her, 'I'm having an affair.'

She blinked with shock, then a trace of anger edged into her face. 'Why?' she asked me. Not 'who' but 'why'?

'I don't know.' And the downside of it all, the nervous guilt, the scorching shame opened up in me. A pit of my own making. I tried to explain to Jane but my account sounded shallow. It was the first, the only time, I'd met with her disapproval and I resented her for it.

'I don't love him, it's just a fling.'

She was quiet and I spoke to fill the space, asking about her holiday, their house-hunting. The dislocation in our friendship was horrible. Jane genuinely couldn't understand my behaviour. Later, when it was all over and we were able to talk about it, she said it would have made sense to her if I had loved Jeremy but to risk so much just for sex seemed self-destructive.

Three years after that Mack left Jane for another woman. Someone he had already been seeing before he married Jane – and he'd just kept on seeing her. I wonder if Jane hadn't had some premonition, some sixth sense that behaviour like mine and Jeremy's would hurt her.

Was I being self-destructive? Having an affair because I knew I didn't deserve the security I had found with Neil? Because I knew that one day he would leave me, like my father had left, so I beat him to the punch? Maybe there was an element of that, kicking down my own sandcastle, but I also believe it was a fluke of circumstance. If any other man had opened the door of that apartment, I wouldn't have lusted after him so foolishly.

After three months my design brief for Jeremy and Chandi was almost completed. Contractors would be carrying out the work to my specifications, but that was delayed as the construction of the building was behind schedule. I hadn't thought about what would happen after my part in the project was done. It was like being a child again, living only in the here and now, with no thought for the consequences.

It was the middle of winter, the last time I saw Jeremy. Temperatures had dipped and the side-roads glimmered with black ice. The air was cold and foggy, washing everything monochrome. We had fixed a meeting first thing in the morning; I had other clients to see later in the day. Jeremy had the heating on full whack when I arrived. Their lounge felt airless and dry. I peeled off coat, gloves and scarf.

'Don't stop.' His voice thickened. He was sitting on the couch in his jogging pants and a sweatshirt, his hair still damp from the shower.

I glanced at my portfolio.

'We can do that after.'

He reached out a foot, ran it up the inside of my leg, above my knee. Heat pulsed through my veins like hot syrup, making my skin rosy and my breathing quicken.

I took off my cardigan, unzipped my boots and pulled them off. He watched as I slid down my trousers and stepped out of them. He pulled his sweatshirt over his head and dropped it. I unbuttoned my blouse, then the cuffs, let it fall open. Enjoying his excitement, the irresistible burn of sexual appetite.

That was when Chandi walked in. Fresh from work, where the boiler had packed up and her appointments had been cancelled.

She took in the sight of us, me in my shirt and sheer underwear, her husband half naked on their couch, and she gave a little dry laugh. Like she'd known all along – like here was another fuck-up to add to her bloody lousy day. 'You fucking bastard,' she said to Jeremy.

He had the grace to redden and began to apologize to her. I said nothing, pulled on my trousers, stuffed my feet into my boots, shrugged my coat on and scooped everything else up. Chandi began to shout at him. Without a word I walked out, my heart thundering and my legs trembling.

A week later I got a cheque for my work. I never knew whether they had gone ahead and used the designs, if they had stayed together and completed their home. But wouldn't it rankle if they had? Each time anyone commented on the grey-green of the curtains or the wood-burning stove, wouldn't it be like heat on a burn?

Three weeks after that I told Neil what I had done. There was no need to, no one else would have spilled the beans, but I found that carrying the betrayal was souring my love for him. I needed his forgiveness. I got an inkling of why Catholics go to confession.

He was very hurt, very angry. Then he cried. He wouldn't touch me. That was the worst thing. When he still hadn't come near me after three days, I surveyed the wreck I had made of our marriage, faced the prospect of losing him for good and asked him to come and see a counsellor with me. I was desolate and couldn't see how we could rebuild our relationship without outside help. How could he forgive me? If the tables had been turned I would have rent him limb from limb, kicked him out and built a prison on the moral high ground for myself and the children.

The next year was very painful, though our counsellor was a brilliant and highly skilful woman and the work we did with her was far more intellectual than I had expected. She encouraged us to examine in depth the patterns of communication in our families, the use of power and control, of emotional life, and to look at what we had brought with us to our own marriage. Again and again I came up against the wounds left by the loss of my father, and my mother's distance, which was a loss of sorts. Perhaps for the first time I mourned him properly, grieved for her and for the mother I never had.

I think it took several years more for Neil to really relax into the relationship again. I don't think he ever loved me the same. I'm not saying he loved me any less, but differently – it might even have been stronger because of what we had weathered, but it was less innocent.

As for trust, that grew with time. The years flew by and the children grew and I never strayed again. Of course, trust was part of the equation at the end. Could he trust me to do as we had agreed? Sometimes I think that mattered more to me than the love. After all, my love might have led me to deny his request, arguing that I loved him so much I was not prepared to spend one day less with him. That would be love as need – love as taking not giving. Trust had a more practical dimension. Trust was a question with a yes or no answer. It was one-sided, one way. Could Neil rely on me to do his bidding?

Perhaps if I hadn't had the affair I wouldn't have needed to prove I could be trusted with this most onerous of tasks. Perhaps I'd have held out longer and forced him to see that there was another way. That he could die peacefully, with dignity, without hastening the process.

Instead, when he asked me for the third time, I thrashed about like a landed fish for long enough and simply caved in.

Chapter Fifteen

When Neil got his diagnosis in 2007, the neurologist told him about the local MNDA branch and offered to put him in touch with them. Not long afterwards he had a phone call from someone there. They talked for quite a while and then she sent him a folder full of leaflets and information on different aspects of the disease. She also invited him along to the next branch meeting. Neil procrastinated. He told her he would think about it. When I raised it with him, he said he didn't feel like going. 'I need a bit more time to get my head round it.'

Now I wonder whether even then he had made the decision about his death and therefore thought joining the Association wasn't an option for him. Meeting other people with the disease, getting advice and support and a sense of solidarity might compromise his position. If he made friendships there, gave or received succour and then arranged an early demise, how would those other people and their families feel?

So we never really got involved. Should I have pushed him more, early on, when his resolve hadn't hardened? Then he might have found some hope, another way of looking at things, won more time with us and taken advantage of hospice care. But now that I knew his days, his hours, were already cut so short, there was no way I could pressure him into spending time on anything he wasn't eager to do.

We did take charge of one of the breathing space packs and followed the advice in the Association's leaflets to help us talk about the situation with Adam and Sophie.

On my own behalf I rang the MNDA helpline several times. Sometimes I needed space to be angry, to vent the why us, why him, why me questions with someone who understood. Sometimes I needed to clarify the information in the leaflets, about Neil's symptoms or the care he was getting. Other times I wanted a place to be miserable, someone to know how sick I was about the whole bloody mess. Allow myself to weep on the phone to one of those anonymous volunteers. Open my Pandora's box and pull on a cloak of bleak despair, wrap scarves of fear tight about my throat, veil my face with sheets of white-hot grief and weep for my loss. Unlike Pandora, my demons went back into the box and I did what anyone in that position has to do: I soldiered on with a brave face. Ms Practicality.

I'm sorry for myself. Then and now. Sorry for all of us but, yes, sorry for myself. That the Fates dealt me this hand. I imagine them prowling on the sidelines, outraged that I have interfered, that I cut the thread of life before Neil had lived his allotted span. Three blind women sniffing out my treachery and preparing to cut me down. When Asclepius dared to interfere with their hold on life and death they persuaded Zeus to kill him with a thunderbolt.

Tomorrow in court I face Veronica. I see us like two hyenas, tearing at Neil as if he were a fresh kill, so much dead meat, competing first for his love and then for his corpse. Time and again, I remind myself that as a mother she feels the same about Neil as I do about Adam. She is not the wicked witch of the north. She is not Medea slaying her children to get back at her erring spouse. She is a seventy-four-year-old woman, a former nurse with all the bossy practicality that denotes. Happily married, a marvellous cook. She likes to drink martinis and can still jive. In the 1950s she left her family in Ireland to come here to work and never looked back. When Sophie was four, she saved her from choking with the Heimlich manoeuvre. She babysat for us at the drop of a hat. She had a breast cancer scare in her sixties. When I was depressed, after my own mother's death, Veronica helped a great deal, cleaning the house when I could barely get out of bed. Popping in with home-made fruit pies and chicken casseroles. Taking Adam out for treats and giving me space.

Why was I always so prickly around her? Why does she still make me feel like a stroppy adolescent? I'm a fifty-year-old woman. Would it have been any different if my own mother had been warmer, more nourishing?

Veronica's unwavering faith, her religion, has always unnerved me. In the heady days of university, when Neil told me about his upbringing and some of the rules and regulations, I found it hard to credit.

'They'd soon have me burned at the stake,' was Jackie, the Cleopatra look-alike's comment when a few of us were sitting around one night in our university days, playing Risk, drinking cider and sharing a spliff. 'Unnatural practices.' She inhaled from the joint she held, grinned and let the smoke curl out of her mouth.

'You can't go on the pill because that's interfering with God's will,' I declaimed, pretty drunk by then. 'Then if you do get pregnant you can't have an abortion. It's condemning women to be baby machines.'

'Don't look at me.' Neil laughed. 'I didn't invent it.'

'Does your family know you don't go to church any more, that you're an unbeliever?' I asked him.

'A heathen,' said Jane.

'Yep. But they don't like it much.'

Later, as I got to know Veronica, I was shocked at how abruptly her manner would change if there was any challenge to her religious beliefs. It was like throwing a switch and she'd be mouthing brisk homilies, steel in her tone.

I read in the papers about Catholics who had challenged the orthodoxy, those who campaigned to change the dogma, who wanted sexual emancipation, who made a connection between poverty and female oppression. At uni we even had a small group of revolutionary Catholics come on the abortion rights marches. Then there were all those who found their own compromises. Millions of Catholics used contraception, including the pill. In Veronica's home country, Ireland, contraception was being smuggled in and secretly given to girls and women desperate not to have another baby.

Veronica had seen it all, the poverty back home, the ill-health of women coming into hospital worn out by bearing and raising children. She must have known and maybe treated those who had survived botched abortions and I couldn't understand why that life experience didn't lead her to question the diktats that gave women so little choice. I soon learned that there wasn't any point in trying to talk to her about any of these issues. And I'm sure I came across as opinionated and self-righteous and wilfully provocative.

She came to see me when I was expecting Adam. She had known Neil would be teaching. It was an unusual situation, the two of us alone together. I made a cup of tea and we chatted about the baby.

'I've brought you this,' she said softly, and pulled a parcel wrapped in tissue paper from her plaid shopping bag. 'Here, open it.'

Puzzled, pleased, I unfolded the tissue paper to find a long, cream satin christening robe with seed pearls around the neck and cuffs. It was beautiful.

'I wore it,' she said, 'and Neil wore it.'

Words stuck in my throat and a flare of irritation shot through me. Veronica knew we had no intention of getting the baby christened. We weren't going to raise the child in any religion. Neil was adamant. He was an atheist now and he'd no intention of being a hypocrite. He had already told her this; they had argued about it. Now here she was ambushing me in my own kitchen.

While I was searching for a response that wouldn't completely destroy our fragile relationship (I didn't think, 'You sly old bat, if you think you can guilt trip me into this then you don't have the measure of me yet' set quite the right tone) she followed up with her *coup de grâce*. 'It would make Michael and me so very happy to pay for the christening party – our present to the baby.'

'We're not having it christened,' I said rudely, my cheeks aflame with embarrassment and irritation.

'Well, who else will use it?' she cried, a spark of temper from her and a swift nod at the gown. She took a quick fierce breath, the prelude to a scolding, but said nothing. She picked up her shopper, pausing at the door. 'What harm can it do?' she demanded.

She left the robe on the table, like an accusation.

Later Neil was sure she'd whipped the holy water out at some point and done a DIY baptism on the babies, protecting them from limbo if they died. She would have believed implacably that our selfish defiance, as she saw it, robbed both of our children of the prospect of ever entering heaven.

Jane was nonchalant about it when I told her the story. 'If you both think it's a load of old tosh,' she said, 'then does it really matter if the baby gets baptized or not? Isn't it an irrelevance? And if it makes them happy . . .'

I stared at her. 'Neil won't do it in a million years. And I don't like the idea. If she practised voodoo or was a Moonie or a Jehovah's Witness and she wanted me to initiate my child in the one true path, then what would you say?'

Jane waggled her head, screwed up her mouth, allowing I had a point, maybe. 'You could do your own thing – a naming ceremony or something.'

I groaned. 'That would be like rubbing their noses in it. Besides, I don't want to do anything. I want to have this baby and it to be all right and just leave it at that.'

Of course, we won. There was no way Neil was going to cave in to his mother's pressure. He told her himself that he wasn't going to change his mind. After that she never mentioned a christening. Neither did she make any suggestions about schooling when the time came to put Adam's name down for a place. By then it was clear that we weren't part of her community. As the children got older and stayed with her and Michael, she would take them along with her to mass. They were fascinated the first couple of times, coming home full of questions that we had to answer tactfully, qualifying many of our explanations with 'Grandma and Grandpa think . . .' or 'Grandma and Grandpa believe . . .' and often ending with 'and other people don't'.

Whatever our religious differences, the children brought us closer. The four of us shared the love and pleasure of Adam and then Sophie, and had so much in common there, a mutual sense of joy and privilege and a similar way of caring for the kids that, thankfully, overrode those divisions.

Day three of my trial and the drizzle has cleared: a fierce wind has pushed all the clouds away and the sky is a piercing blue, bright enough to sting my eyes as I'm transferred from the prison to the van.

Travelling into the city centre, I look up out of the small rectangular window in my compartment at the buildings. I spy the light grey modern British Telecom building, at Castlefield near the Mancunian Way, and then the imposing brick bridges that carry the railways across the end of Deansgate. The railway arches have been converted into bars and clubs. Further along, there are old banks and warehouses, insurance companies and office blocks, most of them raised in the Victorian era during the cotton boom. They bear witness to the craft of stonemasons, with their fine carving and columns, finials and trims. The window is too small for me to see the top of the Hilton skyscraper. Halfway down Portland Street and way up high on one building, I notice words, cast in brick, bas-relief: 'honesty' and 'perseverance'. Admonitions to the city's workforce. I don't know whether to laugh or to cry.

And then we are at Minshull Street and pull up alongside another prison van. The back entrance that we use is solid oak, studded and imperious. Either side of it frolic gargoyles and demons, legs splayed like lizards, faces contorted with sadistic glee.

Today I am in a different cell at the opposite end of the corridor. It is ten o'clock. The courts begin each day at ten thirty. There is a lot of waiting about. Between the paralysing tension of the courtroom there are interminable stretches of dead time when it's hard to find anything to do. I should like to sketch but I am not permitted to carry a pen or pencil in case I use it as a weapon against myself or someone else.

Tension gathers in my back. I stand and stretch and roll my shoulders to try to release it. I am on my feet doing side stretches when the viewing panel in the door slides back and the guard tells me Ms Gleason is here to see me.

We sit on the bench.

'How are you?' she asks. 'Did you get any sleep?'

'Some,' I answer.

'We're expecting Mrs Draper this morning and possibly Dolores Cabril. It'll depend on when the judge decides to break for lunch.'

Dolores Cabril is the psychiatric expert for the prosecution. She is my greatest threat. If she convinces the jury that I was sane when I helped Neil die, they will have to return a guilty verdict. Dolores is aptly named as far as I'm concerned – Spanish for 'sorrows'. She threatens to bring me grief. But at the moment I am more worried about facing Veronica.

'And that'll be the end of their witnesses?' I check with Ms Gleason.

'Yes.' Her clothes are smart today. She's made an effort, or perhaps just had a chance to do some ironing. There are a couple of short white hairs on her lapel. When did I get to be so fussy? What does it matter? Compared to Mr Latimer and his scuzzy wig, Ms Gleason is perfectly groomed. Should I point it out? I do.

'God,' she huffs. 'My dog's moulting. Black's a nightmare.' She picks the hairs off.

'Does anyone ever wear anything else?'

'At their peril.' She releases the tips of her thumb and finger, lets the hairs float to the floor. 'Tradition is all,' she drawls, in her laconic, fruity Bolton accent.

When she has gone, the usher sends for me and a guard escorts me up to the courtroom. The barristers are already there, like so many crows pecking over their papers and dipping their heads together for a quick confab.

Glancing up to the public gallery as I make my way to the dock, I see Adam and Jane in their places. Then my eyes fix on the row behind. There is Sophie. Sophie and her grandpa, Michael. A pain burns in my heart and for a moment I lose my balance, stumble slightly by the steps. I think I might faint but the dizziness eases and I am left with nausea. The back of my neck and the back of my knees are damp.

It hadn't occurred to me that after giving her evidence Sophie would attend the trial. And why shouldn't she? She wants justice for Neil. I have no idea where Michael stands in all this, whether he agrees with Sophie and Veronica's desire to see me prosecuted.

And my children? How are they faring? Sophie has her grandparents and Adam has Jane. Looking at him now, Adam's face is like thunder. Is this because Sophie is there or because his grandma is due on the stand? Or is it nothing to do with the trial? Maybe he's getting ill again. I feel so bloody helpless and make a mental note to ask Ms Gleason if she can find out how he is. While I am on trial I cannot have visits so I won't be able to see him for myself.

Chapter Sixteen

When Adam first became ill, he was in the third year of secondary school. He was fourteen. The change to a bigger school had seemed to go fine at first. Neither of us expected him to be top of the class – he was too lazy, too disorganized, to be a high achiever. The school had a programme in place to support his dyslexia and although he muttered darkly about being bunched in with the other special needs 'saddos', his reading and writing were clearly improving. He had friends too: Jonty and a bunch of others, who steered a careful line doing just enough work to avoid trouble and spending every waking minute they could hanging out with each other. They moved from household to household, grazing through the freezers, a lanky, clumsy, well-meaning, deodorant-drenched herd. Now and again, I smelled smoke on Adam, but I hoped he was only trying it out and would outgrow it. Then in the third year, year nine, as Neil would remind me it was now called, the glow went out of Adam. We heard from school that he was missing days. When we challenged him about it, he was surly and close-mouthed.

'Adam,' I insisted, 'we need to know what's going on.'

'Nothing,' he repeated.

'You should be in school,' Neil said. 'And if

there's some reason why you're deliberately missing it then tell us about it.'

'It might be something we can sort out,' I added.

Adam raised his eyes long enough to shoot me a look of utter disdain, then let his head fall back down between his shoulders. We got nothing out of him but things seemed to settle for a week or so. Then I came home at midday, after a meeting with a client, to find him in bed.

'I feel sick,' was his excuse.

I didn't believe him. 'Have you been sick?'

'No.'

'Well, don't eat anything and we'll see how you are in the morning.'

He languished in his room till we were all in bed and then I heard him roaming round the house. Was he becoming an insomniac like me? The next morning he was still 'ill'. I decided to test him. 'I'll make a doctor's appointment, shall I?'

''Kay,' he replied dully.

Halfway through the morning, I went into the house to empty the washing-machine and called up to see if he wanted anything. My own behaviour was lurching from maternal to authoritarian and back. Did he need nurturing or a kick up the bum? I'd no reference points. My own adolescence had been trouble-free, as far as my mother was concerned. She'd had no idea what I got up to outside the house and I was canny enough to keep it concealed from her. As for my brother, Martin, he didn't have a disruptive bone in his body. He was shy, very reserved, anxious only to blend in. The childhood memories I have of my big brother are of helping him with one of his methodical games, lining up toy soldiers in serried ranks, the way his face clenched if

I knocked any over by mistake, though he never said anything by way of reproach. Martin didn't like dirt or clutter or playing with other kids much, while I was never happier than when I was breathless, my windpipe burning and cheeks hot from running, mud-smeared, twigs in my hair, the glory of a day-long game of cowboys and Indians. Building dens from giant stalks, beating them hard to dislodge the earwigs. Martin was happier with his books and his Airfix kits and he cherished the daily routines that I carped against. We were like lodgers sharing a home but each independent of the other.

When I got no reply from Adam and found his bed was empty, I was puzzled. What was he playing at? He waltzed in at half past five that afternoon, his eyes bloodshot. When I tried to remonstrate with him, he began to giggle. He was stoned. Without even waiting to consult Neil, I told Adam that he'd get no pocket money until his behaviour improved and he was in school for all his classes.

He shrugged and went upstairs.

That night he prowled the house again. I got up to investigate. He was by the back door when I went into the kitchen and whirled round, startled.

'It's only me,' I said. 'What are you doing?'

He looked pale, bleary with tiredness. In an old 'And on the sixth day God created Manchester' T-shirt and baggy pyjama trousers, his hair tousled, he was my little boy again. 'The police,' he hissed at me.

'What?'

'They're outside the house, out there.'

I went towards the hall but he called after me, 'No, the garden, they'll be waiting in the garden.'

Ice froze my spine and chilled my guts. 'Adam, it's all right, there's nobody there.'

'There is!' His teeth chattered and he gave a little jig of fright.

'I'll check.'

'No! You can't open the door – you can't! Please, Mum, please.' The terror in his cry tore at me.

'All right.' I held my hands up to placate him. 'Come and sit down.'

My mind was whirring. He was being paranoid. It reminded me of student days: a girl at an all-night party had dropped some acid and spent hours insisting the SAS were on the roof, and the more wound up she got about it, the more inane giggling she received from the others. I tried to calm her down, tried to get her outside to fresh air, but she wasn't having it.

Was Adam tripping?

'Have you taken anything, Adam?' I held my voice even.

'What?'

'LSD – acid?'

'No.'

'Dope? Cannabis?'

He didn't reply.

'What was it? Grass, sputnik, what?'

'Just weed.'

'It's making you anxious, that's all.'

I stood up.

'What are you doing?' Panic in his voice.

'I'm making you some hot chocolate, and toast and honey. Eating might help.'

He ate and drank. I asked him whether he had felt like this before. He swung his head away from me. 'I don't want to talk about it. It just makes it worse.'

'Okay. But I want you to see the doctor.'

Later that morning he was at it again: checking

doors, peering out of curtains, under siege from his nightmares. It took another week to get him to the GP. Andy Frame referred him to a specialist, who told us that Adam had cannabis-induced psychosis.

We'd not heard of it. There were various theories about the phenomenon. Some people were thought to have a predisposition to mental illness and the use of cannabis triggered biochemical changes in the brain that prompted the illness to develop. Then there was talk of the modern-day strains of the drug being much stronger than in the past.

It was hard to believe that the drug Neil and I had enjoyed with impunity, that had a reputation for being benign, soft, non-addictive, that was linked to peace and love, John and Yoko, festivals and Rastafarianism, to fits of giggles and the munchies, was the same drug that had so damaged our son.

The judge comes in and everybody stands. Once he is settled he invites Miss Webber to continue with her evidence. 'Will the court please call Veronica Draper,' she says.

The usher walks to the door, 'Call Veronica Draper.'

The witnesses wait in a room set aside for them. Veronica comes in and all eyes are on her as she makes her way to the stand. She is straight-backed but the pace she moves at and the way she lists to one side betray her age. Her hair is iron-grey, styled to give it some volume and rolled under in a short bob. She wears a pleated navy skirt and a cream blouse with a cream cravat. She looks tiny on the stand. When she swears on the Bible her voice is tremulous. I see she is terribly nervous and I feel a rush of sympathy, even though I'm angry that she is speaking against me. That brisk efficiency has vanished. Here, in an alien domain, in an agonizing situation, she is passive, a victim.

'Mrs Draper,' Briony Webber begins, 'can you tell us how you first heard the news of your son Neil's death?'

'Sophie rang me.' Her voice is soft; her Irish accent blurs the consonants and we strain to hear.

'Sophie rang you, not Deborah Shelley?'

'No. It was Sophie.'

'And you went immediately to the house?'

'That's right. We were in Tesco's at the time and we just walked out.'

The judge leans forward. 'Mrs Draper, can you speak up a little? It is difficult to hear you and it is extremely important that the jury hear everything you have to say. And if you can direct your answers to the jury instead of to Counsel.'

Expressions of sympathy ripple across the faces of Hilda and Flo, the Cook and Mousy. I'm sure they imagine themselves in her shoes – having to speak about terrible things in front of strangers.

'And when you called at the house on the fifteenth of June, what did Ms Shelley say had happened?'

'She said she'd gone upstairs and found Neil, that he was dead.'

'Was this a shock to you?'

'A dreadful shock.' Veronica loses volume on the last word and her mouth spasms.

My guts clench as I will her not to break down.

'At that stage did you have any doubts about what Ms Shelley told you?'

'Not then, no. It was just the shock of it, you know, that's all there was then.'

'Some days later, on the twenty-fourth of June, your granddaughter Sophie came to visit you.'

'Yes.'

'What did Sophie tell you?'

'She said she didn't know what to do. She thought her father hadn't died of natural causes, that unless he had had a heart-attack he couldn't have gone so quickly.'

'And what did you tell Sophie?'

'That perhaps that's what did happen – a heart-attack.'

'Was she satisfied with your answer?'

'No. She said she thought her mother had helped him take his own life.'

'And what did you say?'

Veronica pauses, struggling to speak. 'I slapped her,' she says quietly.

My hackles rise, a rush of heat at the thought of her striking my girl. Hurting her.

'You slapped her?' Miss Webber echoes, in case any of us missed it.

'Yes. It was an automatic reaction, from the shock. I couldn't believe what she was saying, that he would be part of something like that. It's against everything we believe.'

'You are a Catholic?'

'Yes.'

'And Neil was raised in that faith?'

'Yes.'

'Was he still a practising Catholic?'

'No.' She hates to say it.

And if he had been we wouldn't be here today, in this God-awful mess. Nine of the jurors swore on the Bible. I wonder if any of them are Catholics too, and if that will influence the way they view the evidence.

'Please tell the court what happened then.'

'I said I was sorry to Sophie, but she must have got it wrong. Then she told me about the things she'd seen.'

'Like what?'

'Her mother had been on these websites on the computer about mercy killings and so on. And there had been morphine in the house, which was missing.' Veronica goes on to repeat more of what Sophie said yesterday: my insistence that it was too late to revive him, Neil's health that morning.

'And after this what did you think about Sophie's view of the situation?'

'I thought she was right. It made sense.'

'And you were there when she first contacted the police?'

'Yes.'

'And you accompanied her when she went to the police?'

'I did.'

'Mrs Draper, you have known your daughter-in-law how long?'

'Thirty years.'

'Did she confide in you about her health?'

'Too vague, Your Honour,' Mr Latimer interrupts.

'Sorry, I'll rephrase that,' Miss Webber says swiftly. 'In 1993 when Deborah was suffering from depression after her mother's death, did she confide in you?'

'Yes. She told me about it, and said she was under the doctor.'

'Can you think of other examples?'

'Yes, she told me she thought she was getting an ulcer, one time. When she was stressed.'

'Can you remember what year this was?'

'2005.'

It was when Adam had become ill.

'Any other examples?'

'Just after Neil got his diagnosis, that first Christmas, when we'd all got together.'

All? All of us? It sounds like a great clan gathering – there were six of us.

'That was in 2007?'

Veronica agrees. 'Deborah told me she was thinking of seeing a therapist. She said she felt very low – they'd had all the business with Adam being taken into A&E, then Neil's illness, but she didn't want Neil to worry.'

'Did she speak to you about this again?'

'I asked her the next time we met and she said she was feeling much better.'

'Mrs Draper, did Deborah tell you she was mentally or emotionally unwell after that, at any time before Neil's death?'

'No.'

'Nothing in the next eighteen months?'

'No.'

'Did she appear to you to be mentally unwell?'

Veronica's chin goes up a fraction and she says, 'Not at all.'

'Did you ever ask Neil about her well-being?'

'Oh, yes. He said she was doing really well, amazing, he said.'

'On the day of his death, how did your daughter-in-law seem to you?'

Veronica hesitates. Surely they will have rehearsed such a crucial point. Has she simply forgotten her lines? 'She seemed reserved, withdrawn.'

'Depressed?'

'No. Just quiet.'

'And in the following days?'

'The same . . .'

I want to yell across at her, 'How should I have seemed? Incapable with grief? Blubbing in your arms as though we loved each other instead of loving the same damn man?'

Veronica carries on. 'Usually Deborah is quite chatty—'

Chatty? I have been many things but chatty is not one of them.

'—forthright. But she only spoke if she had to.'

She is painting me as sly and secretive, retreating into my shell after the hideous deed. My grief questionable.

'Can you tell the jury whether you saw a change in Ms Shelley's behaviour in the time before Neil's death and afterwards?'

'Just that she was quieter afterwards.'

'No sign of agitation?'

'No. She was fine,' she says. She swivels her head from the jurors to make eye contact with me, for the first time during her testimony. Her gaze is an open wound. It hurts me to see.

As Miss Webber regains her seat, the jury shuffle about and prepare for Mr Latimer's cross-examination. What do they make of us? Mother and daughter-in-law at odds. Does Alice know about that? Or PA? Has she got a mother-in-law? The Artist coughs, a dry, rackety sound. He takes a sip of water and clears his throat. Does he go home and paint after a day here? Has our story inspired him to get out the oils and stretch a new canvas? I resist a smile, catching myself out – he may be a postman or a vet or a physicist.

Mr Latimer has only a few questions for Veronica.

'Would you describe your relationship with Deborah as close?'

'Not really.' At least she is being honest.

'Did you and Deborah ever spend time together separately from any family visits when your husbands or your grandchildren were present?'

'No.'

I try to imagine it. We would have been awkward, out of place, each itching for the time to pass and to get into more comfortable company.

'Did you chat on the phone?'

'No.'

'Deborah knew your views on the sanctity of life?'

'Yes.'

'If she was being pressured by her sick husband to help him die, if she was cracking under that pressure, do you think she would have confided in you, knowing your views, knowing this was your son asking her for help?'

'She could have.'

It is a weak answer, with a touch of petulance in her tone. I feel perhaps Mr Latimer has taken the sting out of some of Veronica's account.

'But she didn't?' he presses.

'No.'

He seems satisfied and there are no further questions.

As Veronica leaves, I see Michael touch Sophie's arm and rise. And I feel the tug of jealousy. He must be meeting Veronica. Will they go home now? Or will they come back in to hear Dolores Cabril give me a sparkling bill of health?

At the end of the day, Ms Gleason had warned me, it'll be a battle of the shrinks. Here we were poised for the bell, the big match, the first round seconds away.

175

Chapter Seventeen

My mother's death seemed brutal. There were times when it was hard to tell what was actually killing her: the cancer or the treatment. Perhaps if she'd had my father to support her, or a close friend to weather the journey with her, it would have felt less bleak.

Martin was there to ferry her to the clinic and run errands. He lived about ten miles away from her, in a flat above his business: an insurance brokerage. He lived alone. There were girlfriends from time to time but nothing ever developed. At weekends, when I would drive over and visit, our paths would cross but our exchanges were exclusively practical and we were rarely out of earshot of our mother.

Invariably I would return home from those visits feverish with resentment, feeling cheated and miserable. Cheated because I was waiting for death's drum to make my mother dance to a different beat. I longed for the illness to bring us closer, for her distance and reserve to melt away and for her finally to open up, to share her feelings with me, to acknowledge the difficulties we had had and at last, with the end in sight, to be able to love me. I wanted to be able to tell her I loved her, without feeling it was a love born of obligation not pleasure, that I was sorry we hadn't shared much enjoyment in life, that we both deserved some reconciliation before the end.

Now and again, I'd make crass efforts to pave the way for this transformation. I would talk about my feelings for Adam or my anxieties about the coming baby and then refer to her own experience. Or I'd ask leading questions about her upbringing. She would always deflect me, never giving an answer but finding some little task for me to perform: switch the TV on, check the thermostat, top up her tea, take a note for the paper shop. Distraction techniques. The sort of thing you try on a toddler in a tantrum.

One day my patience snapped. Wretched with lack of sleep and frightened by how sick she looked (the whey colour of her skin, the peculiar smell, like sour fruit, that came from her), I challenged her outright. When she blocked my opening gambit with some flummery about the fuel bill, I rounded on her. 'Mum, can't we just talk like normal people for once? About something other than the bloody gas meter? Can't we talk about us, about what's happening?'

She blinked; dots of colour stung her cheeks. 'I don't know what you mean.'

'We never talk about ourselves, about the past or our problems or how we feel. It's like we're strangers.' Tears unshed pressed behind my eyeballs. There was an image in my head. Motherhood idealized. She who would laugh with delight when I appeared, who would drink me in with warm eyes, listening to news of my triumphs and disasters. She who would celebrate my pregnancy and touch my belly, enthralled at the quickening ripple of her grandchild-to-be. She'd sit up late regaling me with tales of life with my father, of my own childhood, confiding in me her own disappointments and regrets. She would send me to bring out the photograph album and demand the latest photos of Adam for her bedside.

She frowned. 'I don't—' She broke off, an expression of defeat on her face. 'You're here, Martin comes. That's not strangers.'

A quiver of frustration vibrated through me. She didn't get it. Or maybe she pretended not to get it. Could she really think this was enough? Either way I never found the intimacy I craved with her.

The night she died, I was driving to the hospital and my thoughts were circling like vultures, picking over the remains of our relationship. I'd been trying to tell myself that she'd had no choice in how she acted, that her own upbringing, about which I knew little, had made her like this. But in my heart I blamed her. Oh, yes – I had her strung up and crucified with my childish rage.

She died before I reached her. No last words of redemption for me. She lay there, frail and pale, like the husk of something, and I was sad. Not for what I had lost but for what we'd never had. For the absence in our lives.

When it came to my trial they would argue that the spectre of my mother's painful illness and death, the stress of watching her wither and die, had contributed to tipping me over the edge into killing Neil. That I couldn't bear to see another person close to me go through that.

They didn't understand that it wasn't her death that haunted me. It was the cold embrace of her life.

Dolores Cabril is a small plump woman with protruding teeth, fine brown hair the colour of walnuts and a husky smoker's voice of a darker shade. She wears a black trouser suit with a tan

Paisley blouse, an ensemble that serves to emphasize her short stature. We have already met. She visited me in prison to assess me and to come up with her expert opinion as to whether I was firing on all cylinders when I helped Neil die.

I notice that the jurors are a little more uncertain about her than they have been about the previous witnesses – it's in the postures they adopt. Mousy's chin drops lower so that she has to cast her eyes upwards slyly to see the stand. Freckly Alice on the back row has lost her smile and three of the men, smart Media Man, the Cook and Callow Youth, have folded their arms. I assume a mistrust of shrinks is behind it. Perhaps a fear that Dolores Cabril is going to march into uncomfortable territory, spouting about penis envy and incestuous desires, or a notion that she has delved into the nastiest recesses of my mind and is going to drag out the ghastly entrails and drape them round the court.

This defensive reaction is not necessarily good for me because later the weight of my own defence will rest in the arms of my own expert psychiatrist. It is fine if the jury mistrust or dislike her, even better if they dispute her opinion, but if they simply despise the profession then I am way up the creek.

Dolores Cabril is dwarfed by the stand. We can just see her head and shoulders. She raises her hand to the good book and swears to tell the truth. Her voice is alluring. If you close your eyes and listen you might imagine it emanating from a six-foot siren who has wandered out of the steamy Havana of a Graham Greene novel. There's a tinge of her Spanish mother tongue in the smoke, audible in the way she pronounces 'truth'; a hard *t* at the end.

Briony Webber makes a meal of establishing her credentials: the degree from Cambridge, the MA and PhD, the years spent working as a psychiatric consultant, the books, the papers, the time as a forensic psychiatrist at Broadmoor high security hospital, her role as chair of the working party into human rights and mentally ill patients, her position on this and that select committee and the number of court appearances she has made. The MBE.

Hilda and Flo flicker into life at this last revelation and the Cook relaxes his arms and appears to revise his opinion. Beside him the Artist rolls his eyes – a republican I guess, given that the honours system and royalty are still so closely bound together.

Miss Webber continues: 'Professor Cabril, you first met Deborah Shelley on November the eighth last year. Can you tell the court the purpose of this visit?'

'This was an opportunity for me to assess Ms Shelley's state of mind.'

'Would that be her state of mind on November the eighth?'

'Yes. And also to hear about the circumstances surrounding her husband's death and to draw conclusions about her state of mind then,' she explains.

'And after meeting Ms Shelley you drew up a report for the prosecution?'

'That's right.' She gives a sharp dip of her chin.

'Was that report based solely on your meeting with Ms Shelley?'

'No. I also had access to police interviews and witness statements.'

Miss Webber nods and smiles, giving us the impression that she is pleased with the amount of care that Professor Cabril has put into the case.

'How did you find Ms Shelley to be at your meeting last November?'

'Functioning well, displaying normal reactions to her bereavement and incarceration.'

She imbues the last word with the tang of Spanish and I imagine Styal transformed, sweltering in a sun-baked landscape, dried mud walls and a corrugated-tin roof, the whine of mosquitoes, pitiless thirst, cockroaches and screams from the 'interview' room down the end of the corridor.

'Can you please take the jury through the summary of your findings on page three?' Miss Webber gives Professor Cabril the report and clears it with the judge. 'Your Honour, I am now passing Professor Cabril a copy of the report that is included in the case papers.'

The judge grunts, shuffles through the pile on his bench, and unearths his copy.

Professor Cabril reads her summary: 'Having reviewed the evidence provided and the account given to me in person by the defendant, and taking into account her prior medical history and her behaviour before and after the incident, it is my considered opinion that Ms Deborah Shelley was of sound mind and that she was not suffering from any abnormality of mind that might have resulted in diminished responsibility. Overall Deborah Shelley enjoys a well-balanced mental disposition.'

A pit opens in the bottom of my stomach. They have warned me to expect this description but her certainty, her brio, as she pronounces the phrases 'sound mind' and 'well-balanced', are overwhelming.

'In fifty years she has only once sought psychiatric support and that was in the classic situation of losing a close family member, namely her mother. In her behaviour preceding the event I have found no evidence of abnormality of mind. To all intents and purposes Deborah Shelley was coping admirably with a demanding situation.'

Coping. That bloody word again. I want to yell, 'What else could I do?'

'In the planning and execution of Neil Draper's death, Deborah Shelley exhibited a considered and rational approach. In the aftermath she was able to maintain a version of events constructed to evade prosecution. These are not the actions of someone suffering from an abnormality of mind. Setting aside any consideration of motive, which is beyond my remit, but focusing solely on her state of mind, it is my considered opinion that Deborah Shelley was mentally responsible for her actions and that her behaviour was consistent in this regard.'

It's all a bit wordy and the jury react. Media Man grips his forehead, hiding his eyes – all the better to think about something else. Hilda gives a slow blink and fiddles with her necklace. The Callow Youth casts his eyes skywards, consumed with interest in the chandeliers that hang in the vault of the ceiling.

'Thank you,' Miss Webber says. 'As this expert testimony is crucial to the prosecution case, I am concerned to ensure that the members of the jury fully understand your report and its implications.'

Professor Cabril gives a quick nod. She is the final witness for the prosecution, and the most important. Miss Webber must milk her for all she's worth.

'In my opening speech, members of the jury, I outlined for you the legal basis for this trial. Namely that Deborah Shelley faces a charge of murdering Neil Draper and that you will find her guilty or not guilty of that charge. You may find her not guilty of murder but guilty of manslaughter, due to diminished responsibility. This is the crux of the matter.' Miss Webber turns back to her witness. The lawyer's eyes are bright, her expression alert. She has an air of competence, of energy. This is what she does, and she does it well.

'Professor Cabril, you say Ms Shelley enjoys a good overall standard of mental health.'

'Yes, she does.'

'And does her behaviour in the period immediately before her husband's death show any deterioration of her mental health?'

'Nothing of any great significance.'

'Does her behaviour in the period after her husband's death show any deterioration in her mental health?'

'Nothing beyond the normal grieving process.' A roll on the final *r*, a flourish.

'In your expert opinion . . .'

I notice Dolly give a little huff. She doesn't like all this expert business. Or maybe she's already grasped the point and finds the repetition patronizing.

'. . . is there any evidence other than her own version of events to suggest Ms Shelley was suffering from abnormality of mind when she administered a fatal overdose to Neil Draper?'

'None at all.' Complete confidence.

No shred of doubt. I'm holding my breath. The tension burns in my neck.

'With your extensive experience, did you find any evidence that Deborah Shelley had impaired mental responsibility when she used a plastic bag to hasten her husband's death?'

I don't like to think of this. It makes me nauseous. Sophie bows her head and Adam sets his jaw. I force myself to keep looking ahead, then up to catch his eyes. I may regret what I have done but I will not be shamed. At last his gaze flicks my way and my pain softens a touch. He gives a wobbly grimace, trying for a smile.

Professor Cabril is answering: 'Not at all. Her actions were those of a mentally responsible person.'

'Professor Cabril.' Miss Webber pauses, lowers her voice a touch, drawing us in. Her words are measured, solemn, laden with gravity. 'When Deborah Shelley killed Neil Draper, was the balance of her mind disturbed?'

'No. She was fine, healthy, responsible.'

It's a neat last line. Succinct, deadly. The room is still, silent. The implication of her opinion hanging there, shrouding us all. Murder. My eyes are hot, my mouth dry. There's a fizzy sensation at the back of my skull as if I might faint.

Quietly, with a reverential nod and a whispered, 'Thank you', Briony Webber leaves the floor.

It is Mr Latimer's turn and he is on treacherous ground. He must attempt to discredit Professor Cabril's opinion without compromising the jury's view of the profession – for it won't be long till his own expert shrink is trundled out for more of the same.

'Pr-Pr-Professor Cabril. Your testimony here today is an opinion, is it fair to say, not a fact?'

'Yes, an opinion based on facts.'

'But an opinion all the same?'

'Yes.' She gives a tight smile.

'And opinions, particularly opinions about human behaviour, may vary?'

'Yes.'

'So the jury here will have to try to decide which expert opinion best fits the rest of the evidence?'

I think of the trail of lies, stitched to my widow's weeds, and shudder inside.

'Please can you tell the court how Ms Shelley herself described her state of mind immediately before her husband's death.'

Professor Cabril appears to fish for recollection. Mr Latimer is quick to prompt. 'In your report, paragraph four on the first page. Please can you read that for us?'

'"Deborah Shelley reports feeling under great pressure. She states that she felt trapped into agreeing to help Neil but was very anxious about that agreement. She also reported panic attacks and insomnia."'

'Panic attacks, anxiety, insomnia? Are these indicators of a healthy mental state?' Mr Latimer could be scathing but he's careful not to ridicule the witness.

'No, but they should be taken in context.' She takes a breath to expand, but Mr Latimer cuts her off.

'I am keen that the jury should understand this apparent contradiction.'

The Cook smiles and glances at the Artist. He's enjoying the jousting.

Professor Cabril lowers her shoulders, clasps her hands together, an unconscious attempt to regain equilibrium. 'Deborah Shelley reported these symptoms but my opinion rests on her behaviour. Her actions were those of a coherent and fully responsible individual.'

And we all know actions speak louder . . .

'That is your interpretation?'

'Yes. I am not saying there were no stresses whatsoever. She was faced with a difficult situation but her actions – the research she carried out in preparation for the event, the careful planning, the collected way she behaved afterwards. This is hard to square with her own description of her state of mind at the time.'

I am a liar. Mr Latimer must navigate carefully. Here be monsters.

'But another person,' Mr Latimer says reasonably, 'knowing how trapped Deborah Shelley felt, hearing of her panic attacks, her lack of sleep, her anxiety might formulate a different interpretation?'

'They might,' she allows.

'They might deduce that Ms Shelley was driven to the brink by the appalling situation she found herself in. That, racked by anxiety and paralysed by panic attacks, she lost the ability to distinguish right from wrong. That she became disturbed to the point where she bowed to the pressure of her husband's pleas. The husband she loved. A man she had been with for more than thirty years. Her husband of twenty-four years. They may well deduce that?'

'They may,' Professor Cabril says drily. The subtext: they'd be a fool if they did. 'In my experience,' she goes on, her dark eyes glinting, 'people who commit acts of this nature while the balance of their mind is disturbed find it impossible to sustain normal behaviour for very long. Like a pressure cooker, the cracks are there—'

'Professor Cabril.' Mr Latimer tries to shut her up.

'Let the witness finish,' insists the judge.

'Your Honour, my client's liberty, her reputation, her freedom are at stake here,' Mr Latimer says forcefully.

'Let the witness finish,' the judge repeats, frowning.

'Your Honour—'

'Mr Latimer!' The judge slaps him down. I sense

186

the gathering clouds, the swell of disaster dark on the horizon.

Dolores Cabril inclines her head by way of appreciation, 'If Deborah Shelley had been as vulnerable as she reported then it is my opinion that she would have swiftly broken down after the event. She would not have had the resilience to stand any scrutiny of her behaviour, to maintain her composure, and certainly would not withstand the police questioning she underwent. The need to confess, the relief she would seek from her situation, would have been paramount.'

'In your opinion,' Mr Latimer repeats. It is the best he can do and it is nowhere near good enough. I feel cheated, stuck in sinking sand with the waters rising. He walks back to his table and sits as Briony Webber leaps up for a last bite of the cherry. Mr Latimer has tried to introduce the spectre of doubt and she is keen to repair any damage.

'Professor Cabril, if Deborah Shelley actually did suffer from some anxiety and insomnia, if . . .'

Each 'if' is dripping with scepticism.

'. . . she had some panic attacks as she reported, would these symptoms constitute severe abnormality of mind sufficient to substantially impair her mental responsibility?'

'No, they would fall a long way short.'

'Thank you.'

So, even if I was having the odd wobble, I wasn't mad enough, according to Professor Cabril, to be guilty of the lesser charge of manslaughter. For that I'd need to be completely deranged. If I'm just a bit freaked out, it's murder. A bit of a conundrum, really.

'Your Honour,' Miss Webber addresses the judge, 'that is the case for the prosecution.'

Chapter Eighteen

Although I am hungry, when I try to eat my lunch my mouth floods with saliva and I feel sick. Mr Latimer will open the defence case when we resume and I will be the first witness. He is limiting the defence witnesses to the bare minimum. 'Less is more,' he pronounced, when he explained it to me. 'The jury wants the essential facts, not to be alienated or, worse, bored by an endless procession of faces all chipping in their two-penn'worth.' After I've given my evidence, he will call my neighbour, Pauline Corby, and then Don Petty, our shrink. We will all be saying variations of the same thing – that I was out of my mind when I agreed to Neil's request and off my rocker when I went ahead.

Earlier on I had thought about asking Jane to testify. She'd have had no qualms and she probably knows better than anyone how I had struggled through the first half of last year. But if Jane had been a witness she would not have been able to attend much of the trial and Adam would have been on his own if he chose to come. It was better for Adam and better for me if Jane was there to support him.

I have rehearsed my testimony with Mr Latimer, and he and Ms Gleason have drummed into me the pitfalls to avoid when I take the stand, especially during cross-examination. No losing my temper, no backhand remarks or trite put-downs, no evasion. I must keep my tone level where I can but not appear cold. My demeanour, my character, will have more impact on the jury's verdict than any other aspect. I must make them like me, or at the very least not dislike me. For someone who has never sought much approval from people, never wanted to be popular, rarely worried about what others thought, this is a tall order.

'We want them to step into your shoes,' Mr Latimer said, 'to think that in your situation they may well have responded in the same way.'

Cast reason to the wind and lined up the drugs. Lost their marbles and prepared a last drink.

Throughout the whole of the trial we must quash any debate around the notion of mercy killing (or assisted suicide or whatever label we use), any whisper that this might be a rational, humane, tenable course of action. The trial is not about Neil's right to die, it is not about my right to help him, it is solely about one question: was I responsible for my actions? My role is to play the madwoman – now recovered and remorseful.

The third time that Neil asked me was in April 2009. We were at home. He had stopped teaching: he no longer had sufficient strength or mobility. He was occasionally breathless. Trips downstairs were quite an effort and I was wondering whether we should convert the dining room into a bedroom. That way he would remain part of the household without being stuck upstairs like some benign Mrs Rochester. We never used the dining room for eating: the computer table was in there, lots of books and a second TV, which Adam used to play games on. But the computer and TV could easily go in the lounge for the duration. Not for ever, I thought, and the notion seemed awful and funny and poignant all at the same time. Neil would still need to get upstairs if he wanted to shower or bathe; we only had a loo on the ground floor. He was finding it harder to get in and out of the bath. His arms were worse than his legs, and the weakness was debilitating. We had to remember simple things, like giving him smaller, lighter mugs so he could lift them, and using tops and T-shirts that had a front opening so he didn't have to raise his arms above his head, which he could barely do.

The day before, Neil had seen the neurologist. The consultant recommended a wheelchair and suggested talking to the GP about medication if the pain in his shoulders got any worse. I say it was the third time but the question had hung between us ever since Barcelona. It was there in Neil's glances and silences, between our phrases as we discussed his symptoms and how we managed them, in each kiss. A briny tide lapping at my ankles, eroding the honesty between us. I knew he wouldn't give up on the idea but, like a child, I hoped that if I ignored the issue it would go away.

We were in the kitchen after breakfast. Sophie had gone into school and Adam was still asleep after a late night working at the airport bar. Neil was still eating – everything was taking longer – and I was loading the dishwasher.

'I was thinking about moving our bed,' I said, 'bringing it downstairs.'

Neil went to pick up his coffee and stalled, his arm shook and he lowered it to the table.

'Tired?' I asked.

'Deborah.'

I could hear it in his voice, hear it coming and taste it in the air between us. Like the ominous drop in pressure before a storm. I tried to escape. 'I need to leave soon – my meeting's at eleven.'

'Please,' he said, 'sit down.'

I made him wait. Stood, sullen and scared, like a teenager, for a few beats then slid on to a chair, sat with ill grace.

'I'll get weaker. I won't be able to walk. I might not be able to swallow.'

'I'll look after you.'

'That's not what I want.'

'If this is about pride . . .'

'No.' He stopped me.

'I don't want you to die, Neil. How can you ask me—'

'I am dying. One way or another.'

'Wait.' I felt jittery, buffeted by his arguments. I pushed myself away from the table, shaking with emotion, mainly anger. Cross that he was asking again. Furious that he wanted to leave me. I snatched the book I wanted from the dining room, thumbing through to the page I remembered on my way back to the kitchen. I read it through clenched teeth. '"Medical advances mean many of the symptoms of MND can now be treated and with planning and support patients can enjoy a good quality of life and a peaceful death."' I looked across at him, said fiercely, 'You're not going to lose your mind, you're not going to become incontinent, you're still going to be you . . .'

'So I'm lucky? Please, Deborah, this isn't a whim. I know it's a lot to ask.'

'You want to leave us . . . me, the kids.'

'Just a bit sooner. I could have another year, maybe two, with my world shrinking, getting frightened, depressed, helpless. I don't want to go on to the bitter end.'

'It might not be bitter,' I insisted. My throat ached, ringed with grief.

'I'm happy now, still. I love you, I love Adam and Sophie.'

'You don't want to be a burden?'

'It's not that. I want to go while it's still good.'

Like leaving a party before the end.

I shook my head, pressed my palm to my mouth, unable to answer. I looked across at him, my eyes blurring. Thought of the boy I'd seen at uni, making his friends laugh, his long legs and mischievous eyes, of the man who had led me round the Acropolis spinning stories, who had wept at the birth of his children, who had never belittled me or neglected me, who had encouraged me in every venture, who had never cheated on me but had had the generosity of heart to forgive my transgression. The man who could still set my pulse singing with a certain look, whose touch was balm and spice. My man.

'See a counsellor,' I said.

'What?'

'Talk to a counsellor, one of the people the consultant told us about, or someone at the MND Association. Talk to them.'

'I won't change my mind.'

'But you will talk to someone?'

He dipped his head. 'And?'

'Then if you still feel the same . . .' I couldn't continue. Dread stole into my heart, the shriek of fear chittered in my ears, claws of panic scrabbled at my scalp. I felt my nose swell and tears start. He slid his hand across the table. I held it. His grasp was weak but it was there. I wiped my face and moved around to hug him.

And then, after a while, I washed and dressed and went to discuss floor tiles with a ceramics company in Cheshire, having just agreed to kill my husband.

Depression swallowed me in the months after my mother's death. Martin made most of the arrangements and I recall very little of the funeral, other than it was a suitably bleak affair. The March wind nipped at our wrists and ankles and a squall of hail greeted us at the hillside grave. My great-aunt nodded with approval towards the valley. 'She's got a grand view.' My mother was joining my father in the same plot. Twenty-four years he had waited for her. Twenty-four years she had slept in their marriage bed alone. I stood dry-eyed throughout, my back aching with pregnancy and the chill.

A few weeks later Martin and I met up at her house to sort out her things. He had already made a start, boxing up crockery and linen, emptying the fridge. There was a pile in the lounge of any items we might want to keep: paintings, ornaments, clocks and mirrors. All I was interested in were the photographs, the two heavy albums and the box of loose prints. I gestured to them. 'We could share them out?'

'You take them for now,' Martin said. 'I've a couple at home as it is. We don't need to do that yet. But I thought – her clothes?' He tilted his head in the direction of the stairs. 'Anything decent can go to the charity shop. I don't know if there's anything you'd wear.'

Not bloody likely. I smiled, nodded, immensely grateful that Martin was here to do this with me.

'I'll have a look.' I wriggled out of the chair. Six months pregnant with Sophie, I felt enormous.

Reaching my mother's bedroom door, I was assailed by a lurch of fear, sulphur in my nostrils, tendrils on my neck. A trick of grief. Taking a deep breath, I opened the door. No corpse, no zombie, no chattering whispers. Just the still-life of her room: the rose-coloured duvet cover, the small chintz bedside lamp and old mahogany wardrobe. On her dressing-table was her brush, grey hairs still tangled there, her makeup, jewellery box, the Yardley perfume she wore on special occasions, her hand cream. A school photograph of Martin and me. We must have been five and six. Daddy would still have been alive. Was she happy then? Did she laugh and make jokes? Did she play with us? Games and make-believe? Tickling, hide and seek? Fishing for memories, all I came up with was the well-worn one of her singing while my father played the piano. A number from a musical, 'Baubles, Bangles and Beads'. She had been happy then, I thought, with him, but when he had gone we weren't enough.

'It's not fair.' I spoke aloud, frustration tight in my throat. 'It's not bloody fair.'

I yanked open the drawers and began to sling her things into the bin-bags Martin had provided. Underwear for the tip, scarves and jumpers for charity, throwing them in any-old-how, trying to convince myself that I was simply being efficient. I flung open the wardrobe doors and stared at the contents. Her woollen camel coat, a polyester jacket, dresses in navy and cream and burgundy, blouses, the faint floral smell of her hand cream and perfume.

Once my father's things would have hung at one side of the space. How long had she waited to do this with them, packing away all trace of him? She'd kept nothing. Why not? Hadn't she wanted reminders of the shape and smell of him? Was it anger, at losing him, at being cheated of a future together that had made her erase him as she had? The same anger that chilled her heart and smothered her love of life?

I hauled the coat out of the wardrobe and put it on. It dwarfed me, the cuffs covering my hands, the waist hanging by my hips. I stuffed my hands into the pockets but they were empty. What had I expected? A secret note? Clues to our past, to her innermost thoughts? Even while I ridiculed the notion, I rifled through the shoeboxes at the bottom of the wardrobe, then the bedside cabinet. And came away empty-handed.

I was numb, chilled through. I slid the rest of the garments from their hangers in the wardrobe and laid them one on top of another on the bed then rolled them lengthwise into a bolster. Climbing on the bed, I nestled into the bulk of the bundle. I spoke to her, muttering and carping at first, trying to voice the cold anger inside me. And then, halting, by way of apology. Because I hadn't loved her enough – I hadn't loved her as a daughter should. I had failed her. I spoke to her through slow, hot tears and shuddering breath, my nose thick and my lips dry. Swimming upstream after my mother. Never catching up.

In time, the sensation of being submerged, of weight and incapacity, and the waves of panic grew worse. At two and a half, Adam was lively and incessantly active, and the demands of looking after him became harder. Neil did all he could, but he was at school every day. My emotions were so close to the surface that I could no longer bear to watch the news or read the papers. I also became fearful that something would happen to the baby and I was dreading the labour. Reluctantly, I mentioned some of this to the midwife who was visiting me at home in preparation for the birth. She strongly advised me to see my GP. Andy Frame prescribed anti-depressants. He told me that while there might be some side-effects there was little risk of harm to the baby. There would be great benefits in treating the depression and he said he would be very concerned about the consequences if I didn't take them.

The pills gave me a slightly giddy feeling, the world became gauzy and my capacity to cry at the slightest prompt diminished. Still my limbs felt leaden, my self soiled and raw and scared.

Believing it would help me to confront my sadness rather than try and escape it, I spent hours poring over the family photographs. I wasn't considering them from a professional point of view – I had no interest in the focus of the shadows, the composition or contrast or depth of field – but hunting for understanding, for memory and meaning.

My father rarely appeared. Too often behind the camera. There was solace in the thought that I had inherited that skill from him. That I, too, had adopted that role. Among the portraits there were several black and white still-lifes and landscapes: a wrought-iron balcony in fierce light, the shadows inky against the smooth rendered wall, stormclouds above a winter field of stubble, a basket of fir cones and, my favourite, a yacht cutting through a glimmering ocean. He had written on the back, in neat print, *White Sail – Whitby, '61.*

Peering at the family groups I scouted for signs of love and affection. Felt relief when I found my mother's smile, her hand on my shoulder. Near the bottom of the pile of loose snaps there was a small, square picture, which must have been taken on the box camera they had then. A man in dark dungarees holds a wallpaper brush, his head flung back in laughter. Beside him on a step-ladder stands a small child, her face creased in glee. My father and me. Did my mother take it? Or a friend calling by? What was so funny? I love the picture. I crave memories to match it.

Sophie was born four months after my mother's death and I was still depressed. The contractions started before dawn and I sat by the lounge window, rocking when the pain came, and watched the pale February sun climb the sky before rousing Neil. We called the midwife and Neil took Adam to his mother's – luckily she had the day off – and returned to find me pacing the bedroom, restless and out of sorts. The labour was so different from Adam's, quicker and more violent. After only four hours in the first stage, I was ready to push, the overpowering urge forcing me to the floor, clinging to one corner of the bedstead, the midwife hastily rearranging the plastic sheets, and the doctor arriving as the head crowned.

The midwife spoke tersely, telling us the cord was tight around Sophie's neck. The atmosphere in the room changed, a vortex of panic sucking the air. There was a whirl of activity as they readied instruments, told me not to push and prepared to cut the cord. I had read enough books to know that the cord was the baby's lifeline and that if she didn't get out quickly now she could be in trouble.

As soon as the cut was made I was instructed to push. I strained and groaned, the pain tearing through my vagina and bowels. With the second push she slithered out. She was paper white, her lips and eyelids blue like a fish. In the heartbeats it took to revive her, I was falling, falling through the back of my skull into the velvet dark, falling away from everything to my own deep retreat. Her cries: a mewl, a creak, caught me. Held me, pulled me up. That, and the hot splash of Neil's tears on my forearm.

If we had not got her out in time she would have suffocated. Her lungs filling with amniotic fluid. Drowning. Like my father. Choking on brine. Like Neil did, the alveoli filling with the salty fluid from his body. Drowning in his tears.

Chapter Nineteen

They call me to the stand. They are all in the public gallery: my children, my in-laws, my friend. For a stupid moment I wonder where you are, Neil. It's an error I want to share with you. I heard somewhere that it's good to talk to the dead and sometimes I do. Murmur news of my day behind bars to you in the dim, dry, stifling night.

Mr Latimer stands up and addresses the jury. It is his task to convince them that I am no feminist harridan with a smooth tongue who would perjure herself, but a loving wife and mother driven demented by circumstances, pushed to the giddy limit and beyond, now drowning in regret and desperate for understanding.

'Members of the jury, you have now heard the case against Deborah Shelley. A case which rests on one, and only one, question: was Deborah Shelley suffering from diminished responsibility when she helped her husband Neil die? The answer to that is yes. And we will present evidence from Deborah Shelley to support that. We will hear from Deborah how living with Neil's terminal illness affected her own mental health, leading to insomnia, panic attacks, anxiety and depression. Her situation was made even worse by concerns over the well-being of her son Adam. Things reached the stage where Deborah was no longer able to act responsibly.'

Adam colours but keeps looking at Mr Latimer. I had discussed with the barrister whether we had to drag Adam into it but he made it plain I needed all the help I could get. And a drug-addled teenager who had had spells in a loony bin would score plenty of Brownie points. Though he had a more elegant way of putting it.

Mr Latimer goes on, 'Deborah's neighbour and the expert psychiatric witness for the defence will describe to you a woman who, weakened and isolated, was faced with a tremendous pressure that she was incapable of resisting. Deborah Shelley broke the law because she could no longer differentiate between right and wrong.'

He turns to me and gives the tiniest of nods, a little jerk of his scrappy wig, to calm me. It will be all right, he is saying, you will be all right.

'Deborah,' he will make a point of always using my first name – humanizing me for the jury, 'your husband was diagnosed with motor neurone disease in September 2007?'

'Yes.'

'What impact did that have on you?'

'I was numb at first, it was such a huge shock, and when we learned that there was no cure, that Neil would get progressively worse and then die, well, it was shattering.'

I let my eyes scan the jury. Dolly, jaunty today in pillar-box red, draws her mouth tight in a shrug of regret. And I see the Cook's face soften in sympathy – or I think I do.

'But you were able to carry on working and looking after the family?'

'Yes. I had to. In that sort of situation you cope, you carry on. That's all you can do.'

'Some years earlier your mother had died?'

'Of cancer, yes.'

'Would you say that she had a good death?'

A torrent of emotions unseats me. I feel my face heat up. 'No, not at all. She was in a lot of pain. It was horrible. She was on her own at the end. No one ever seemed to talk to her, or to us, about what was happening.'

'Her death affected you deeply?'

'Yes, I became depressed.'

Hilda and Flo exchange a look. They know something of this. What? Depression, losing a parent, cancer? Live long enough and I guess the odds are good for all three.

'And around this time you and Neil had your second child, Sophie?'

'That's right.'

'W-was the d-depression,' he starts to stutter and segues into the chanting delivery that eases the flow, 'severe enough to warrant medical attention?'

'Yes. I saw my GP and he put me on medication. Anti-depressants.'

'Did these help?'

'A bit. Not a lot. Mainly it was the time that helped. The passing of time.'

'How long did this period of depression last?'

'About a year.'

'And when you knew Neil had a terminal condition did you think you might become depressed again?'

'No. Not at first. I was upset, angry – it just felt so unfair.' It still does. His illness was unfair, his death too. I want him back. Perhaps this is the denial stage. People write about the different stages of grief but I haven't a clue where I'm up to. He wasn't dead three weeks when they locked me up. Arrested development.

In the second row of the jury box, the Sailor nods. I'm relieved at his empathy until I realize with a rush of outrage that he is dozing, nodding off. Too big a lunch, perhaps. Not on my watch, matey. I give a sharp cough and he startles awake, rubs his face and rolls back his shoulders.

'And after the initial shock?'

'Then I was more worried about Neil, how he would deal with it, and the children too.'

'Had you any particular fears regarding the children?'

There's the taste of coins in my mouth as I reply. Blood money. 'Yes, my son Adam had been having problems. He isn't well – mentally.'

'Please can you tell the jury what is wrong with him?'

I cannot look at Adam or I will cry. I want to fend the question off. Tell them what a lovely child he was, how he delighted in the world, show them how beautiful he still is, how he has his father's eyes and a kindness, a naïvety, about him. Holding my jaw taut I tell them, 'Adam suffers from delusions. He gets panic attacks and sometimes becomes paranoid. The doctors believe the illness was triggered by using cannabis.'

Even as I say the word I see the Prof and Mousy stiffen, Hilda and Flo shuffle uneasily. A generation thing, I think. The older members of the jury probably see little distinction between cannabis and heroin. I assume those under fifty have at least tried it – even if they didn't inhale. As for Media Man, in his sharp suit, the Artist, and the PA with her lovely tan and flawless makeup, I bet they've hoovered up plenty of coke in their time. The Sailor's probably seen it all – a new drug in every port, though the ruddy complexion, the road map of capillaries, suggests a lifetime's acquaintance with the bottle, too.

'I'm told some people are more susceptible than others,' I continue speaking.

'And at the time when Neil was diagnosed, how was Adam's health?'

'Not good. Adam had taken an overdose just before.'

'And as time went on and Neil's health deteriorated how was Adam's condition?'

'Variable. The hardest thing was really not knowing whether he'd be okay or not. It was so unpredictable. He had a couple of hospital stays, in 2008, as a voluntary patient.'

Callow Youth looks anxious. Perhaps he likes to smoke weed but gets edgy. The Prof continues to look remote. Surely he's come across drug use with his students. I wonder what his poison is. Fine wines? Then I remind myself he may not be the academic that I imagine. He may be a catalogue buyer or a window cleaner or a brickie.

Do any of them blame the parents? See in Neil's and my treatment of Adam the seeds of his destruction? Are they judging me? Well, duh! The absurdity of the question threatens to make me smile. Not good body language as Latimer walks me through my descent from grace.

'At what stage did you become ill yourself?'

'I think the anxiety was there all along but I tried to ignore it. Then when Neil began to talk about—' I can't say any more, a ball of grief chokes me. I grip the edge of the stand. There's a humming in my ears.

The judge leans forward. 'Ms Shelley, this is obviously very difficult. Would you like a break?'

I shake my head. Find a word. 'No.' Fumble for the current of my thoughts. 'Sorry.' Good, Deborah, humility, weakness, that's the style. 'When Neil said he wanted to plan his death, it began to get worse.'

There is a rush of interest in the court. I see it in the way the PA's sharp face narrows with interest and the Cook's head whips up. See it in the way the press reporters at the side begin to scribble. The truth stalks closer.

'When was that?'

'In March 2008. About six months after his diagnosis.'

'And he asked if you would help him?'

'Yes.'

'What was your answer to him?'

'I said, no, I wouldn't do it.'

'Why?'

'Because I didn't want him to die. I wanted as much time together as possible. And there was help available. Ways of making sure he had a good death, when the time came.'

'Were you aware that he was asking you to break the law?'

'Yes – well, I checked actually. I wasn't sure, but when I looked into it, it was clear.' Sitting by the computer, scanning the Internet, clicking back and forth, my stomach plunging as I found the same stark answer time and again. Now moves to change the law were gaining ground but too late for Neil. For me.

'Did Neil raise the subject again?'

'Yes. We had a holiday together in Barcelona, that September. He asked me then.'

'And what did you say?'

'We argued about it. I couldn't agree to do it. I was angry that he'd asked me again. And I was sad. I'd hoped he'd changed his mind. Given up on the idea.'

Is Sophie hearing this, taking it in? Does she understand that this was not my will?

'How was your own state of mind at this time?'

'Shaky. I wasn't sleeping well and I'd lost weight. I was depressed.'

'Did you see your doctor?'

'No.'

'Why not?'

'I didn't think there was anything he could do, really. I just had to keep going. Neil was the one who was dying. I had to be strong for him.' This is the truth, not an embellishment to prop up my defence. I had felt frayed and woozy; my hold on everything was brittle.

'Did you ask anyone for help?'

'I rang the MNDA helpline a lot. Let off steam. But there didn't seem to be any point in seeing a doctor. Nothing could stop the inevitable. It was something we had to live with.' Die with.

'And did Neil ask you to help him end his life a third time?'

'Yes.' There's a wobble in my throat and I sound feeble. What might have happened if you hadn't? You might still be here, loved and looked after. The three of us round your bedside. A Walton family death. 'Bye, Pa. 'Bye, Adam. 'Bye, Pa. 'Bye, Sophie.

'And what did you say?'

'At first I said no, again. But he was begging me. Pleading with me. He wanted it so much and I was so confused. I told him to talk to a counsellor. He said he would.'

'How was your state of mind at that time?'

'Worse. I was getting panic attacks.'

Late April and I am in the workshop. Dawn and the birds herald the sun, the raucous sparrows in the eaves, the liquid song of the blackbird. I am kneeling rigid on the rug, one arm wrapped around my chest, my hand at my throat. Pain radiates from my heart, robbing me of breath; my throat is sealed, skin slick with sweat. My mind is diving through the groundswell of terror, seeking to break through to the surface. Even in this wilderness I am able to appreciate that if this kills me I will not be able to help Neil. But it is not a heart-attack: breath comes, and the pain seeps away, leaving an imprint to haunt me.

'I wasn't sleeping properly and I felt sick all the time. I couldn't concentrate on anything.'

'So you agreed to his request?'

I can't speak. I press my tongue against my teeth, dam my tears. The moment stretches out. Mr Latimer waits.

'Yes,' I whisper.

'In your statement to the court you have admitted administering drugs to Neil and then putting a plastic bag over his head, is that correct?'

'Yes.' An eddy of guilt rocks me.

'How long after agreeing to do this did you carry out his wishes?'

'Ten weeks.' Oh, I wish it had been longer. Another day, another week. I miss him so. I want him back now. Sick as a dog and weak as a kitten, I would take him in an instant, sit in vigil until the only muscle moving is his heart. Relishing the breath of him and the feel of his palm and the smell of his hair.

'And having made the agreement, presumably you and Neil talked further about how to carry out his wishes?'

'Yes.' Oh, those macabre discussions about methods and dosages, cover stories and timing. We went over it again and again. Me rooting out objections, obstacles, dangers. Neil persistently working it through.

Neil had spoken to a counsellor as promised. Now we had to plan his death. Spring was unseasonably warm, that day a cloudless sky. I was supposed to be working on some designs for a new apartment block but I couldn't settle. I went upstairs to see if he wanted to come down and have lunch in the garden. He liked the idea. Once we'd got him into his shorts and shirt, I helped him to the top of the stairs. There, he lowered himself to the floor. It was easier for him to shuffle downstairs on his bottom, with me yanking his legs or shoving his back when he seized up.

Sophie came in when he was halfway down. 'You ought to get a stair-lift,' she said. 'They said you could get one, didn't they?'

'Yes.' And there was a six-month wait. 'Yes, I'll give them a ring.' Sophie got a text message and before long her friend called round and the two of them went out. Neil and I had lunch, our talk desultory. I cleared the plates and looked out at him. He was settled in the patio in a high-back chair that supported his neck and arms. His face was in repose, his expression reflective. The ache of knowing I was losing him bloomed in my chest. I fetched my camera from the dining room and photographed him from the kitchen window, zooming in to get a closeup.

I took drinks out and joined him. Propped a long

straw in his beaker so he could hold it in his lap and still sip it.

'How?' The taste of fear made me bark the question. 'How do you plan to do it? How do we avoid being found out?'

'An overdose.'

'There'll be signs, won't there?'

'They won't necessarily do a post-mortem.'

I shivered in the heat. 'Neil, I don't know whether . . .'

'Ssh!' His look was gentle, indulgent, his olive eyes calm.

'And what do we use, what drugs, how do we get hold of them?'

He didn't say anything.

'Could always ask Adam, I suppose,' I muttered.

Neil laughed and I began to giggle, my anguish punctured. We couldn't stop and then I was crying too but trying to hide it because I didn't want to let him down.

'Might give the game away,' he said, his chest still heaving.

Rage flared fresh in my belly. *It's not a game!* I wanted to scream at him. *It's your life. It's my life.*

I stood up.

'Where are you going?'

'The Internet. Marvellous what you can find.'

It wasn't, as it happens. There was information about the methods used in the Swiss clinics, doses of barbiturates preceded by a strong anti-emetic to stop the person throwing up the drugs. How would we get those? Anti-emetic. Would travel pills help? Sophie always got car sick and we gave her tablets, which seemed to help – but whether they treated the symptom or the cause I'd no idea.

When I typed *suicide* and *overdose* into the search engine it threw up everything from paracetamol to heroin.

Rejoining Neil, I told him what I'd read. 'So we could try a packet of Joy Rides followed by sleeping pills but (a) we'd have to get hold of the stuff first and (b) if they did a post-mortem it'd be an obvious deliberate overdose.'

I felt giddy talking like this, as if in a fever, the garden gleaming in the sun, the scent of cut grass and the bony claws of death crawling up my spine.

'We need something that could be accidental,' he said quietly, 'in case anyone does get suspicious.'

'Could shove you downstairs.' I groaned. 'I can't believe we're having this conversation.'

Neil reached slowly across and put his hand on my knee. I turned his hand over, pressed my palm to his, locked fingers, willing him to leave it now, to shut up.

But he carried on: 'Or something I could have taken myself, without your help, without your knowing. Then, even if it does come out, you're okay. There's no risk.'

'Something you're already taking?'

'Would Zoloft work?' he asked. At that stage he had been prescribed Zoloft for depression.

'I'm not sure.'

'Morphine,' he said. 'It's in the breathing kit.'

'A dose. Not enough to kill you.'

'Andy Frame will give me some for the pain – the consultant suggested it. It's also used for breathlessness.'

'You're not breathless.'

'I could be.' His voice was quiet, delicate.

'And save it up,' I said, cottoning on. 'The syringes—'

'I think they do liquid, too. To drink. If it's hard to swallow, to get solids down.'

It seemed so simple. I coveted his equanimity. But there was a backwash of resentment, too, slapping inside me. I gazed at the crimson and yellow splashes of primula, at the buds on the maple. I drank in the sweet, creamy fragrance from the magnolia tree. This, I thought, is what's hard to swallow. That you want to go and leave me here. You can still talk and laugh and kiss and come. Okay, so we'll never dance again but you can still breathe and swallow, and yet you want to go.

'Did you ever consider reneging on your promise?' Mr Latimer savours the verb though I see Alice's eyes narrow as she puzzles it out.

'All the time. I went round and round it in my head, like a maze. I kept hoping he'd die before it came to it. Or he'd change his mind. I dreaded it. I was frightened all the time but I couldn't see a way out. Most of the time I just pretended it wasn't really happening. I'd get these panic attacks when I found it hard to breathe, this terrible dread like a paralysis.'

'Yet you were helping Neil to acquire the medicines you used?'

'Yes. I thought I was going mad.'

Mr Latimer guides me through the sequence of events, a quadrille of question and answer. Neil's complaints to Dr Frame and the prescription for liquid morphine. The medicines hidden in his bedside table. One, then the other. More than a month's supply.

Mr Latimer asks me about the children. I recall one conversation, early evening, Neil in bed resting, me putting clothes away. The banality of it. We'd already agreed to conceal his intention from the children. Knowing how horrific the burden was for me, I could not countenance imposing it on Adam and Sophie. Neil felt the same. It was too much to bear – they were kids.

'What about afterwards? What do we tell the children?' I asked Neil.

'Nothing.'

'Is that fair?'

He glanced away, then back to me. 'If we organize it properly, everyone will think I just died sooner than expected. The kids included. If anyone suspects otherwise you could be in trouble. It wouldn't be fair to ask them to keep that sort of secret.'

I nodded. Neil had redrawn his will and written letters for Adam and Sophie, love letters for them to keep.

At each turn of the dance, Mr Latimer stops to ask me about my state of mind. I tell the court about prowling the house. About the nightmares that waited for me to lower my guard and succumb to sleep. About being unable to share meals because of the way my throat sealed as I raised my fork, nausea gushing through me at the smell of food. How practised I became in hiding my disintegration from the world, from my family, my friends, my clients. Neil was the one who was dying. I was just dropping to bits.

'On the twenty-sixth of May last year,' Mr Latimer prompts, 'there was an incident involving your neighbour Pauline Corby. Can you tell us what happened that day? Perhaps you could start by telling us how Neil's condition was.'

Dolly perks up, flicking her tongue round, licking her lips. I make a quick assessment of the jury. Half of them have crossed arms, a bad sign, closed, defensive. What they're about to hear won't improve matters. What's important is that they think of me as mad, not bad, and material like this could go either way.

'Neil had lost a lot of movement in his arms. It seemed to get worse quite suddenly so I was having to do more for him. Feeding and toileting.'

Alice pulls a wry face. Has she known this? An aged parent, a disabled sibling?

'The neighbours have this cat,' I go on. 'It uses our garden sometimes. We tried everything. I was feeling very tired, very tense, and I saw the animal soiling' – I use 'soiling' instead of 'shitting' so I won't offend anyone – 'in where we have the herbs. I filled a bowl with water and drenched the cat. Mrs Corby had seen me and she came round. She knocked on the back door and said it was outrageous and unnecessary.'

'And how did you respond?'

'I lost control. Completely. I was shouting abuse and screaming at her. She threatened to call the police and I – I threatened her with a hammer. I'd been fixing cables to the wall with it. I said I'd hit her with it.' *Stove your fucking skull in*, had been the exact turn of phrase.

'What happened then?'

'She went back inside.'

'And what did you do?'

'I got drunk.' Sat in my workshop and polished off half a bottle of gin. Hiding from Neil, hiding from the children. Wanting to smash something with the hammer but knowing if I started I might not be able to stop.

'Had you ever behaved with such enmity, such aggression before?'

'Never.'

212

'Looking back now, how would you describe that outburst?'

'It was out of all proportion. I lost control. I wasn't myself.'

'And how did you feel afterwards?'

'Frightened. Like I was cracking up. I didn't know what I was going to do next.'

Mr Latimer pauses so they will have a chance to absorb this. Then he makes a move in a new direction. 'Had you and your husband discussed when he would take the overdose?'

'No.'

'You never asked him?'

'No. I hoped he'd change his mind, or be too scared to go through with it.'

'What happened on June the fourteenth?'

'We had a quiet day. We had a take-away dinner. Then Adam helped me get Neil back to bed. The children went out. Then Neil told me.' My voice cracks. I freeze again. Feel the dread across my shoulders like a clammy shawl.

Mr Latimer waits. The courtroom ripples. Faces loom at me, then retreat. I am given a cup of water. The judge asks if I am able to continue. I've started so I'll finish. My voice sounds dry, rustles. 'Neil said he wanted to do it the following day.'

I can hear the suck of excitement from people.

'Were those his exact words?'

'No. He just said, "Tomorrow." And I knew.'

'Did you try and dissuade him?'

'No.'

'You were happy to go ahead?'

'No. No – I was devastated but I had to . . . I couldn't . . . I had . . .' I'm inarticulate, words spilling out like broken teeth.

213

'Why had you to?'

'Because I'd promised. Because I loved him. And I didn't know what was best any more. I was so confused.' I have been coached to end on this sentiment. It is crucial. My motives may have been of the highest moral order but my actions were illegal. The only defence I had, the only defence the law of the land allowed me, was a lack of reason, a loss of judgement.

'I didn't know what I was doing,' I say plainly.

'And do you regret what you did?'

'Oh, yes. Every minute.' I mean it.

There is a sound from the gallery and my blood leaps in consternation. Sophie is crying. Oh, my sweet girl. What have we done? I stretch my throat, raise my eyes to the ceiling and blink. But nothing stops my tears spilling.

The judge instructs an adjournment for the rest of the day. The jury file out. There's a sombre, shaken atmosphere now. And everyone knows what tomorrow will bring. They know I admit to killing him; they know what I used to do it. But until they hear the details of it from me, they can only imagine what it must have been like.

Chapter Twenty

The journey back to Styal takes for ever. We have to call at courts in Wigan and Stockport and Bury. It is rush hour so the traffic is appalling. I hear the security guards talking about an accident on the M60, which has gridlocked half the region. Snow starts to fall, looking dirty against the sky, then rain so the tyres make a slushing sound on the wet roads.

Once back in Reception, I am strip-searched again. I feel the familiar slow burn of humiliation and try to disguise it. When I get back to my pad, I make a cup of tea in the house kitchen. Sitting on my chair, I close my eyes, sip and listen to the sounds in the place. A telly still on, a jangly tune. Someone shouting. There is always someone shouting here.

As I get ready for bed, it is snowing again. The flakes are fat and soft and coat the limbs of the trees and the steeply pitched roofs of the houses. The place looks like a scene from a snow globe – stick in a horse and carriage and it could be a Victorian Christmas scene, as long as you photo-shopped out the fences and wire in the background and the bars at every window.

One Christmas we rented a cottage in the Lake District. Adam was ten and Sophie seven and they were happy to go along with it, as long as we did a 'proper' Christmas. That involved taking our tree decorations with us as well as materials to make some new ones on Christmas Eve. And a boot full of presents. I thought we should take a tree too, but Neil laughed. 'We're going to the Lakes,' he said. 'Half the countryside is forest. We can just pick one up.'

He was right. As we left the motorway nearing our destination, there were signs saying Pick Your Own. And the kids were giddy with excitement at the prospect. The four of us wandered through the plantation with a leaflet and a saw, arguing amicably over choices. Adam wanted the biggest possible tree but Neil explained that it might not fit in the cottage. Sophie, coming out for the underdog, was drawn to the spindliest specimens. I was after symmetry. We agreed at last on a five-footer and took turns to wield the saw. The sharp scent of pine sap was delicious in the air, the trunk sticky with drops of amber resin.

The cottage was low and cramped but the living room was cosy: the owners had left a great fire banked up and we were able to keep it lit for the whole week. In the bedrooms the sheets were cold enough to make us squeal and there was frost inside the bathroom window in the mornings. Out the back there was a view of the hills above Grasmere. Snow fell on the third day and we bought sledges at the petrol station on the main road. The man told us where the popular local runs were.

I recall careening down the slope with Adam, who was yelling like a banshee, and racing against Sophie and Neil, or Neil and I rollicking down together, travelling faster with our combined weight, Neil whooping and me laughing uncontrollably. Later, peeling off sodden gloves to reveal bright pink fingers, Sophie whimpering as her hands stung from the cold, then dunking shortbread in hot chocolate, feeding the fire shovels full of tarry coal and growing dopey in the heat.

Once the children were asleep, Neil and I sat reading by the fire, sipping Famous Grouse and cracking open walnuts and hazelnuts. I was curled in an armchair and he sprawled on the floor, his back against the chair opposite, relaxed and tipsy with whisky.

When I put down my book, I looked across to find him watching me.

'Fuck me,' he mouthed, and his eyes danced.

Turning I switched off the table lamp, casting us into firelight. While he watched, I stood and undressed, the air against my back and buttocks cold from the draught at the door. I knelt beside him and took his face in my hands. Kissed him soft then harder. Pulled away as he reached for me. I took off his fleece and then his T-shirt, licked his nipples and the hollow of his throat. I unbuttoned his jeans, moved his underpants aside and let his penis spring free. I straddled him and he ran his hands flat and smooth down my shoulder-blades and my back. He pulled me closer, eased me on to him. I felt the depth of him fill me and my sex quickening. I rode him as he bent his head to reach my breasts, his mouth hot, his breath more ragged with each rocking motion.

I came, shuddering and pulsing, and reared back, releasing him, the tremors travelling to my forearms and fingers, to my scalp. With a few quick strokes Neil came too, arching his back and groaning and spraying pearls onto his belly and my thighs. We lay together afterwards and I listened to the hiss and pop of the coal and the thud of his heart.

The next day our winter-sports antics were cut short when Adam fell off the sledge and started screaming. A high-pitched animal sound that cut to my bones. He had broken his wrist. We spent a couple of hours in A&E and got back to the cottage in the dark, the street in the hamlet empty, the air full of oily coal smoke, the sky a dense black and the stars crisp as ice.

It's a time I revisit as I lie down in bed and wait for sleep, forcing myself to take it in sequence. I usually reach the part where we make the decorations: the table covered with newspaper; Sophie, her tongue between her teeth for concentration, sticking black beads onto her snowman bauble; Adam, his good hand thick with glue and glitter, daubing at a reindeer that looked more like a rat; Neil telling us all stories about the olden days here, who would have lived in the cottage and how they would have worked, children and all, in the local slate mines.

I never get to Christmas Day.

I was happy. We were all happy then. I'm sure we were. I thought I'd got away with it. That Neil and I had weathered the damage done by my affair and survived. That the worst was over and my family still intact. That everything would be all right from now on.

That night, halfway through my trial, I dream that I am in the snow. We have been building an igloo and I am inside it but I can't find Neil or Adam or Sophie. I have lost them. There is a shore nearby, a lake frozen, and I run to the edge, knowing they are trapped under the ice. Walking out on to it, I see shadows, pewter-coloured, twisting beneath. On my knees I hammer at the blue-white crust but it is as hard as stone, inches thick, and I can make no headway. Knowing I must get help, I spy a dwelling on the horizon. There may be people there. I get to my feet but when I try to run my legs don't work. No power. I can barely lift my foot off the ground. No matter how hard I try to force myself forward, my lungs bursting with effort, my legs are as weak as dried grass stalks. The soles of my feet are stuck to the ice, which is growing through my heels and the pads of my toes, forming crystals in my blood. Then I hear banging. They are breaking the ice, something is breaking the ice, and I am sliding in fast, sinking down, the water shocking, cold and heavy as lead.

I wake, my duvet on the floor, the prison officer hammering on my door again, calling at me to get up, the transport leaves at seven.

I am reluctant. Today I will have to tell them things that I would rather not remember.

When I had been on remand awaiting trial in Styal for two weeks, my brother Martin came to visit. We hadn't seen each other for years, drifting apart in the wake of my mother's death and with nothing in common other than our childhood. He was patently ill-at-ease. I was still shell-shocked, I think, both with losing Neil and with the horror of being incarcerated. He was sitting in the visitor's centre when I walked in. He rose as I got close. We exchanged a clumsy hug, talked numbly about him finding the place, and sat. There was a stilted pause punctuated by a child's laugh. Nearby three youngsters were visiting their mother.

'Dad and now Neil.' Martin shook his head.

Halfway through grunting in agreement, I stopped short. Dad and now Neil, he said. Why Dad and not

Mum? Her situation was closer to Neil's: the illness, the diagnosis, the decline.

'Dad?'

He gave an odd twitch of his head and blinked, a sign of embarrassment.

'Martin?'

He raised his hands then, palms towards me: leave it, forget it.

My mind scrambled for explanations. Men I'd lost as opposed to women?

'Was Dad ill?'

He gave a great breath out. 'Maybe now's not the time.'

'No,' I was cross at his prevaricating, 'now is the time – now is precisely the time. When better? I've nowhere else to be, nothing else to do. Dad – it was an accident.' The clothes folded on the sand. I waited for him to agree, to explain, my face hot, my breath trapped in my chest.

His eyes, a lighter blue than mine, slid down, a slow blink of denial.

'What then? Was he ill?'

Martin hesitated. I wanted to reach across the table and throttle him.

'Not physically. Look, I don't know all the details.'

'You know a fuck of a lot more than I do.' He flinched at the steel in my tone. 'Martin, please, just tell me.' I tried to rein in my agitation. There were prison officers up on the dais monitoring the room. Any argy-bargy and they would clear the place, send us all in.

'He was depressed,' Martin said.

Time ran slower. Disbelief clutched my throat; the hairs on my arms stood up; my scalp tightened. 'What?'

Every image I had of my father threatened to dissolve with the onslaught of this new truth.

He was folding his clothes, slipping the watch from his wrist and tucking it into his shorts, laying the towel over the neat bundle. Shivering in the dawn wind, indifferent to the bone-deep ache as he waded out, driven by a greater pain.

The sea is cold around the British coast, even with the Gulf Stream, cold enough to induce hypothermia. Was that what he had done? Float? Memory jolted me rigid. Daddy supporting my back at the lido while I tried not to sink, my arms flung wide. Did he do that? A human star, limbs splayed as he bucked the waves, as the cold settled in his tissues and his teeth chattered and the sky rose and fell. Or did he hurry, diving down and filling his lungs with brine, searching for Charybdis to suck him under, snorting and choking and gulping in more?

'Mum said it was an accident,' I persisted.

'Well, we can't know for sure.' Martin, who had always been so good and dull and ordinary. Who had toed the line and smiled politely as he did so. Who never seemed to have adolescence or any rebellious phase. Was this why? Had he carried this all those years? Not a cross to bear but a trim grey suitcase anchoring him to the known and safe?

'Apart from the depression?' I wanted evidence, facts and figures. Prove it.

'He'd never done that before,' Martin answered, 'gone for a swim so early. He knew he'd be alone. He'd been drinking a lot, whisky with everything, sleeping it off in the afternoons.'

The taste of whisky, bitter in my throat. I stared at Martin, incredulous. Were we talking about the same holiday? I didn't remember any of this.

'They'd been rowing, arguing. Things were very rocky. Not just between them. Dad was in line for redundancy – Pendle's was being taken over.'

The name brought back an image of a warehouse up a cobblestoned hill, near the edge of town. I don't recall that we ever went inside but occasionally Dad would have to call in *en route* to some family outing. Pendle's was a fancy-goods wholesaler. Now and then Dad would bring home some new item from their range (inflatable plastic photo frames, fibre-optic lights, luminous doorbell push), which we'd admire before they ever got into the shops.

'But you can't know for sure,' I echoed his words. 'Mum thought it was an accident and the police must have done.' Even as I spoke a hot wash of anger flooded through me. He had left me on purpose. I'd always known my fierce independence, which I used to thwart my fear of abandonment, was rooted in his early death. But he had *chosen* to leave. Scylla, the sea-monster, had not robbed me of a father. My father had not loved me enough to stay. Was this how Sophie and Adam felt about Neil? Unfairly abandoned?

Martin cleared his throat. 'When Mum was ill, I asked her.'

The air between us crackled with tension. I could feel my pulse in my ears and the burn of adrenalin about my neck and wrists.

'She lied to the police?' Obviously a family trait.

'She didn't tell them about the problems. They didn't probe too deeply. Suicide back then, there wouldn't have been any insurance.' He fell quiet.

I kept my gaze steady. Suicide: illegal, shameful, dirty work at the crossroads. In Dante's Hell, the suicides are imprisoned in trees, immobilized so they

222

can hurt themselves no more. The Harpies roost in their boughs and rip off twigs making the trees bleed and the souls within moan.

She lied to me. 'Why didn't she tell me?' I demanded.

Martin shrugged awkwardly. 'You had Adam, you were expecting Sophie, you were travelling fifty miles every few days to visit.'

'Why didn't you tell me?'

'I agreed with her. You'd such a lot on.'

Arguments crowded into my head, batting around like moths to a lamp. 'Since then?' I spoke sharply. 'She's been dead for fifteen years. Haven't I a right to know what happened to him? He was my father too.' There was jealousy clawing in my gut, the loneliness of having been left out. She'd told him but not me. And still the gnawing ache that he had left us, folded his clothes and left us for the dark, cold sea.

A look flew across Martin's face, guilt, then his features fell. 'I shouldn't have said—'

'Yes, you should – you should have said years ago.' And I turned my face from him and wept.

Once I had learned from Martin that my father had committed suicide, I found it hard to stay afloat. I'd been punctured, my history, my childhood leaking away. My grief had doubled. I requested a doctor's appointment; I'd been warned it might take ten days to actually see someone. While I waited to hear, I felt raw: a layer had been peeled back to expose my vulnerability. At night I'd go over and over it, vitriolic with anger at my father, raging at my family's duplicity. Sleep eluded me – nothing new there – but the acidic fury I felt exacerbated the physical discomforts of sleeplessness. My muscles ached dully, I was dehydrated, my skin and eyes itchy, dizzy, and a headache lapped at the back of my skull.

By day I stuck to the timetable, kept my head down and struggled to cope with the tears that would spring to my eyes at the slightest thing. One afternoon Patsy, a woman I was teaching to read who also lived in my house, came in with a letter from her daughter. Would I read it to her and help her write back? It was mundane stuff, family news and local gossip, nothing overtly sentimental, but as I read on, I broke down. She rushed to comfort me, which made it even worse.

'Aw, darlin', what's wrong? What's to do?'

'I lost my husband,' I spluttered, 'I miss him so much. And I lost my dad and now I feel as if I'm losing my mind.'

'We all feel like that sometimes,' she said. 'That's why there's so many girls cutting up.'

Self-harm is commonplace. Some people cut or burn themselves; others swallow dangerous objects or even find ways of breaking their bones. The prison librarian told me that forty per cent of the women inside have a mental illness, and eighty per cent have a serious drug or drink addiction. Most have been convicted of crimes linked to their addiction. Counselling is practically non-existent – lack of resources. Women speak of waiting nine months, a year or more to see a therapist.

'You want to see the doctor,' she told me, 'get some meds.'

I nodded, wiping my face. 'I've put in for an appointment.'

And then I helped her write the letter.

If I had known that my father had killed himself, if I had experienced the bewilderment, the anger and hurt of that abandonment, would I have even entertained Neil's request, knowing what it might feel like for his children?

Chapter Twenty-one

'Deborah, will you please tell the jury what happened on the fifteenth of June 2009?'

'The children went out, Sophie first to school, and then Adam.'

I had made a point of asking each of them if they had seen Neil before they left. One of the clues, perhaps, that had made Sophie doubt my story later that day.

'I sat with Neil in our room until about one o'clock.'

Adam had gone by then. I felt sick. Sick and shaky and terribly frightened. It was the fear of nightmares, visceral and inescapable. Neil seemed calm, resigned to his decision. I wanted to savour our last hours and minutes together. It was a beautiful day, a good day to die. But my mind was fractured, panicky, skittering away from the deed that lay ahead. Would he want to eat? The notion of all these 'lasts' – a last meal, last kiss, last breath – was intolerable to me. I said very little. I lay beside him. Should I have made more of it? Brought in flowers and put music on? Songs to end a life to? I did none of these things because until the end I was hoping it would never happen.

'And then what did you do?'

'I got us a drink.'

Are you hungry? I had said. Perhaps if he ate a

good lunch he would be sick and the whole thing would fall apart, a débâcle that would set him straight. Neil had shaken his head: I'd like a drink. Some wine.

I thought of his Greeks and his bloody Romans, drinking their flagons before falling on their swords. I smiled at him and went downstairs to cry. I'm sure he knew how distressed I was but he didn't say anything when I returned except 'Thank you.' What was he thanking me for? The wine or the rest of it?

'A drink?' Mr Latimer wants the details.

'Some wine.'

Red wine. The colour of blood. Ruby staining his lips, his tongue.

'And then?'

'It all happened so quickly,' I say. Tears start in my eyes, but now I will say my piece. I'm damned if I'll collapse again. 'We hadn't even finished the bottle and Neil said my name, he touched my face. And I knew what he meant.'

'What was that?'

'That it was time.'

'Thank you. Please tell the jury what happened next.'

'I got the morphine bottles and opened them.'

My hands were shaking and my heart hurt in my chest, a profound pain, as if a fist was squeezing it. I thought how fucking ironic it would be if I had a heart-attack before I could give him the drugs. End up dead and Neil forced to live on.

'Neil drank one. I kissed him and told him I loved him. He told me the same.' My voice is uneven, fluting with emotion. In the jury box Alice is crying silently, her hand over her mouth, her eyes closed and her wide face flushed.

'Then I gave him the other bottle. Then I think he had some more wine. Then the last one from the breathing space kit, or it might have been then that he had the wine. I can't be sure.'

'How long did it take Neil to drink all the medicine?'

'About five minutes.' It was so quick.

'And then?'

'He fell asleep.' His eyes closed, his hands relaxed, his breathing altered.

'What time was this?'

'It was almost two o'clock.' I remember looking at the alarm clock and thinking that when it next rang Neil would be gone. That I'd be getting up on my own. It seemed unreal. Preposterous.

'And what did you do then?'

'I lay down with him. And waited.'

'How long did you stay like that?'

'Half an hour. Neil was still breathing. I didn't know what to do. I knew Sophie would be home soon. I tried to wake him. To see if it was too late.' As I talk, I can't catch the rhythm of my own breath. There is no oxygen in it, I am choking. Pushing at Neil, shaking his shoulder, slapping his cheek. Neil, Neil, wake up. Please, oh, God, please.

Mr Latimer waits, hoping to settle me.

'I couldn't wake him up. I had the plastic bag.' Sweat breaks out across my body. I am trembling. 'I put the bag over his head. He jerked and made this sound, this awful sound. I held it tight. Then he stopped breathing.'

'Would you describe what happened as a good death?'

'No,' I whisper.

It had been horrible. It hadn't been dignified – not from my point of view. How could he have pressured

228

me into it? The worst moments, the drumming of his heels on the bed, the strangled murmur that might have been 'Stop' or 'Help', the bubbling breath, the way his body bucked, the smell as he emptied his bowels. They pulse through me time and again in waves of shame and revulsion.

'What did you do then?'

I cursed him. 'I took the bag and the morphine bottles, along with the breathing space kit, put them in an old carrier bag in the wheelie-bin, then emptied the kitchen bin on top.' My knees threatened to buckle as I went outside. I felt eyes on my back, expected someone to come up the drive any moment. Pauline to trot round with a complaint.

'I went back upstairs. I needed to make sure he was still there. Still . . . dead.'

Flo, in the back row of the jury, blanches and looks down.

When I cupped his face in my hands I thought perhaps he was slightly cooler. I traced the lines on his brow with my thumbs, rubbed the heel of my hand against the stubble along his jaw. Speckles of silver in there with the black. He had never grown a beard, not even a moustache. He looked worried in death. His mouth turning down. His lovely eyes marbles now.

'Wake up.' I tested him. 'Neil, come back.' All I heard were the birds outside and the hammering from down the road where they were converting the loft. I wrapped one palm around his throat, over his Adam's apple, absorbing the absence of motion, the lack of rhythm in his blood. I wanted to clean him up, bathe him with libations, oils and tears. Like the godly women who laid out the dead. We no longer had that skill: death, like birth, had been hived off to professionals, to antiseptic corporate enclaves far removed from the glory and filth of the real thing.

'Then I rang the ambulance. And I left a message for Adam on his phone. And I rang Sophie,' I tell the court.

'What did you tell her?'

'She guessed. When she got back I told her that I had gone upstairs and found he wasn't breathing.'

'When you and your husband planned his death, you hoped to evade detection?'

'Yes.'

The Prof settles back. I sense disapproval. Dolly glances his way and behind them the Artist scratches at his neck, a leisurely move that seems foreign in the circumstances.

'And did you discuss what you should do if any suspicions were aroused?'

'Yes, if it came to it, I was to say that Neil had taken an overdose, that unknown to me he had hoarded his medication and that I had no idea what he was planning. And that I had then hidden the evidence to spare the children.'

'But you didn't do that, did you?' Latimer asks.

'No.' Because once I knew Sophie was caught in the undertow with me, only the truth would do. 'When I heard that Sophie had gone to the police, I just wanted to stop all the lies. To tell her the truth. Her and Adam. To help them understand. And also because I'd had to use the plastic bag, and they'd found evidence of that in the post-mortem, well, it made it less likely that Neil could have done it all himself.'

The bag was strong, clear plastic. It had once held some fabric samples in it – for some curtains in the Arts and Crafts style I was working on. I had

230

gripped it tight under his chin. His breathing was shallow and the bag compressed in tiny, incremental stages until it lay plastered and creased against his forehead and cheeks, sucking against his nostrils. His face darkening and then those dreadful pitiful movements he made. The brief clamour for life that had me leaping out of my skin. The appalling stillness that followed.

'Why didn't you tell Sophie the truth?'

'I wanted to protect her, and Adam. I didn't want them to know what we had done. Neil wanted them to believe he had died naturally from his illness.'

'And why didn't you tell the police what you had done when you were questioned?'

'The same reason. Because of the children. Because I had broken the law and Neil was dead and I had to be there for our children.'

'What do you think now about your actions?'

'I never should have done it. It was awful, the whole thing. If I'd only been stronger and kept refusing him.'

'Why didn't you?' Mr Latimer sounds almost harsh now.

'I couldn't think straight. I couldn't work out what was best. And Neil was so clear, so sure. I was absolutely exhausted and losing my mind and he kept on at me until I couldn't say no any longer.'

'How do you feel now about agreeing to his request?'

'Terrible.'

I look across to Sophie, willing her to face me but her head is bowed, her hair a veil.

I wrote to Sophie from Styal. Ms Gleason cautioned me that I ran the risk of being accused of exercising

231

undue influence on a prosecution witness but I promised that there would be nothing inflammatory in my letter. The prison monitored communication anyway. I wrote to say how sorry I was. To tell her how much I loved her and how I never meant to hurt anyone with my actions. And that, whatever happened, I would never stop loving her. I told her that Neil loved her too. Also I promised that if she ever wanted to ask me about Neil, about his life or his death, whatever she needed to know I would tell her. There was one thing I didn't write that needled at me like a toothache. I left it out because it might have seemed too harsh and because this wasn't the place to pose that question, because she was my daughter and only fifteen. What would you have done? That was what I really wanted to know. If it had been you, and you loved him as I did, then what would you have done?

When Briony Webber stands up and launches into me she is crisp and professional, just the right side of hostile. 'Ms Shelley, you say you feel terrible about your involvement in your husband's death. Is that because you were caught?' There's an intake of breath from someone in the gallery.

'No.' My cheeks glow with heat.

'If you'd got away with it, would you still feel so terrible?'

'No. Yes. It's not like that.'

'I think we'll let the jury judge for itself what it's like, whether the picture you paint of someone driven to lose reason is only that, a picture, a fiction.'

Mr Latimer bolts to his feet: this sort of language should be saved for the closing speeches but Miss Webber's ahead of the game and moves on. 'Tell me,

Ms Shelley, you were still working in the weeks leading up to Mr Draper's death?

'Yes.'

'Did any of your clients complain about your work?'

'No.'

'Anyone cancel a project, dispense with your services?'

'No.'

'Did any of your clients give you bad feedback about your attitude or behaviour?'

'No.'

'So, as far as your clients were concerned you were performing your work perfectly well.'

'Yes.'

'And home. You were still looking after your house and family?'

Someone had to. 'Yes.'

'And apart from a spat with your neighbour we have nothing to indicate you were not in sound mind and coping admirably with a difficult situation? Is that true?'

'I don't know.' It's a weak answer and my mind darts about, desperate for a better one.

'Oh, I think you do, Ms Shelley. Let me take you back to the events of that fateful morning. According to your own testimony, your husband did not specifically ask you to do anything that morning, did he, apart from fetch some wine?'

'Not as such.'

'But you inferred that he was desperate to commit suicide?'

Her tone riles me and I feel a tide of anger mounting beneath my fear. 'He had said, "Tomorrow." I knew what he meant.'

'Did you check? Did you ask him outright?'

233

'No.' My blood boils.

'You just chose to interpret it that way.'

'Why?' I yell, knowing as I do that this is folly. 'Why the hell would I want to do that? I wanted him to live.'

In the aftershock there is a deep silence. Briony Webber doesn't reply but pauses, gives a tight smile of forgiveness before she sallies forth. 'I put it to you that you knew full well what you were doing. That you believed your husband had a right to die and that you supported him to the hilt.'

'No!' My face is hot, my composure lost.

'And that when the medicine failed to work as quickly as you expected, you had the plastic bag at hand to complete what you had started. Is that not the case?'

'I didn't know what I was doing.' I force down my fickle temper, mute my tone.

'I say you did. And having carried out your promise to the bitter end, you then made every attempt to cover your tracks, did you not?'

'Yes.' I can hardly say otherwise.

'You hid the evidence. You lied to your family, then to the police. I put it to you that had you been incapable of responsible thought, as my learned friend suggests, you would not have then had the wherewithal to maintain this fabric of lies. You knew exactly what you were doing when you fed those drugs to your husband, when you selected that plastic bag and held it over his face until he suffocated. When you hid the evidence.'

'No. I was wrong. I was so mixed up.'

'Ms Shelley, you were able to withstand hours of questioning with little evident distress. How do you account for that?'

I wear it well, I want to say, but simply shake my head. The more I say the more she will devour me.

'Only when the evidence against you became overwhelming, when you were told that your own daughter was a witness for the prosecution, did you even admit to any complicity in Mr Draper's death. I suggest your change of tack was simply a tactic to try to save your own skin.'

Of course it bloody was, you daft bitch. What else could I do? There is no other defence they will let me make. 'I'm telling the truth,' my voice rings out, a tremor of rage in it.

'Now, when it suits. But we have heard different versions of events. You lied in order to acquire the drugs in the first place, you lied to your own children, to Neil's parents, you lied time and again. If you lied then, how do we know you are not lying now? Lying to the court, lying to this jury. There is precious little in what we have heard to suggest you are a credible witness.'

I look directly across at the jury, feeling miserable, bullied. 'I'm telling the truth,' I say to them.

Mousy drops her gaze, most of the others look away but some people meet my eye in that moment: the Cook and Dolly. And that humanity helps ground me.

Miss Webber finally drops me, a dog tired of its chewing slipper. She leaves them with the accusation 'liar' pervading the air. This is the word stamped on each of her bullets, carved on the shafts of her arrows, engraved on her knuckle dusters. Say it enough times and it will gather weight, gain credence.

A shaft of light, pale golden sunshine, gains admittance through the large window high in the walls and floods the ceiling. My neck is fused with tension. I can smell my own terror, a sharp musk.

There is a brief pause while Mr Latimer confers with Ms Gleason. From the gallery Jane smiles at me, an open, warm smile. The worst is over. Is it? I bite my tongue and suck in my cheeks.

Mr Latimer calls my neighbour Pauline Corby. There was never any love lost between us, though relations were more or less civil until the hammer incident. My defence team think this distance will give her testimony clout, as it were. This is no fawning friend or loyal relative but a mere acquaintance who can tell it like it is, no punches barred. And Pauline Corby does her stuff. Particularly when Mr Latimer asks her about my aggression.

'She was like a mad woman. Completely off her rocker. I thought we should get the police, have her sectioned.'

'And when later you heard that there were suspicious circumstances surrounding Neil Draper's death, what did you think?'

'I wasn't surprised. I'd already said as much to Barry' – Barry is a short, fair Londoner with all the social graces of a wasp – '"The woman's not safe. She'll swing for somebody."'

Hah! A hundred years ago I would have swung for this. Women standing here, men too, would have been taken from here to the gallows at Strangeways prison. That please you, Neil? A little historical perspective? My skin feels clammy as though the ghosts are with me now pat-a-caking my arms and cheeks, grinning slyly with black, bloated tongues and blood-red eyes.

If they find me guilty how will I bear it?

'Was her behaviour out of the ordinary, different from normal?'

'Oh, yes. She was like a different person. She was just crazy.'

'And apart from this incident did the situation return to normal?'

'Hardly. She was always wandering about the garden at night, going out to her conservatory.'

Workshop, Pauline. Workshop.

'The security light would come on and wake us up. I don't think she ever slept after that. We didn't know what to do.'

Miss Webber thanks Mr Latimer and approaches the witness box.

'Mrs Corby. It's true, is it not, that you have had previous problems with your neighbours and their children?'

'Some.'

'Could you give us an example?'

'Well, the son Adam, he damaged the car. We had to ask for money to get it fixed.'

Adam, stoned, had found it amusing to walk over the Corbys' Golf. The dents in the roof cost a small fortune to repair. 'It's only a car,' Adam had protested, when Neil and I had hauled him into the kitchen to sort it out. 'It's not like I barbecued the cat or something.'

'Anything else?' Miss Webber asks.

'We had to complain about the noise sometimes. Loud music going on half the night.'

'And wasn't this incident simply one more confrontation in the series?'

'No,' Pauline says stoutly. 'This was different. She threatened me with a hammer. She was abusive.'

'Did she raise the hammer?'

'A little.' She sounds defensive, unsure. 'She was off her head.'

'You're a housewife, Mrs Corby?'

'That's right.'

'Do you think that qualifies you to assess someone's mental health?'

'Maybe not,' she says bluntly. 'But I was a psychiatric nurse before I got married and I reckon that does.'

Oh, bless you, Mrs Corby.

There's a moment's silence, then the court erupts with laughter. Dolly cackles and Hilda and Flo giggle and Alice whoops. Even Miss Webber has the grace to smile and gives up on Pauline before she digs a deeper hole.

The judge decides we will break for lunch. I realize, with a swirl of vertigo, that by the end of the day my trial will be over. There is only Don Petty, my shrink, to give evidence and then there will be the closing speeches. As the jury file out, I watch them go, the Callow Youth hunched but any attempt at looking cool compromised by his gait – he bounces on his toes like a kid as he walks. Flo has to help Hilda up. I see them as lifelong friends, like Jane and me. But they met for the first time last week, selected at random. The Sailor wears the same clothes again. It strikes me that I have never heard any of these people speak. They are silent in the court, eyes and ears. Once out of the room their chatter will flow, conversation and anecdotes with which they oil the lunches and coffee breaks, the times they wait for the call of the ushers, the partings at the end of the day.

I have absolutely no idea how we are faring. When the court is almost empty Mr Latimer comes over. 'That was a gem,' he tells me. 'She doubled the weight of that witness's evidence.'

'Can you tell,' I ask him, 'what the jury are thinking?'

He shook his head. 'Never can. Not worth a moment's speculation. Only time I ever did, I was wrong.'

'I'm sorry,' I said, 'for shouting.'

He dipped his head. 'Hard to resist. Could have been worse.'

'I could have gone for her with a hammer,' I murmur.

His eyes glint. He purses his lips. The smile is in his voice. 'That would never do. I will see you after lunch.'

Chapter Twenty-two

D on Petty, the shrink for my defence, is a tall gangly fellow, close to my age, I guess, with a bald head, beaky nose and an insignificant chin, giving him the cast of a tortoise. He speaks in a precise Edinburgh accent and never smiles (now, I have to appear suitably glum and contrite but surely he could afford to crack a grin now and then).

Mr Latimer establishes his manifold qualifications and his extensive experience. He has been selected as our expert witness because he measures up to Dolores Cabril and then some. Though not, I fear, in the personality stakes.

Now Mr Latimer winds him up and sets him off, asking him about his assessment of me.

'Our mental health operates in similar ways to our physical health,' Don Petty begins. 'And the two are closely intertwined. The balance of health can be compromised by sudden attacks to the system such as bereavement, redundancy, the end of a relationship. These are the equivalent of the broken leg or the heart-attack. But mental health is also undermined where there are ongoing long-term factors – say, an unhappy marriage, a stressful job, a lack of self-esteem. In addition, there are the factors we inherit. Just as some cancers or allergic complaints run in families, so do mental health diseases.'

'And h-how does this relate to Deborah's situation?' Mr Latimer asks, with a flourish of his arm in my direction.

'Inheritance first. Deborah's parents both suffered from depression.'

I am surprised to consider my mother in this light. But it makes perfect sense. Her cold reserve, her distraction, her continuing failure to engage with me, with the world, her disaffection: these could all be symptoms of depression. Had she ever sought help herself? Gone to the doctor about her nerves, exhausted by the heavy cloak of misery she carted about? Should I have seen this? Understood it, done something about it? Always too lost in my own disappointment with her, I'd not had the objectivity to do so. How different things might have been. Perhaps I could have forgiven her, absolved myself. But the past is done. The tide went out, leaving us marooned on opposite sides of the same island. Cast away.

'Her father was also an alcoholic,' Don Petty carries on. 'This alone predisposes Deborah to depression. On top of that, the death of her father at a formative age would have been a huge shock to the system. The loss of a parent in childhood remains the single most influential factor in the development of mental illness.'

Adam and Sophie are teenagers: when does childhood end? Will Neil's death add to the risk for them? Does the cruel snare of depression lie in wait for Sophie? And Adam, who has been amazing in these past months, functioning better than I could ever have hoped: as time passes, will Neil's death magnify his problems?

'The loss of her mother and Neil's diagnosis were two other significant attacks on Deborah's mental health,' says Don Petty.

'But her mother died many years ago,' Mr Latimer points out – best to get that cleared up before Miss Webber gets her claws out.

'True,' says Mr Petty. 'However, Deborah's relationship with her mother was a troubled one. Difficulties within it were neither addressed nor resolved and this can arrest the grieving process and store up problems that later emerge at stressful times.'

'It was then, after her mother died, that Deborah sought medical help for her illness?' Mr Latimer asks.

'That's correct. And her GP was concerned enough to treat her for clinical depression by prescribing anti-depressants. So we have a prior incident of serious mental illness. Now, more recently, the constant strain of caring for her terminally ill partner while also coping with her son's mental illness, and dealing with her own insomnia and panic attacks, caused Deborah to become seriously ill.'

'Ill enough to lose the ability to distinguish between right and wrong?'

'Yes,' confirms Don Petty. It's a bald reply and I expect him to elaborate but he just stares impassively at Mr Latimer.

'The insomnia,' Mr Latimer asks, 'how would that affect Deborah's state of mind?'

'Insomnia has a direct adverse impact on the amount of stress we experience, and how we cope with that stress. It also makes it hard for people to concentrate, to think rationally. In more severe cases insomnia can lead to delusions and other severe mental states. We now know insomnia can increase the risk of depression and contribute to recurrent depression.'

'And the panic attacks?'

'These episodes are extremely frightening for anybody: palpitations of the heart, inability to breathe, feelings of terror, of losing control. They are disturbing, debilitating and would have increased her sense of being out of control.'

Mr Latimer nods thoughtfully, 'So, given her history of depression and insomnia and the other stresses in the family, when Neil repeatedly asked Deborah to help him die, her mental state meant that she was not able to make a sound judgement?'

'Not in the end. Though she did refuse him twice, which indicates that it was the mounting pressure and the deterioration of her own mental health that destroyed her ability to make a reasoned decision.'

'And her actions afterwards,' asks Mr Latimer, 'her attempts to conceal the facts of the situation?'

'Deborah would be the first to admit that she was horrified, sickened by the reality of Neil's death. The nightmare had come true for her. Grief-stricken and depressed, she did all she could to minimize the damage to her family. She knew that she had done wrong and was desperate to protect her children.'

'Was Deborah Shelley mad when she helped Neil die?'

'Mad isn't a word I would use but the balance of her mind was disturbed to such an extent that she could not be held responsible for her actions.'

Cross-examining, Miss Webber picks away at him like some starving crow. She starts by trying to get Don Petty to admit that my actions before, during and after Neil's death would equally well fit the profile of a sane woman who simply believed in her husband's right to die, and who, however reluctantly, went along with it.

243

He's having none of it. 'In such cases,' he expounds, 'the person responsible makes no attempt to hide the matter but freely discloses their involvement to the family and to the authorities. They are morally secure and prepared to risk prison for their convictions.'

She comes at him from another angle. 'Deborah Shelley agreed to her husband's request on Friday, the third of April, is that your understanding?'

'Yes.'

'And on the fifteenth of June she went though with it: administering a massive dose of morphine and then smothering Neil Draper with a plastic bag?'

Again and again the plastic bag is raised, flagged up and waved in the jury's faces. An obscene image. Each time, I see Neil's face darkening, feel that sickening panic, the terror in my bowels, in my heart.

'Ten weeks separate those dates,' she presses on, 'during which time Ms Shelley continued to care for her children, run a household, attend meetings with her clients. Are you seriously suggesting that Deborah Shelley was mentally incompetent for ten weeks and yet no one noticed?' Miss Webber's voice rises with incredulity.

'That's not what I said,' he barks, and flushes, angry. It is not a pleasant sight. I feel embarrassed. How will the jury take it?

'Was the balance of Ms Shelley's mind disturbed when she agreed to assist her husband?'

'I believe so. From her account, it is my opinion that Deborah was under great pressure and agreed to placate her husband. Had she felt stronger she would not have agreed. She hoped it would never come to pass.'

'And when she set off to research methods of killing someone, scouring the Internet for deadly information, when she plotted to hoard drugs and lied to their GP, was that to placate Neil? Was the balance of her mind disturbed then?'

'She was confused—'

'I certainly am,' Miss Webber says swiftly, and some people laugh. 'Please, Mr Petty, answer the question.'

'It is often the case,' he sounds petulant, his Scottish accent suddenly echoes with peevish grievance, 'that a person can be suffering mental disturbance yet appear to function quite well. I believe she went along with it, still hoping it would never happen,' he says stiffly.

'So she was sane, then?' Don Petty frowns at that and Miss Webber adds, 'She was mentally responsible during those weeks?'

'No. Mental health fluctuates as does physical health. It is a spectrum, not a fixed state.'

'Exactly,' pipes Briony Webber, 'quite fluid – certainly in this case. Seems to come and go to suit the occasion.'

'Miss Webber,' the judge growls.

'Withdrawn.'

I catch a look between Mr Latimer and Ms Gleason. Dismay. My cheeks burn. Oh, God. This is the battle of the shrinks and Don Petty is supposed to be my champion. I want to stand up and yell at him, grab hold of him and slap him into shape.

'And was Ms Shelley mentally responsible when she performed the fatal act?' Performed: there's a pornographic slur in the way she articulates the word. I am beginning to tremble. I stare at Don Petty, willing him to fight for me. To show them how it was – or, rather, how we want it to appear.

'No, she was no longer mentally responsible.'

'When did the change occur?' Miss Webber demands. 'That morning, the week before?'

'It is my opinion that the weeks leading up to that day saw an increasing deterioration in Deborah's mental health. The evening before June the fifteenth was the tipping point, when Neil named the day. The balance of her mind was so disturbed that she could no longer be held responsible for her behaviour.'

'Really?' she says drily. 'And after the murder of her husband did not Ms Shelley perform perfectly well, fooling family, friends, medical staff, even the police until her lies were exposed?' Now she makes me an actor, all mask and makeup, mouthing my lines by rote. 'I put to you an alternative view – that Ms Shelley is a clever and calculating woman who knows her only chance of evading a prison sentence is to spin this tissue of lies and fancies. Asking this jury to believe that on April the third she lost all reason and said yes to Neil Draper, that ten weeks later on June the fifteenth, again all sense deserted her as she helped him die. Yet she was able to recover amazingly quickly, hiding the evidence, trotting out a story, covering up the murder of her husband.'

'Is there a question for the witness?' Mr Latimer complains, the tail on his scrappy wig shivering furiously.

'Do you have children, Mr Petty?' asks Miss Webber.

'Sorry?'

'Is this relevant?' Mr Latimer demands.

The judge nods for Miss Webber to continue.

'You have any children?'

'Yes, two.'

'Keep you awake at night?'

'Sometimes.'

'Broken sleep affects most parents, would you say?'

'It's not my area of—' He's beginning to fudge.

She cuts him off. 'Oh, come on, we all know what it's like. New parents barely get any sleep but they don't become unbalanced, they don't lose the capacity to distinguish right from wrong. Yet you claim that Ms Shelley's insomnia left her so sleep deprived it made her sick?'

'It's a contributing factor.'

'So you say.' Her retort drips sarcasm. 'Another factor was the strain of the problems with Adam Shelley: his mental problems, his drug abuse.'

'That's right.' His words are clipped, defensive now, mealy-mouthed.

'And Adam had been a voluntary hospital patient on occasion in 2008? And had received counselling?'

'Yes.'

'But since then he had been settled at home?'

I see Mr Latimer close his eyes slowly: he knows this is heading nowhere good.

'That's right.'

'There had not been any serious incident with Adam in the year leading up to his father's death? Is that correct?'

'Yes.'

'So, it would appear that the situation with Adam had improved significantly, that Ms Shelley might have taken consolation from the fact that things were so much better, that there was much less pressure in that quarter. In effect a respite? Would you agree?'

I close my own eyes for a moment, shake my head a little. She is demolishing my defence, peck by peck. I hear Don Petty clear his throat. 'It may appear like that but the reality of living with a child with these sort of issues creates long-term stress.'

She ignores him. She has made her point and moves on. 'We have already heard that Ms Shelley did not see her own doctor in 2009 or ask for any help. That is your understanding?'

'She used the MNDA helpline.'

'Though she did not call them to discuss Neil's request or ask for help in those final ten weeks? Is that right?'

He pauses but there's no way out. 'It is.'

I can see Jane, her face set, wary. She too must feel that any sympathy in the room has melted away. I do not dare survey the jury. Briony Webber walks to the benches.

'And we have heard that only once in her life did Deborah Shelley ever seek professional help for depression, in . . .' she makes a show of checking her notes '. . . 1993. Sixteen years previously. No sign of depression for sixteen years.' She weighs each word, heavy with import. 'Do you agree?'

'It's possible to have the illness but not seek help.'

'And you believe that's true of Deborah Shelley?' The subtext is 'poor misguided fool'.

'I do.'

'So we have a woman who you claim lost all reason on June the fifteenth and acted while the balance of her mind was disturbed. What about when she researched those very methods, scouring the Internet for websites about suicide? When she went over with her husband how she would conduct herself after his death?' Her voice gains volume, filling the court, the catalogue of my misdeeds bouncing back from the high ceilings, the far corners. 'When she planned with him what she would say if any suspicions were aroused? Was the balance of her mind disturbed on each of those occasions?'

I chance a glance towards the jury. Alice, resplendent with a black hairband and strange blue pinafore dress, bows her head, studying her hands. Discomfited or disillusioned.

'In my opinion the preparatory acts made by Deborah Shelley were on a par with the act itself – they were carried out under enormous emotional pressure and in the desperate hope that they would be superfluous at the end of the day.'

'And after the deed was done?'

'I have already said—' Don Petty complains.

'I would like you to repeat your assertion, for the sake of the jury, because quite frankly it beggars belief.'

'Badgering the witness!' Mr Latimer shouts. He has gone very pale and his lips are taut with displeasure.

'Your Honour,' says Miss Webber, 'this speaks to the very core of the defence. I must be able to test the witness rigorously.'

'Proceed with caution,' the judge tells her.

She swivels back to Don Petty. 'And afterwards a remarkable recovery, wouldn't you say? As soon as she despatches her husband, Ms Shelley sets to work. How was her state of mind when she cleared away the drug containers and the plastic bag, when she told the ambulance man that her husband's death was expected, when she told her daughter that she had found him dead in his bed, when she accepted condolences and placed the death notice in the paper, when she played the innocent as the police asked for the truth? All very logical acts if you are trying to get away with murder, would you agree?'

'She was trying to save her family,' Don Petty says. 'To salvage something. She was in denial.'

'I don't think she's the only one.' There's a gasp at Miss Webber's insolence. 'No further questions.' She swoops back to her seat.

I am gutted. She has laid me out and torn me open. Carrion. The trembling is worse. I am trembling inside, an ague, cold and bone deep.

Once Don Petty has gone there is a pause in the proceedings. The judge consults with the lawyers. He decides that it would be better to hear the closing speeches in the morning. Court is adjourned for the day.

Sophie stands up, making to leave and bends down for her coat. Our eyes lock. She doesn't look away. She doesn't glare or narrow her eyes. She just looks raw and shattered. Then the moment is gone.

Chapter Twenty-three

The wind is fierce tonight. You could mistake it for a jet engine. It sweeps the clouds across the dark sky. It shakes the limbs of the lime tree and snatches at doors and windows. Anything unanchored is hurled up and down the avenues.

They say the prison houses are haunted, ghosts of women who've died there, and the orphans before them. I am not afraid of ghosts. I am afraid of just about everything else. All day long my stomach is cramped with dread. I am afraid of the jury, of the power they hold, of remembering Neil's dying seizure. I am afraid of losing Sophie for good. I am afraid of being summoned to the office to hear that Adam has joined his father and grandfather. I am afraid of staying here: of going mad, of locking myself in and copying the other lost souls, with a lighter to my bedding or a knife to the long blue vein that pulses through my forearm. Of diving down into the cold, dark embrace of the river Styx, feeling the silt and the water fill my lungs.

I must have slept because I wake at six, my head feeling fuzzy and my skin chilled, covered with goose-bumps. I get ready quietly; the other women still have an hour before roll call. I cannot face any breakfast but drink a little milk. Even that turns to curds in my mouth. The prison officer takes me over to the gatehouse. I am strip-searched again.

251

It is only just light as the van arrives at Minshull Street. Ms Gleason comes in to see me in the court cell. She has coffee in one of those enormous polystyrene beakers, which she leaves with the guard. Enough caffeine to strip half your stomach lining.

When she asks me how I am, I shake my head. She places her hand on my shoulder. The touch is such a comfort.

That's something I crave: physical intimacy. Not the sex, though if Neil were raised from the dead I wouldn't think twice. No, it's the everyday contact, the hugs and pats, kisses and strokes, the hand-shakes. They shrank when Neil died and disappeared almost completely when they locked me up.

In the closing rounds, Briony Webber gets to go first.

'Members of the jury, British law does not permit us to assist in the taking of life, no matter what the individual circumstances. So-called mercy killing is illegal under our law. It is murder. That is why Deborah Shelley lied so brazenly: to her children, to the ambulance crew, to the police, to Neil's GP. She lied before the murder and after. She is lying to you now. Don't be fooled. She knew that what she was doing was wrong. She knew it was murder. Ask yourselves this . . .' She pauses and I swallow. My view wavers, the light dims, the jurors on their benches swim closer, then retreat.

'Why did Ms Shelley change her story? She changed it because she got caught. Because the police evidence, the forensic evidence, demonstrated be-yond any doubt that Neil Draper died an unnatural death. Since that point everything Deborah Shelley has said has been with one end in mind – that she get away scot free. That she get away with murder.'

She swings around and her black robe billows out, then she strides over to her table and examines her papers. But not for long.

'My learned friend is arguing that Ms Shelley lost use of her reason under pressure of the strain of her husband's illness and conceded to his wishes. I ask you to consider this: there were ten weeks between her agreeing to his request and carrying it out. Ten weeks during which time she competently set about preparing for the event, gathering information, stock-piling morphine, practising her lies. You have heard Ms Shelley's account of the terrible events of June the fifteenth. But consider this: Neil Draper was still alive when Deborah Shelley pulled a plastic bag over his head and held it tight, hell bent on finishing what she had started. If she really was as distressed and ill as the defence claims, wouldn't you expect her at that point, with her husband unconscious, when she tells us she was panicking, to collapse in defeat? To cry for help? No. Not only did she hold the bag over Neil's head while he fought to breathe but she then hid everything – the bag, the evidence of the drugs – and set about creating a sham, a charade for the whole world.'

Mute and mutinous, I listen to her singing my sins, feel the breath stutter in and out of my windpipe, the beat of blood in my ears.

'Deborah Shelley is an intelligent woman, a university graduate, a businesswoman. She knew how to seek help, she was articulate, financially secure, she knew the law, she knew . . .' Miss Webber turns and stares at me, nodding, calling me a liar. I will not bow my head. '. . . yet she chose to go along with her husband's wishes. Her intentions may have been honourable but her actions were not. What she

253

did may have been out of loyalty but her motive was sadly mistaken. She murdered her husband. Neil Draper's mother wants justice for her son. Neil Draper's daughter, who has spoken so bravely here in court, needs to know that you will recognize her courage and heed the truth.

'The victim is not here. He cannot speak and tell us what transpired. If he were I have no doubt that he would tell you he begged his wife to help end his life. No one disputes that. What is in dispute is whether Deborah Shelley knew what she was doing. Do not be fooled by her lies. She has shown she can be fluent in her explanations, but no matter how smoothly she tells it, her account is a fabric of falsehoods and deceit. I believe there can be only one verdict returned on the basis of the evidence you have heard. And that is guilty, guilty of murder.'

Miss Webber returns slowly to her seat and the room is still.

Mr Latimer takes a sip of water and gets to his feet. When he speaks his voice is soft, just audible and he sounds regretful.

'When Neil Draper asked his wife to help him die, she refused. He asked her again months afterwards and a second time she said no. But in April last year, when he asked her a third time, Deborah had become seriously ill. Her life was unravelling. The depression that had numbed her in the months after her mother's death returned with a vengeance. She had no faith in anti-depressants. She didn't believe anyone could help. Deborah was unable to sleep, her son Adam was a constant worry, known to be suffering from cannabis-induced psychosis. Deborah herself was having paralysing panic attacks. She could no longer hold everything together. The child of two depressives, one of whom took his own life while she was still small, Deborah had fought hard to cope. It's what women do, as mothers, wives, workers. They soldier on, they cope with crises, and they clear up the messes.'

It's a lovely, generous speech, and the jury are captivated.

'But Deborah could no longer manage. Her savage attack on her neighbour is testament to how disturbed she was becoming. W-w-weakened and terrified of what lay ahead, Deborah was unable to resist her husband any more. You have heard her say that she thought it might not happen even as she hoarded the drugs, that it might not happen even as she planned what to say if anyone grew suspicious, that it might not happen even as she poured Neil his last glass of wine. Her grasp on reality was loosening. Like a child who will hide behind his hands and imagine he can't be seen.' He dips his head for emphasis; the scrappy wool gives a little shiver, like a stiffened, shrunken lamb's tail.

'When Deborah gave Neil those doses of morphine, when she then suffocated him, it was because she was literally out of her mind. She could no longer tell right from wrong. She loved him and wanted to help him but she knew that by helping him she would be committing murder. The fear of what would happen added to her mental collapse.'

I hold myself tight, bound up, hands grasping each other, mouth rigid, frightened of flying apart, of unravelling before them.

'Deborah Shelley was sick. She could no longer be held responsible for her actions. She acted while she was unfit to judge. Now you must judge her. The burden of proof is on the prosecution, which means that they must prove to you beyond all reasonable doubt that Deborah Shelley murdered her husband, fully aware of what she was doing. Ask yourselves: are you one hundred per cent certain that this was the case? One hundred per cent,' he says again. 'When she lay beside her husband on that early summer day, when she told him she loved him, was she fully aware of what she was doing? In the midst of the horrendous pressure she had been under, was she still completely responsible for her actions? If you have any doubts you must find Deborah not guilty of murder. Deborah Shelley was not flouting the law, she is not an advocate of mercy killing. She is a woman who, in the height of her sickness, got swept along by her dying husband's pleas. She did wrong and has admitted it. All we ask now is that you bring your intelligence, your common sense and your humanity to consider the evidence. And find Deborah Shelley innocent of the charge of murder.'

The judge has the last word. He must interpret the law to the jury.

'This has been a very sad case: a terminal illness, a life cut short, children left fatherless. But now you have one task ahead. That task is simple yet arduous. On the evidence you have heard, and only on that, you must judge whether Deborah Shelley was mentally responsible for her actions, whether or not the balance of her mind was disturbed on the fifteenth of June 2009 when she helped her husband die. If you find the evidence shows that she was of sound mind, then the verdict must be guilty of murder. If, however, you believe the balance of her mind was disturbed to such an extent that it diminished her responsibility then you must find the defendant not guilty of murder but guilty of man-slaughter due to diminished responsibility.

'You have heard experts give opposing views of Ms Shelley's state of mind. This court now entrusts you with the duty of considering all the evidence and deciding who to believe. And I must remind you that if there is any doubt in your minds then you must find her not guilty of murder. Thank you.'

There is no knowing how long they will take. The hours drip by as I sit in the court cell but I would stop time. Because when they call me again my fate will be sealed.

Neil is with me now, his long legs stretched out, crossed at the ankles, his black hair tangled. He is reading. He looks up when he feels my eyes upon him and his own green eyes meet my gaze. They are merry and mischievous. He sets his book down, his movements fluid, and reaches over, cups his hand around the back of my neck.

'Deborah.' Three syllables savoured.

He bends to kiss me. His lips are smooth and warm, his tongue gentle, and I kiss him back, soft at first then harder.

We are floating, a long way from the shore. The water is balmy. I can taste the salt and smell the brine on the warm breath of the wind.

We swim on together; we will always be together. The sun is high. It glances off the water, fracturing into a million diamonds.

Neil holds my hand, palm to palm, his slim fingers entwined with mine.

Deborah.

Three syllables.

They call me back.
The jury have their verdict.

My jaw is rigid, my guts churning, my ears buzzing as I enter the dock. My breath is erratic and I'm aware that people can hear the stutter of it and see me fight to control my facial muscles, my movements spastic. I am so cold. I think my teeth must shatter, my skin harden and crack.

I want to be strong, for Adam, for Sophie and Jane, but it is beyond me.

They have chosen PA as the forewoman. I am surprised: she seems so young, with her neat ponytail and her tidy clothes. Is she a teacher, has she demonstrated some sort of leadership that influenced them to pick her? She's shown little emotion during the trial – I've had no sense of empathy from her.

'Have you reached a verdict?' the court clerk asks her.
'Yes, we have.'
'Is that a verdict upon which you are all agreed?'
'Yes.'
'On the charge of murder how do you find the defendant? Guilty or not guilty?'

I cannot hear, the buzzing in my head swells, I gulp to try and clear my ears. Dizziness spins me round, bubbles in my blood. I am choking.

I see Adam leap to his feet, and Jane. Sophie blanches, clutching at Veronica, who falls forward a little as though someone has punctured her, and Michael's hand sweeps his face but his expression is relief, I think, not dismay.

Paralysed, petrified, I watch these motions, unable to translate. Sound is muted, stretched. I am very far away, shrinking, disappearing.

Then I catch the words. 'Not guilty.'

Tears spill down my face and I gasp and cry out, a great howl of release.

There's a pause and people sit again. I am huffing and puffing, the handkerchief that I've used already a wet ball.

'And on the charge of manslaughter on the grounds of diminished responsibility, how do you find the defendant, guilty or not guilty?'

'Guilty.'

The judge thanks the jury for their service. Hilda and Flo look pleased with themselves. Dolly is crying and the Prof puffs out his cheeks and messes with his glasses.

Ms Gleason's eyes are shining and she is beaming at me.

Someone at the side, a reporter I think, dashes out. I will be on the teatime news.

In Styal, Prison Officer Clarkson is in the house office. She asks me how I've got on, and congratulates me on the verdict. I am drained, punch-drunk with relief. Upstairs is quiet. The shower is empty, still steamy from the last occupant. I stand under the jets and savour the warm spray on my eyelids and lips, turn and let it pour through my hair, drumming on my shoulders and down my spine. Sluicing away the grit and grime and sweat of the long day.

I put on my pyjamas and dressing-gown, go to get a cup of tea.

The women from my house are crowded into the kitchen. They let out a cheer when I come in.

'We made you a cake,' says Patsy.

They're nudging each other and grinning, banter slipping back and forth. On the table is a glistening chocolate cake. I can't speak.

'Put the kettle on,' someone yells, 'she's gasping. Aren't yer, Mercy?'

I smile and nod, then sit at the table while mugs of tea are made and the cake carefully divided.

'Did yer faint?' Patsy asks. 'I got a not guilty time before last, nearly keeled over.'

I lick the sweet, dark crumbs from my fingertips. 'Nearly,' I admit.

I will be back to Minshull Street for sentencing in two weeks' time. The women speculate as to how long I will get. Estimates range from a suspended sentence to five years. But it is much more likely to be the former, as I was not responsible for my actions. And I will be free.

They swap war stories, verdicts and surprises, reversals of fortune. Their voices blur and swell, salted with laughter. I let it all wash around me. I feel a rush of love for these women with their chaotic, fractured lives, the grim burdens they bear and their sparky, bloody-minded, frail resilience.

It is almost seven thirty and PO Clarkson comes to remind us she needs to lock up soon.

Patsy and I clear the plates as the others drift away with words of congratulation and jokes; the atmosphere in the house is warm with good humour.

'So the jury believed yer?' Patsy says quietly. 'That you were off yer head when you did it?'

'Yes.'

'But yer weren't really, were yer?'

I freeze, my hand on the cupboard door. A prickle of fear needles through me. Will she tell? Could they try me again? My mind soars back to that summer afternoon. I look her in the eyes and I trust her.

'No, I wasn't.' I was in a hard place.

She wipes the sink. 'You were just being kind, really. Anyone'd do the same, if they really loved someone. It shouldn't be counted like murder.'

She is right.

I leave my curtains open and watch the tree. A pitch silhouette against the luminous sky. The moon is almost full and hangs fat and low, blue-white like milk. I long to be home, to be gone from here. Home, where I will roam the house and garden, drink in the sight and smell of my son, begin to find a way to bring my fine fierce daughter home.

I peel back the sheet and mattress cover. Take a black felt pen. Add my own mark: *Deborah Shelley and Neil Draper*. Our names will always be linked. Not just in private but in the public domain: on search engines and in legal casebooks, in people's memories. The dying man and the wife acquitted of his murder, her reason lost. The ill-starred lovers.

But I am not going to climb on any more pyres for you, Neil, not hurl myself from a tower or slip my neck in a noose. What you have put me through has been more than enough for a lifetime. You will have to wait for me. I will rewrite our ending. We will be Baucis and Philemon, beloved wife and husband, who give shelter, food and wine to the incognito Zeus when others shun him. Rewarded, we are led from disaster and granted a wish – to stay together for the rest of our lives, to die together. And then we become two trees, an oak and a lime, side by side, our roots tangled in the earth, our branches inter-twined, our leaves kissing in the wind. For ever.

Discussion Points

(1) Did you have a view on assisted suicide before reading *The Kindest Thing*? Has reading the book changed your opinion at all? Did Neil have a 'good death'?

(2) Deborah describes herself as a 'back-chatting bitch'. Is this a fair description? What did you think of her as a character? Did her personality affect your ability to empathise with her situation? Which other characters did you like most, and why?

(3) Adam and Sophie have very different responses to Neil's death. Why do you think Sophie testifies against her mother?

(4) Prison life and the workings of the criminal justice system are described in some detail. Did this interest you? Were you surprised by anything?

(5) Sex scenes are notoriously difficult to write. How do you think the author acquitted herself with the scenes in the book? Did they bring anything to the story?

(6) While waiting for her trial, Deborah learns the secret behind her father's death. In turn, she and Neil kept their plans secret from Adam and

Sophie. Should parents keep secrets from their children? Do secrets protect us or are they ultimately destructive?

(7) The narrative switches between the stages of the trial and Deborah's past life. Was this way of telling the story satisfying? Did you ever get confused? The author also switches between present and past tenses for the different sections. Apart from differentiating the time period does the use of different tenses add anything to the flavour of the prose?

(8) Mental health is one of the themes running through the novel. Did you find the depiction of Adam's problems and of Deborah's grief and her anxiety realistic?

(9) Deborah insists on sharing domestic chores and childcare equally in the marriage. The arrangement apparently works. Why do you think it works? Do you find this believable?

(10) Deborah's relationship with her own mother is very difficult. In what ways does this influence her own attitudes and behaviour as a mother? Do you consider Deborah and Neil to be good parents? If not, why not?

(11) How did you feel when you finished the book? Do you think the jury were right? Were there any memorable scenes or images that have stayed with you?